W9-CNR-121

"Stay in character. Always,"
Eric said, his voice barely
audible.

"Do not forget you're my Andorran wife." He drew back, still holding her, and gave her a tight smile. Tension played between them like a high-voltage current.

Dawn became more aware of his hands on her, the subtle catch in his breathing, the intoxicating sandalwood scent of him this close to her. His gaze prowled over her like a hungry lion.

Suddenly he released her and left her there alone.

Something had happened in that brief span of time and Dawn could not explain it. Sexual attraction peaking big-time, of course, but more than that. It was as if she had felt his thoughts, his worry, even a fear that he was getting too close to her and yet not close enough.

Or maybe she was projecting her own thoughts....

Dear Reader,

The operatives who work behind the scenes, gathering and analyzing information and acting on it on behalf of our country, deserve much more praise than they get. We hear about their mistakes and failures but never do we learn much about the extent of their success. I would like to thank them here for their contributions to our security.

My fascination for the various agencies grew out of a close association with individuals involved in the intelligence community. I witnessed firsthand how their jobs, frequent travel and the secrecy required of them impacted on the agents and on their families. I saw the courage of spouses who wait and the ones who go out, the camaraderie between those who watch each other's backs in the field, and the personal and professional pride in a job well done even when they aren't allowed to discuss it.

Though the characters I write about in my SPECIAL OPS stories are strictly imaginary, they meet the same real-life problems, the hopes, disappointments and dreams that our friends in intelligence encounter. Life is lived on the edge. Love is precious, yet too easily lost by a shift in priorities. Trust in a partner, on the job or at home, is not only nice to have, it is crucial.

So, that said, I hope you enjoy this tale set in the Greek Islands where the incredible sun-kissed beauty of the surroundings contrasts with the dark side of terror that brings Eric and Dawn to paradise on their mission.

Here, have a little mystery and watch love ignite under pressure....

Lyn Stone

STRAIGHT THROUGH THE HEART

Lyn Stone

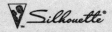

INTIMATE MOMENTS™

Published by Silhouette Books

America's Publisher of Contemporary Romance

If you purchased this book without a cover you should be aware that this book is stolen property. It was reported as "unsold and destroyed" to the publisher, and neither the author nor the publisher has received any payment for this "stripped book."

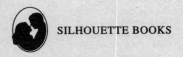 **SILHOUETTE BOOKS**

ISBN 0-373-27478-5

STRAIGHT THROUGH THE HEART

Copyright © 2006 by Lynda Stone

All rights reserved. Except for use in any review, the reproduction or utilization of this work in whole or in part in any form by any electronic, mechanical or other means, now known or hereafter invented, including xerography, photocopying and recording, or in any information storage or retrieval system, is forbidden without the written permission of the editorial office, Silhouette Books, 233 Broadway, New York, NY 10279 U.S.A.

All characters in this book have no existence outside the imagination of the author and have no relation whatsoever to anyone bearing the same name or names. They are not even distantly inspired by any individual known or unknown to the author, and all incidents are pure invention.

This edition published by arrangement with Harlequin Books S.A.

® and TM are trademarks of Harlequin Books S.A., used under license. Trademarks indicated with ® are registered in the United States Patent and Trademark Office, the Canadian Trade Marks Office and in other countries.

Visit Silhouette Books at www.eHarlequin.com

Printed in U.S.A.

Books by Lyn Stone

LYN STONE

is a former artist who developed an avid interest in criminology while helping her husband study for his degree. His subsequent career in counterintelligence and contacts in the field provide a built-in source for research when writing suspense. Their long and happy marriage provides firsthand knowledge of happily-ever-afters.

This book is dedicated to Karla and Dawn,
two mischief makers who inspired me to write this one.
Thanks for your enthusiasm and support!

Prologue

Amazing what a paper clip bent into the right configuration could do to a lock. More amazing still, the fact that there was a paper clip in such a paperless environment.

The desk drawer scraped as Dawn drew it out, the sound echoing in the darkness. She hissed in a breath and directed the beam of her penlight over a couple of unopened packages of snacks and onto the lone, small notepad in one corner.

With gloved fingers, she turned it over. There were three eight-digit passwords scribbled on the back. She committed them to memory.

She glanced at the computer, now dark and in rest mode. Did she dare take time to boot it up and see what she could get into? No, it was enough to know she could if she wanted to.

What would Daddy think now of his helpless little princess if he could see her in action? His incessant coddling had nearly ruined her for doing anything useful with her life. Maybe her size or the way she moved gave men the impression she needed looking after. God knows, they all tried. But her size and sinuous dexterity made her perfect for this kind of work.

Holding her breath, she gently pushed the drawer closed. It meshed with the front of the desk with only a slight squeak.

Suddenly, calm deserted her and her senses went on high alert. Her skin tingled, her breathing grew shallow and her heart rate increased. Something was not right. The urge to hurry kicked in, threatening her concentration.

She pressed a button on her wristwatch and the luminous numbers blinked on. It was nineteen minutes later than she had planned to wind this up. The outside guard patrol had thrown her off.

No matter. She had what she'd come for. Now was the time to climb back up on the desk, disappear into the vent, replace that panel and get the hell out.

Just as she secured the last screw in the vent's panel and switched off her penlight, the office door opened. The lights clicked on and she heard voices, one of which she recognized immediately.

Dawn froze, peering wide-eyed through the metal slots of the vent.

At first she felt only anger that Paul Bergen hadn't trusted her to do this. After all those instructions and careful coordinating, he had shown up to check on her? It was eight hours too soon for him to be presenting a vulnerability report, and this lab wouldn't be the place for that anyway.

Then she decided he must be working another angle,

another assailable point of entry. She remained silent and still, watching, waiting for the two men to leave the lab so she could make her escape.

Only when Bergen stabbed the technician did Dawn realize what was really going down.

Chapter 1

McLean, Virginia

"So, she's either the hero of the hour or she's facing a rap for treason." Eric Vinland pursed his lips and doodled a little hangman's rope on his notepad next to the woman's name. He was conditioning himself to make the call of guilty if it came to that.

Damn, but he hated it when a woman got herself involved in something like this. Maybe the feeling harkened back to his early training that included looking after the "weaker sex," seeing that none of them came to any harm. Feminists today would rip him apart if he ever admitted that out loud. They'd be right to do that, too. Eric knew from experience that women could be every bit as capable, but also as greedy, sadistic and treasonous as men. "Comes down to him or her," he reminded himself.

"By her own admission, she was there at the scene so that about sums it up," Jack Mercier, Eric's supervisor and the agent in charge of the investigation, agreed. "Let's go so you can determine if she was involved in the theft and establishing cover by killing Bergen, or if she's playing straight with us. You're a hell of a lot faster than a polygraph."

Eric scoffed. "You know as well as I do that she will have been trained to beat a lie detector."

Jack nodded. "Yes, but she won't be prepared for your powers of detection, will she? I wish you'd arrived sooner. Internet sources indicate those plans for the radar shield are already on the block and we need to find out who's doing the marketing. God help us if they decide to download the damned thing to a buyer. It'll be like freeware before we know it."

"Too valuable to risk that happening. The seller will want to deliver and collect in person on this one."

Eric understood the need for urgency. He regretted his delayed flight from Seattle, but it couldn't be helped. At least the investigation there had been successful even if it had run longer than expected.

He followed the boss out of the borrowed office at FBI headquarters, down the corridor to the interrogation room.

"You do the inquisition. I'll observe," Jack ordered. He ducked into the room adjacent to Interrogation that contained the viewing side of a one-way mirror.

When Eric entered the next door, his fellow agent, Holly Griffin, stood propped against the table, speaking to the suspect. "Okay, let's have it again. From the top, please."

Eric's quiet entrance raised no reaction in either woman. Holly kept her eyes on the woman, Agent Moon, who had hers shut.

He zoned in on the redhead seated on the far side of the

table in the uncomfortable metal folding chair. He could read most people's minds like the Sunday funnies, but not this kid's. Not yet, anyway.

Her exhaustion was evident. The incident had occurred around midnight, and it was nearly dawn now. Her defenses should be way down.

She had her arms folded beneath her ample breasts, hands clutching her elbows so tightly her knuckles turned white.

She gave a huge sigh as she rocked forward in her chair. "Not another word without a bathroom break. I *swear* I've told you everything I saw, all I know, all I suspect."

Eric saw no point in torture. He gave Holly a nod when she looked over at him, and she promptly escorted the subject out. Holly, Will and Jack had been questioning her for a couple of hours now. Several empty soft drink cans sat on the table close to where the subject had been sitting.

Holly was the lone female agent in their group and married to Will Griffin, another of their number. Sextant was a tight unit of six, all with particular specialties. Holly's was profiling, combined with an amazing talent for organizing and analyzing gathered data. Though she denied having any extrasensory abilities, she was exceptional at filling in the blanks and hearing the unspoken.

Her husband, Will, was often blessed with remote viewing and occasional empathetic episodes. Joe Corda was psychic to some degree, though still identifying and learning to control what he could do. Clay Senate experienced visions of future occurrences, often hard to interpret, but always interesting to explore. Jack Mercier held it all together and made every attempt to develop scenarios utilizing whatever they were able to provide, however nebulous that input seemed.

Eric's powers had proved the strongest and most reliable

so far. Telepathy was his thing, but he did have sporadic success in other areas.

His fellow agents were thorough, but he had the edge they needed to grasp everything in her pretty head, thoughts she would never speak aloud.

Since he could first remember, Eric had possessed that gift. He'd been hired for the elite Sextant team because of it. Made up of agents recruited from other government agencies, Sextant's mission was to subvert terrorist activities. His academic and professional credentials were very good, but he knew that his ability to read minds had been the kicker when it had come to his being chosen for Sextant. Sometimes he thought Mercier depended a little too heavily on that aspect of him. Eric tried hard not to resent that his other talents were underused.

"Anything yet?" Jack asked over the speaker.

Eric glanced at the mirror. "I'm in the room thirty seconds and you want a conclusion? I haven't even seen her eyes yet. Doesn't take telepathy to sense her exhaustion and frustration, though. Could be she's about to blow."

"Then ratchet up the pressure," Jack said calmly.

Eric nodded and sat down, resting his elbows on the tabletop, and waited, reviewing the little he knew about the subject thus far from her hastily retrieved files.

Special Agent Dawn Moon, five years with National Security Agency, age twenty-eight. Earned a degree at twenty-three, double major in criminal justice and psychology, a master's in the former, trilingual, but mathematically challenged. Eric smiled at the perfunctory, handwritten notation about that last subject.

No outstanding debts, he noted, so she must be able to balance her checkbook. She drove a three-year-old Mazda and lived alone in a modest apartment in one of the less-

desirable sections of Alexandria. She had been on her own
since age eighteen; her only living relatives were her father,
who lived in Charleston, and a male cousin who taught at
Galludet College in D.C.

Eric mentally added that she was really very pretty in a
girl-next-door way. If the girl in question was into crawling
around dirty attics and basements. No makeup. No nail
polish. Strictly business, this one.

She was dressed all in black, right down to her sneakers,
and looked bedraggled after her wild adventure. Her hair
was a mess, the curly red strands tousled and dusty, strag-
gling out of the black scrunchie that held only half of it on
top of her head.

He could picture her yanking off a hood, not bothering
to fix it. That indicated a low vanity score. High in self-
confidence, though, from what he had observed. He liked
that mix, and it was not one he saw very often.

The only motive for a woman like Agent Moon to get
embroiled in a treasonous act like this would be greed. That
just didn't fit.

She returned a few minutes later, entering ahead of
Holly. Without being ordered, Dawn Moon resumed her
seat and immediately locked gazes with him.

That's when Eric first saw her eyes. They were probably
the most arresting he had ever seen. Dark, fathomless and
exotic. She really had the most amazing eyes. And a pow-
erfully indignant glare.

He finally looked away, punched on the recorder that
Holly had been using and identified himself as the inter-
rogator and Agent Dawn Elizabeth Moon as the subject.
He added the date and time. Then he began the questions.
"What happened on the night of June 15 in the R&D lab
of Zelcon Technologies?"

"I was concealed in the air-conditioning vent and I saw Agent Bergen do it," she said in a clipped, determined voice, not frazzled as it had been before. She had collected herself pretty well and in short order.

"Recap for me. I'm new," Eric drawled, watching her sigh with resignation at having to repeat the entire incident yet again to yet another stranger.

"At Bergen's orders, I was to gain entry to the R&D lab, collect proof that I had been there and get out without being apprehended. I should have been off the property by the time he arrived, but I was delayed coming in."

"By what?"

"A complication in getting past the patrol outside. I had to wait for one to stop, smoke a cigarette and carry on a cell-phone conversation before he resumed his rounds."

"When did you first see Agent Bergen that night?" Eric asked.

"When I was replacing the last screw in the vent panel after I had completed my assignment, established the vulnerability in security that Zelcon had neglected to address since our official walk-through and study of the building plans evaluation six months ago."

"And did you participate in that evaluation?"

"Yes." She paused, then took a deep breath and continued, her patience growing thin with all the repetition. "Anyway, I heard voices and I could see through the vent. A minute after the two men entered the lab, Agent Ben Bergen stabbed the tech with a hypo, woke up the computer, plugged one of those little attaché gizmos into a USB port, copied some information, put the thing in his pocket and walked out." She firmed her lips as if holding in a curse.

Eric remained silent for a full ten seconds, attempting

to connect with what she was thinking. Her face gave away a lot, probably distracting him. Attracting him, too, oddly enough. Her face, figure and attitude combined to stir something in him he really didn't want stirred at the moment. Certainly not by a potential suspect. He had to see past all that, get beneath her surface.

When nothing came through on the mental front, he threw out more questions. "But you did nothing to prevent the theft of technology that could be critical to our nation's safety? Isn't that your job, Agent Moon, enforcing national security? That's what you were there to assess, right?"

She calmly placed her hands palms down on the table-top as if she meant to rise, but she didn't. Instead, she spoke calmly, deliberately and in a professional manner. "He had brought in at least one hypo containing an obvious knock-out drug or poison and might have had more, or maybe other weapons for all I knew. I remained concealed because I was unarmed."

Eric picked up sincerity, but he got that from her tone of voice and expression. Nothing from her mind. There were none of the telling mannerisms of a liar present. However, she would know what those were as well as he did. As agents, they would have had virtually the same training, probably by many of the same instructors.

"Why unarmed?" he asked. "You were issued a weapon."

She sighed. "As I have stated at least a dozen times, the vents are a tight squeeze. Inches count, and anything I felt was not needed, I left off. It's not as if I would have been shot if discovered. They would simply have held me until my reason for being there was verified. Please, will you tell me if that tech is dead?"

Eric continued watching her eyes, as open as he could get to receive visuals, feelings, words, anything from her.

He stood suddenly, fairly looming over her, blatantly attempting to intimidate. "What did you do then, inform your superior of what had just happened?"

"Paul Bergen *was* my superior!" She compressed her lips again and shook her head, then ran a hand through her hair, snagging out the scrunchie and tossing it aside. "To answer your question, no, I did not inform anyone at that time. I scrambled out of there as quickly and soundlessly as possible and followed Bergen."

"In your car? You do have communication equipment in your vehicle, do you not?"

"Yes. But I didn't call it in to the duty agent then. What could I have said that would be believed? I needed to find out more. Why Agent Bergen copied what he did and where he was going with it. I saw him deliver it and accept a briefcase. Then the man he delivered it to abruptly shot him two times in the chest, once in the head and took the case back. Then he left in a dark-colored Dodge. I got a partial on the tag."

"Where did this take place?" Eric asked.

"In the parking lot of an apartment complex just outside McLean. I checked to see if Bergen was still alive. He wasn't. Then I immediately phoned our director and waited there as he ordered me to do."

"Could you identify the man who shot Agent Bergen?"

"Yes. He was just under six feet tall, light skin, dark hair, mustache, square jaw. Approximately 180 pounds, late thirties or early forties. No distinguishing characteristics, but I would definitely recognize him if I saw him again. He walked beneath a streetlight as he reached his vehicle. I was less than eight feet away, hidden in the bushes."

"But you didn't try to stop him or follow him?"

She rolled her eyes. "He had a nine-millimeter in his

hand with only three rounds fired. I had a penlight. I'm good, but not *that* good."

Eric concentrated as heavily as possible on her thoughts. That was his primary function in this instance. Maybe he was trying too hard. He couldn't get a thing from her.

She was mad as hell with him and everyone who kept badgering her. Why did they keep harassing her when they should be busy finding that guy who had the disk? It was easy enough to gather all that from her without a brain tap. It was written all over her face.

Suddenly she furiously slammed her fist on the table. "*Do* something about it, will you! Find out what Bergen copied and recover it! Can't you people understand this is crucial?"

"We do." Eric straightened and glanced at the mirror Jack stood behind. "Do *you* know what information was copied?"

"No! How would I know? But it was on a secure computer in a lab that's kept locked. I can't think it was merely a grocery list."

He ignored the sarcasm. "And you're certain you could identify the man?"

"Absolutely." She glared at Eric. "I'd know him anywhere."

Eric looked down at her and smiled. "Thank you, Agent Moon. We will be wanting your help with that. And please don't worry, we are on this, using all the resources we've got."

Her expressive mouth dropped open and her dark eyes widened to the max. His sudden switch to civility apparently shocked her.

He still couldn't read her. Some people were like that, but he was usually able to get around it given a little time and the right circumstances. He wasn't worried.

"Excuse me for a minute," he said, acknowledging both her and Holly with the request. With that he left the room and joined Jack in the next one.

The minute the door closed, Jack asked, "Well?"

"For what it's worth, I believe she's telling the truth, but I have to admit, she's not a good subject. You know as well as I do there are some heads I can't crack. She could be one. Whether that's by chance or her own design is anybody's guess at this point. However, *all* of her physical and verbal responses indicate she's innocent and being perfectly honest. I'd bet on it."

Jack nodded. "I agree. She was the one who made the call even if she was a little tardy about it. Of course, she could be covering her ass by giving us Bergen's. He's dead and can't defend himself."

"But you don't think that's the case," Eric said. "Neither do I. I'd stake my reputation that her story's legit, even if she is a closed book, mindwise."

"It's early yet to be that definite, given that you can't read her thoughts. We can't afford to be wrong about this. Could you try a little remote viewing? See if you can pick up anything on this guy?"

"If I had something he'd touched, it might work, but as it stands, your guess about what's going on is as good as mine." Eric glanced through the mirror at Dawn Moon. "I believe her."

Jack held his silence for a minute. "Okay, I'm releasing her. Let's put her to work with you. She can positively ID the man. I will be Control on this op. Holly, Will and Joe will assist in the internal investigation here at the Bureau. Clay will assist you and Moon. Money was probably Bergen's motive for selling out. The buyers' incentives will be varied. You will be one of them."

"Terrorists will be lined up," Eric said with a sigh. "Al-Qaeda right up front."

"We'll have to work on that assumption. That shield would be perfect for concealing activity in desert training camps. You'll go in as Al-Dayal," Jack said. It wasn't a question. He glanced through the mirrored window into the interrogation room, where Dawn Moon waited impatiently for what would happen next. "Wherever this leads, you'll take her with you."

Eric didn't want to work with Agent Moon, not on this. "I'm best alone on jobs like this, Jack. If I go into it as a potential buyer, that means some high-wire walking with no net. If you insist on my having backup, I'll take Clay. At least he has a working knowledge of Arabic."

Clay Senate was the guy to have at your back, a quiet mountain of bronze muscle with keen intelligence to match his physical strength. His marksmanship skills were legendary, and, even without a weapon, he was lethal. It always amazed Eric how a man of Clay's size and appearance could blend into any environment and go virtually unnoticed until he decided to strike.

Mercier countered the argument, if not the suggestion. "Don't worry, Clay will be involved. A money man like Al-Dayal naturally would have a bodyguard and Clay will fit the bill, but I want Moon with you, too."

"Consider, Jack. If this goes where I think it will, a woman wouldn't be any good to us where meetings are concerned. She'll have to stay secluded in the damn hotel."

"Then you can use a micro-cam and feed her faces to look at. I want her with you. Maybe this shooter is only a thug working on behalf of some organized group, but I have a strong feeling this job is a one-man show. I want that man."

Well, that settled that. One did not argue with Jack's

strong feelings. Also, the agent in charge had the final say. Eric followed Jack's gaze, watching the woman work to control her nerves. "Will you be clearing this mission with her director?"

"Not necessary. For all intents and purposes, Moon's ours until we are satisfied she's given us all she knows, so that won't be an issue. And it could be that Bergen's not the only one in his outfit who was involved in this. Let's keep the whole thing close to the vest until we see how it plays out. You can manage Moon, can't you?"

When you can't read her thoughts. Eric understood the unspoken addition to Jack's question. "Sure. Her face is an open book, even if her mind isn't. If I see any indication that she's a liability, I'll notify you and you can have her yanked."

Mercier nodded. "Fine. I'll call John Q. and have appropriate passports and identification readied since you can't go in as Americans. You might try teaching her a few words of Arabic."

"No, that won't be enough. I guess I could pass her off as my wife. Say she's…Andorran or something. Yeah, that would work since that country is located between France and Spain and she's fluent in those two languages, according to her record."

Fifteen minutes later, Eric returned to the interrogation room where Jack and Holly waited with Agent Moon. She was reviewing photos of possible suspects on Holly's laptop and apparently having no luck.

He entered and approached the table. "I think Bergen sent you on the security gig because he intended you to take the fall for this."

"Why didn't he just steal it and be done with it?" Dawn demanded. "He was perfectly capable. Why set up such an elaborate scheme and involve me?"

Eric explained, "If you look at it from his perspective, it's not a bad plan to get what he wanted and deflect any suspicion from himself. He was too large to crawl through the vents, the one vulnerable point of entry. Obviously you two discussed this hole in security for his report after you did the scheduled daytime analysis with the escort, so you knew exactly how to get inside. That much was detailed in his write-up, very carefully."

"I did get inside. That was the plan. *His* plan."

Eric continued as if she hadn't spoken. "If he had lived, he could have reported that you decided to take advantage of it without sanction, went in at midnight and copied the info. Caught in the act by the tech, you eliminated him and went out the way you came in. You knew the tech's body would be found, the theft discovered, so you disappeared. He would have seen that you did."

"Unless that technician's still alive and corroborates my story, you know I can't prove it didn't go down exactly like that," Moon admitted. "But it didn't."

She remained still as death, her eyes like brown lasers.

Eric agreed that it hadn't. "Bergen entered with the tech's cooperation, unwilling or otherwise. The tech punched in his codes and provided iris and print identification. Bergen would have known how to circumvent the surveillance cameras. No one shows up on those as entering by normal means, even the tech."

"The tech is dead," she said in a small voice.

"Yes. And the surveillance tapes are copies of one night last week when the place was deserted. Bergen was a busy guy."

"So you *do* believe me," she said, exhaling with relief.

"Enough to arrange for your help in the mission. We need to catch the shooter and grab that information before it hits the wrong hands. For the duration of this investigation, you'll be my partner. We're going after this guy, Agent Moon, wherever that takes us."

"Any objections to following through on this?" Mercier stated it like a challenge to her, implying that if she refused, they might suspect that she was in on the theft with Bergen, an accessory to treason and murder.

She'd see it as a test. Eric sensed her hesitation and didn't blame her for it.

He almost hated Mercier for leaving her with that fear, for using it to gain her compliance and take away her choice. This would be a damned dangerous mission. Really dicey. Her training was probably adequate for deep cover work, but according to her file, she had no experience in it at all. Diving in headfirst was a hell of a way to get her feet wet.

She seemed to consider for a few seconds, then shook her head. "No. No objections. I want to do whatever I can." Still, she looked doubtful about why they wanted her in on it.

Eric turned to her and smiled. "The NSA trained all the trust right out of you, didn't they?"

She shrugged and issued a bitter half laugh. "Apparently not thoroughly enough. I trusted Bergen."

"Will you be able to trust *me,* Dawn?" he asked, using her Christian name for the first time, his voice brisk to cover the soft spot developing where she was concerned.

She had been betrayed by one of her own, a man she had trusted implicitly. Eric sympathized. It would be hard to place that much faith in anyone she worked with next.

He glanced at Jack Mercier, his own supervisor, fellow agent and friend, and could only imagine how he would feel if Jack had done that to him.

Dawn Moon stood, her fingertips splayed on the tabletop. The brown eyes hid behind her long lashes and the expressive lips tightened before she replied. "I have no choice but to trust you if I want to vindicate myself completely, do I?"

"None whatsoever," Eric agreed. "The trust has to begin now because we'll be joined at the hip for the duration of this op." He paused for effect. "In case Bergen wasn't working alone on this end, you'll need to stay off the radar. We're going to my place for the first stage of preparation."

She looked warily from him to Mercier and back again. "We'll need to stop by my apartment and pick up a few things."

"No. We'll take care of that," Jack promised. He cleared his throat and looked pointedly at Eric, then at her. "We'll take care of *you*."

"Absolutely," Eric added. He offered her his most confident smile.

Agent Moon was no fool. She knew where the road paved with good intentions led. She also knew there could be giant potholes and detours along that route.

Chapter 2

Dawn woke with a headache. She needed caffeine in the worst way. Sun streamed through the window. Squinting, she propped up in bed on her elbows. This wasn't her apartment. Not her room. Where the hell was she?

She was wearing nothing but her black sports bra and panties. When had she ever slept in a bra?

"Oh," she groaned and collapsed back on the pillow as memory intruded. She was at Vinland's place, an old federal-style house in one of the more exclusive sections of McLean. Though time was of the essence, he had brought her here for a few hours of sleep before they began their mission in earnest.

She didn't want to get up and face more questions. He would probably want her entire life story and everything she'd done since kindergarten. There were certain off-the-record incidents she'd just as soon not recall out loud, especially to him.

Bathroom first, then coffee, she decided. She remembered where the john was. Groggy and grumpy, she crawled out of bed and made it across the room, her bare feet all but dragging. She was incredibly tired.

She yanked open the door to the bathroom and froze. Vinland stood in front of the mirror, a towel around his hips, his face half covered with shaving cream, razor suspended as he stared at her. Looking past him, she saw the connecting door to the other bedroom standing open.

Again she groaned and turned around, pulling her door shut. He grabbed it and swept it open again. "Didn't you sleep at all? You look like hell."

She glared at him from beneath her lashes and growled, "Yeah, and you're so beautiful."

Okay, he *was,* all lean, corded muscles and beach-boy good looks. But male beauty didn't interest her at the moment. "Where's the coffee before I disintegrate?"

"Hallway, go left, downstairs and follow the scent." His sandy eyebrows lowered. "You're not sick, are you?"

That question didn't rate an answer. Of course she was sick. Sick at heart. Bergen's plan had probably ruined her career. This cloud of suspicion could follow her until she was forced to resign or was fired. Or worse yet, arrested and imprisoned.

She plodded to the door across the room and followed his directions to the kitchen. She was nearly naked, but why bother with more clothes? He had already seen her in her underwear and didn't seem greatly affected by it. Small wonder about that if she looked like she felt, and she *must.* He'd even said she looked like hell.

Dawn knew she had no choice but to work with these people, this man in particular. Sure, Vinland struck her as a little too cocky, but the National Security Agency had no place for an agent with a question of treason on her record. She needed to prove beyond a shadow of a doubt that Bergen had intended to set her up. They needed her to identify one of the players. That was the only reason she was getting this chance and she knew it.

Even so, she did not plan to assume an attitude of gratitude with these Sextant agents or simply play tagalong while they solved this. She had a job to do, and they might as well realize that from the get-go.

She wanted to do this for a number of reasons. There was the guilt she felt for not having a clue what Bergen had been up to, even though he had given her no reason to suspect him of anything. No matter how many times she replayed last night's mission in her mind, she could think of nothing that might have alerted her to his intent. Still, she felt a grave personal, and professional, responsibility to ensure that his attempt to sell state secrets did not succeed.

Though she had only known him for a few weeks, Dawn had viewed him as the quintessential agent in charge. All business, no banter, distinguished in both dress and manner, Bergen had neither lorded his seniority over her nor tried to be her friend. He'd simply given her orders and she had obeyed them without question, trusting in what she had been trained to do. Trusting him, simply because he had possessed the experience and the authority to run the operation.

Would she ever be able to obey like that again, without reserve? Not likely. This whole experience could wreck her career in more ways than one.

If the information that Bergen had stolen, ostensibly to sell, remained in terrorist hands long enough to be implemented, it could well be devastating. She had no clue precisely what it was and wasn't sure she wanted to know, but it had to be critically important to rate this much attention from Sextant.

The delicious beckoning of freshly ground coffee beans perking led her by the nose to his kitchen. She inhaled the scent that might make her human again, poured herself a cup and loaded it with sugar. She loved sugar.

Footsteps behind her indicated Vinland was risking contact again. She downed the remainder of her coffee and refilled the mug, pouring one for him, too.

He reached for the cup, and his fingers brushed hers as he took it from her. Dawn made a fist and struggled to ignore the tingling sensation that spread through her from that lightest of touches. The man was lethally handsome. He even smelled terrific. Could be tough or gentle and knew when to be which, a quality that appealed to all women. Small wonder she reacted the way she did. It was perfectly natural, and she could handle it.

She watched as he opened the cabinet and retrieved a box of doughnuts. Uh-oh, the way to her heart. Dawn squelched a smile. Trust him to intuit her weakness.

They took seats at the table where he proceeded to open the sweets. He didn't hurry. It was as if he taunted her a little. He lifted a doughnut from the box and held it out as if anticipating that first bite. "Jack called earlier," he said. "They ran the plates and the car was rented with a bogus ID. He will have ditched it. Soon as it's found, we'll have a lead to follow." Then he took a bite out of a chocolate-covered confection and pointed at her with what was left. "We'll get him."

Unable to resist a minute longer, Dawn reached over and snagged what looked like a lemon-filled doughnut. "Right. I'm sure he left a forwarding address in the glove compartment. Or maybe we can call in the psychics."

Vinland's brow furrowed as he swallowed and thunked down the remains of his doughnut. "Look, we need to get something straight before we get started."

"Oh, spare me the drill. I get it. I *know* you're in charge and I'm not in the habit of trampling male egos. You lead, boy wonder, and I won't even protest. I'll do whatever you say."

He looked a little taken aback, probably because she wasn't bowing at his feet for this opportunity.

"All right, then," he said finally. "Do you want to know what I'm going to do to you?"

That opened her eyes. "*Do* to me?"

His boyish grin didn't sit well with her. "Work with you so you don't sound and look so American. But first I need to talk to you a little more. Get better acquainted."

That might have sounded appealing, except for the way he'd said it. "I thought we did that on the way here." She waved a hand. "So talk."

"Look at me," he instructed, taking the seat across the small table from her. "Take my hand."

"Ha, right. Spare me the lame come-ons, will you?" Dawn scoffed. She didn't want to touch him and feel that tingle again. Or maybe she wanted it too much. Like a third doughnut she knew she'd better say no to. "Just get on with it and ask what you want to ask."

He took her hand anyway. Dawn started to retract it, but decided that so far the gesture seemed harmless enough. Maybe he was only trying to put her at ease. If that was what he had in mind, it sure wasn't working. She tingled in spite of herself. Her skin grew warm, and she was afraid she was blushing all over.

His hand was smooth, the nails clipped straight across and very clean. Calluses ridged the outer edges of his palm and his knuckles were slightly enlarged. All in all, nice hands. Large and warm. Hers felt hot and were probably a little damp.

He gripped her fingers tighter. What was with the hand-holding? If he meant to get any chummier than that, he had another think coming. But when she attempted to pull away, he held her fast, threading his fingers through hers. She glanced up from their joined hands.

His intense look surprised her. The bluest eyes in the world bored into hers as if seeking the secret of the universe. She couldn't look away. Hypnosis? No, she didn't feel the least bit woozy. As a matter of fact, the sugared coffee and doughnut were kicking in and the energy from them had perked her up. Or maybe he did that. The old hormones were alive and kicking, no doubt about that.

Yep, Vinland was a great-looking guy. Exactly the kind she wouldn't trust. She had learned that lesson all too well and twice over. She made herself remember what she'd love to forget.

Her first affair had been with a research assistant in her second year of college. Thomas had had a similar wicked grin, same golden-boy looks as Vinland, same know-it-all attitude, too. She'd found out too late it was a know-*them*-all attitude and ol' Tom was keeping score, a dumping offense if she'd ever encountered one.

Her second lapse of sanity involved a fellow student at the academy. Nice guy, Scott. She had begun to have wonderful visions of something permanent when she found out he had sugared up to her for tutorial reasons. So much for being loved for one's mind. As soon as he passed, she was history.

Given how Bergen had so recently dashed her ability to judge the character of a man, Dawn could no longer trust her professional assessment, much less her personal instincts, when it came to men.

She wasn't falling again, no way.

Vinland equaled danger if she didn't gear down and treat him like artwork. And he was a piece of work for sure.

Finely textured skin, slightly tanned. Those shoulders definitely saw the inside of a gym on a regular basis. His hair gleamed a sort of pale brown with blond highlights. Bottled lights? She wondered. His eyes mesmerized, an almost iridescent blue with long, sexy lashes any woman would covet.

The mouth looked a little too firm at the moment, but she remembered how sensuous it had appeared before when he was more relaxed. Didn't hurt to admire, though doing so did jack up her tension to an uncomfortable level.

Her feeling that way, she understood, but why was *he* so uptight right now?

"Can't you think of anything to say?" she asked. "You're the one who wanted to talk."

He shook his head a little sharply and glanced away from her. "Something's not… Excuse me," he said, releasing her hand and getting up. "I'll be back in a minute."

She shrugged when he left. Maybe he didn't quite know what to make of her. Despite her better judgment, she grabbed another doughnut, a yummy glazed one, swearing to herself that she would work it off later.

He returned in a few minutes clutching her black shirt. Though she was covered better than she would have been in a bathing suit, she *was* sitting there in her undies. Modesty wasn't a big thing with her. Maybe it was with him.

Dawn licked her sticky fingers and reached for the shirt to put it on, but he didn't let it go. Those blue eyes followed her every move.

"Sorry about that," she said with an embarrassed chuckle. Again, she tugged at the shirt. "I'll get dressed now."

"No."

"Yes!" she insisted, snatching the garment from his grasp. "What is it with you?"

Whatever it was, it didn't seem limited to lust. Vinland seemed worried, distracted.

"Would you mind sitting down again?" he asked politely.

"I really need to get some clothes on." She held up the shirt he had brought her. "I shouldn't have come down here in my skivvies. Guess I've lived alone too long."

He nodded relutantly and turned away. "Later, then."

"Is something wrong?" she asked over her shoulder.

He shook his head, but it didn't seem like it was in answer to her question. Instead, he was frowning and looked seriously puzzled about something, and she knew it had to do with her.

Dawn went back to the bedroom where she'd slept and put on the rest of her clothes. Vinland was one strange dude. If he couldn't even get it together to brief her on what they were planning to do, how could she depend on him to run this investigation?

Maybe she should have a word with Jack Mercier about it. Trouble was, she had no idea how to get in touch with his boss without asking Vinland for the number and telling him why she wanted it.

Oh hell, maybe Vinland also just needed a lot of coffee before he could function. She could understand that.

Eric had hoped that Dawn's blocking his attempts at establishing a telepahic connection was a temporary thing, caused by Bergen's blow to her trust. Shields definitely went up at times like that.

That's all it was, he decided. Once she got past that shock and her defenses went down, he'd read her like a novel in oversized print. This morning's repeated efforts didn't signal failure, only delay.

Touching her hadn't helped at all. In fact, it only

confused things more. He hadn't gotten anything from handling her clothing, either.

All Eric had to do today was get their ducks in a row. The first order of business was to get Dawn disguised, brief her about the details of the mission and get her adjusted to him and their new looks. Also, to get himself comfortable with *her,* Eric admitted.

The truth was, he felt a little out of control around Dawn Moon, on both a professional and a personal level. He felt different, less and yet more. Deprived of something, but somehow more complete. It made no sense to feel that way.

He rummaged around in the side pocket of his carry-on bag for the case containing his glasses. Maybe that was the key. He hadn't had his glasses on, either last night or this morning. On the flight into D.C. from Seattle, he had slipped them off to take a short nap and put them away. In his hurry to deplane and report for duty, he had forgotten about them since he didn't need them to see.

Over the years, they had become almost like a light switch that regulated his ability. Though they were nothing but very lightly tinted glass, they had always seemed to block, or at least filter, the thoughts of others that used to bombard him unexpectedly.

He thought back to his arrival at the interrogation. He had immediately picked up on Jack's belief that Dawn was not guilty. He had read Holly's sympathy for Dawn before okaying her visit to the ladies' room. But the inner thoughts of Dawn Moon had remained a mystery.

Since seeing her for the first time, he hadn't read anyone, he realized. There had been a crazy moment of sheer, unadulterated peace. Always, for as long as he could remember, he had endured background noise in his mind, something like constant static. Thoughts of others bombarding him from every direction, held at bay only by doing some blocking of his own. At the moment his eyes had met Dawn's, that had ceased like magic.

He had grabbed it like a blessed reprieve he couldn't bear to give up. It lingered even now. Even when he needed it to go away.

The specs were merely a psychosomatic screen—he knew that—but whatever worked, he had learned to use. He'd put his glasses on now, then take them off after he got Dawn used to being around him. Surely then he would have no problem knowing her every thought.

Eric knew the reasoning was somehow faulty. He also was trying too hard. And maybe loving that clarity of mind and near silence in his head a little too much.

"Hey, Moon, you dressed?" Dawn jumped when Vinland called out to her through the bathroom door. He knocked a couple of times, then opened the door to the guest room.

She was fully clothed, looking out the window, but turned when he entered. "Where are we going?"

"Nowhere, yet."

"Hey, better lose the granny glasses," she suggested. "They make you look like Brad Pitt in that movie where he played a wimp." Actually, he looked too scrumptious for words in those things. The glasses hinted at a hidden vulnerability that made him seem even more approachable, something she did not need at the moment.

He laughed at her insult and reached up, taking off his eyewear. When he had pocketed them, he looked directly at her, his expression growing almost fierce in its intensity.

A few seconds passed and he lightened up, shrugging and shaking his head as if what he saw in her disappointed him.

Damn the man, then. She tossed her hair back with one hand and could have kicked herself for the high-school-ish gesture.

For the remainder of the morning, Dawn shared the tension as they waited on the call from Mercier.

Vinland left her alone for a few hours, but he didn't go out. Instead, he stayed in his home office on the phone and the computer.

The door remained open. She gave him a cursory wave as she passed on her way to the kitchen, but she didn't intrude. What was it that agents like Vinland did to prepare for a mission? she wondered.

He joined her around four in the afternoon in his den, where she was clicking through the TV channels, finding nothing interesting to watch.

"Want some popcorn?" he asked, strolling over to thumb through his DVD collection. "How about pizza? I could order one."

"No way," she said, looking at him now instead of the television. He wore faded jeans and a T-shirt that simply said Navy with a tiny cartoon of a seal underneath the word.

"You don't like pizza? Now *that* is un-American," he stated categorically, shaking a finger at her. "You're obviously some kind of alien. Not a foreigner, but a strange being from another planet."

Dawn laughed and abandoned the remote. "I was going to say you'd better order *two*."

He clutched his chest and rolled his eyes. "Thank God."

With a flourish, he popped in a DVD without asking her what movie she wanted to watch. It was a chick flick, an old one. Dawn smiled at his consideration, though she really preferred action/adventure.

She didn't intend to watch it, anyway. This bit of

downtime was a perfect opportunity for her to find out what kind of agent, and what kind of man, she was dealing with.

So far, nothing about Vinland seemed consistent. One minute he acted stern and uncompromising, the next polite and considerate; then he'd tease her and make her laugh. Who was he, really?

She listened while he joked around on the phone with the pizza person and tried to con them into adding extra olives for free. He quirked an eyebrow at her, as if asking if she approved the request. Dawn nodded enthusiastically. He wound up paying extra, but apparently enjoyed the verbal exchange.

He seemed to enjoy practically everything, she noticed. Only once in a while did he go all serious, and then not for long. One thing about him: he didn't exhibit the wary reluctance to reveal personal things about himself that agents in their business usually did.

He obviously loved his house and spent a great deal on it. Expensive antiques looked very much at home here, complemented by exquisitely framed original art. She noted he preferred realistic to abstract, traditional over modern. Though masculine in tone, the style of the place felt welcoming, warm, friendly. Like Vinland himself. Or, maybe he had simply hired a good decorator, she thought with a shrug. There were photos everywhere, a great many of them of women. Beautiful women.

She pointed to one in particular. "Is that who I think it is?"

He nodded. "Bev Martin."

"The actress?" Dawn was impressed. "You know her?"

Again he nodded and added a grin. "She's a good friend."

More than that, Dawn would bet. Here was a man who had no trouble attracting females. Of all ages, judging by his collection of pictures. The one of the actress she recognized was no publicity photo, but a candid shot of sexy Bev relaxing in the very recliner that sat across the room. "She's very beautiful."

"Yeah, nice person, too," he admitted readily, then promptly changed the subject. Or maybe not. "You going with anyone in particular? I'm only asking in case you need to excuse your absence for a week or so."

"Not at the moment." Not in the last few years, but she wasn't admitting that much to him or anyone else. "What about you?"

"No excuses needed," he assured her without really answering the other part of the question. Maybe Miss Martin understood what he did for a living and knew better than to expect explanations for his absences.

Dawn curled her feet under her on the comfy suede sofa and lay back against the cushions, stretching her arm along the back. "I love your place. Have you lived here long?"

He glanced around. "Almost two years. Bought it just before I left the Navy."

"You're not from here, though," she guessed. His accent was pure Boston. Upper class, too. No doubt an Ivy Leaguer, a Princeton or Harvard man. "Massachusetts, right?"

"Good ear," he said, approving her skill. "And you...let me see...from New Jersey."

"Right," she admitted. "But you didn't get that from my accent. I don't have one."

"Right, you don't," he admitted with a smile. "Read your file." He plopped down beside her, his leg almost touching her knees.

"That is so unfair. I know nothing about you."

"Sure you do." He plucked at the front of his shirt. "I'm ex-Navy. I like old stuff," he said, glancing around at the antiques gracing his den. "Vintage movies and pizza," he added with a nod at the television. "And I've just revealed that I'm unencumbered socially. So what else do you want to know?"

"How'd you get into this business?" Somehow he just didn't seem the intelligence-agent type with that openness of his and the laid-back attitude. Or was that merely a front?

He pursed his lips for a minute, making her stare at their perfection. She hated it when a man made her gawk. He relaxed them and cut his gaze sideways. "Well, I kept getting seasick. The Navy tossed me out and Jack felt sorry for me, cast ashore like that with nowhere to go. Told me if I'd behave like a spy, he'd let me hang out with him and his team for a while."

Dawn laughed. "So you try to behave."

"Sometimes. I keep waiting for him to throw me back, but I guess he'd have nobody to razz if he did."

"Don't tell me you're the team screwup."

"No, but I do believe a sense of humor helps get you through the dark times. Take yourself too seriously and it's harder to roll with the punches, don't you think?"

Dawn did. Odd how he seemed to want her to understand him. He had divulged a lot about himself. "You take the job seriously, though," she guessed.

"Damn straight."

Right. She picked at the luxurious fringe on the pillow beneath her hand and caressed the woven tapestry fabric. She loved this room and everything in it. It suited him perfectly, or at least what she thought she knew of him now. "You have either great taste or a good decorator."

"Thanks." But he didn't indicate which.

Dawn suspected he had chosen everything in his house himself, and did it with an eye for comfort and quality. The painting above the mantel was of a woman who looked a bit like him. "Who's that?"

"My grandmother," he said with an openly affectionate look at the portrait. "Also my favorite person. She died a few years ago and I still miss her."

The woman in the picture told Dawn even more than Eric had. He was obviously from old money and from a family well established in society. She recognized his grandmother from articles in national news magazines and knew why Eric's features had seemed a bit familiar to her.

"Of the Boston Pricevilles," Dawn murmured under her breath, not realizing she had spoken out loud until he replied.

"Mother's people," he said. "The Vinlands are the outlaws."

Dawn laughed at his wry expression, loving the way his brow wrinkled in one spot, right between his golden, perfectly arched eyebrows. "Now that sounds interesting. A mésalliance?"

"A disaster, but that's a story for another day." He pushed up from the sofa, tapped his temple with one finger and headed out of the room. "Pizza's coming up the walk."

How did he know that? There was no window facing the front of the house and she hadn't heard a car outside. Still, the doorbell chimed before he reached the hall.

That was downright spooky, she thought, until the clock on the mantel beneath the portrait chimed, too. Twenty minutes since he had ordered. Of course. He was probably a regular customer. For a minute there, she'd wondered if he was psychic. Not that she believed in such things.

Chapter 3

For the rest of the afternoon and evening, they tacitly agreed to place thoughts of the job on hold and try to relax. The mission would be exhausting emotionally, perhaps even physically, and they both knew it. It paid to go into something like this with a cool head and senses firing on all cylinders.

They talked of their preferences and opinions regarding current events, books and movies, things a couple generally did when getting acquainted. Dawn wasn't certain why that thought came to mind. She certainly didn't want to be half of a couple.

That certainty slid right out of her mind when they called it a night, however. He took her hand to help her up from the sofa where they had been sitting a circumspect three feet apart for nearly two hours. His fingers interlocked with hers, he raised their hands and planted a kiss on the back of hers as their eyes met and held. Her heart stuttered and she leaned toward him, drawn by an unseen force.

Uh-huh, lust, she reckoned when he stepped back and released her hand.

"Good night," he said, gesturing for her to precede him out the door. "Breakfast is at six. Expect a long and busy day."

Dawn felt so rattled, she couldn't say a word. She quickly turned to go up the stairs and didn't dare glance back at him. If she did, she knew she would have a look of invitation plastered all over her face. He might take her up on it, and that would be bad. Then again, he might refuse, and that would be even worse.

She hardly slept at all and when she did, she dreamed of him. As dreams went, these were definitely rated X, fantasies originating in a Georgian town house, sweeping across desert sands and landing in a silken tent with a Valentino-garbed Vinland doing what old silent-movie sheikhs are prone to do. *Prone* being the big word for her, too.

The next morning, Dawn consigned everything that had happened the night before to a file in her mind labeled Forbidden. No way would she take it out and study it in depth, not after what she'd dreamed.

Vinland had only been managing her, she told herself. Mentor to novice, agent in charge to junior agent. If it had been a test, then she had passed, kept her hands and thoughts to herself.

Breakfast proved to be simple. Coffee, cereal chock-full of vitamins, milk and a banana were all ready and waiting for her when she came downstairs. They ate in silence, he as lost in his thoughts as she was in hers, neither mentioning that brief moment when the current of longing had zapped them. She knew he had felt it, and he surely knew that she had.

"Go on upstairs," he said when she had finished. "I'll be up in a few minutes. We need to get started."

She rose and escaped, or that was what it felt like. Maybe a few minutes alone would give her time to shore up her defenses. The man was majorly messing with her hormones, and she resented it.

He arrived ten minutes later, coming through the bathroom that joined their bedrooms.

"First thing we need to do is change your appearance." He held up a kit he had retrieved from his bedroom and plucked out a box. "You want to dye first or shall I?"

Dawn quirked one auburn eyebrow at him and her lips softened into a natural smile. The way he made her feel was not his fault. Vinland couldn't help being as handsome as he was and owning the drawbacks that went with it. She could be kind without losing her head over him. Look at all the practice she'd had.

"I'll go first," she offered.

"Leave your hair wet when you finish coloring it. I'll need to style it."

Somehow she could not imagine him as a hairdresser. "Multitalented, are you?"

"We'll see how you feel about that when I'm done." He grinned and tossed her the box of hair dye.

"Why are you disguising me? The guy didn't see me, I'm sure of that. He'd have killed me if he had. And if someone else at NSA was working with Bergen, they could identify me, disguised or not."

"No one will recognize you when I get through," he assured her. "Besides, no one at your agency will be in on this, except you. They're totally out of the loop until everyone who had contact with Bergen is cleared. Safe to say, you won't be running into any of your fellow agents where we're going."

"Where will that be?" she asked, wondering if he was sharing all he knew.

"Waiting to find that out, but I can almost guarantee it won't be this side of the pond."

Vinland grinned his wicked grin and pointed at the hair dye she held. "It's a good trick when going undercover, a self-perception thing. Changing your looks will alter your whole personality. See yourself differently and I guarantee you won't act the same." He spread his hands wide. "You'll be a blank slate when we're done, and become who I need you to be."

Oh great. "And just who is that?" she asked, fascinated by the concept, if not wild about participating in it.

"Wait and see," he said cryptically. Then he added, "And try to be open-minded, will you?"

Dawn almost laughed, and bitterly at that. He really didn't need to know all the things that crossed her mind when he was around.

An hour later, Dawn realized that her own father wouldn't recognize her. And Vinland wasn't finished with her yet.

Her hair was very dark brown now and straight as a stick. Vinland had expertly trimmed it in a blunt cut, several inches shorter than her former length, and used a flat iron to smooth out every vestige of curl. She'd been trying to do that for years. Amazing man.

She blinked at her reflection, getting used to the style he had created with such dexterity. Their breath had mingled as he'd drawn the scissor-like heated panels of the straightening iron through the sections of hair that framed her face.

He had lingered as he worked, touching her forehead, lifting her chin, caressing an ear. Those marvelous fingers worked their magic, both on her hair and her libido.

He had been so close then, her nostrils flared at the lime scent of his aftershave. And the damn pheromones he threw off along with it. Her cheeks were heated, and so were other parts she didn't want to think about. Five-alarm fire sirens were screaming like crazy in her head.

His hands could be so gentle, she had trouble visualizing them performing anything like defense. But those calluses along his outer palms had not evolved through pampering. Martial arts, probably karate, studied over a considerable period of time would have formed them. Hers were similar, only not nearly as prominent as his.

"You will need to undress," he announced abruptly, all business.

"In your dreams," she replied evenly. "You had your show yesterday."

He held up a spray can, shaking it. "Got to tan you. Don't want to miss any spots."

"Hey, I'm not all that fair. Won't I do?"

"Well, I can't get you any lighter than you are, but the hair change isn't enough. Let's go a bit darker."

Oh well, she could stand that. Obediently, she stripped down to her bra and panties again, praying her nipples wouldn't peak. It was anything but chilly in the room, so there was no excuse. Well, there *was* one, but she didn't want to reveal that to him.

"Straps down, please," he snapped impatiently.

Carefully, Dawn slipped her arms out of the bra straps and hoped the cups would cling to her breasts and not fall down around her waist. Not much chance of that, since she was almost too well-endowed, a fact he was now noticing without trying to be obvious about it. Oddly enough, she didn't mind.

Just for good measure, literally, she inhaled deeply. No reason why she should be the only one suffering around here.

He quickly focused elsewhere. "Okay, hold out your arms," he ordered, his voice gruff as he continued coating her with the spray. Dawn figured he was fighting a little battle of his own now, but she refused to look down his body to check whether he was. Didn't matter.

Did...not...matter.

He crouched and stroked her legs with the spray, clearing his throat as he nudged her knee so he could get to her inner thighs.

Oh...my...goodness.

Dawn felt laughter well up in her throat. She coughed to cover it. This was so ridiculous. Which one of them was more awkward with this? Well, it was Vinland's idea to do it himself. Let him deal with it.

He stood quickly and turned away from her, depositing the can back into his kit that sat open on the bed. "There. All done. In a few minutes, you'll be brown as a berry, a deep Riviera tan with no streaks. Leave your clothes off until it dries."

"Leave my clothes off," she repeated dryly.

"Hey, you can trust me," he replied. "Scout's honor." Grinning, he held up three fingers in the official salute.

"You were a Boy Scout," she deadpanned.

"Oh, absolutely. Got a merit badge for ignoring naked women." He sighed, a woeful sound. "Of course, I was about ten at the time. A couple of years after that, I had to give it back."

"I'll just bet you did." She frowned into the mirror of the dresser and flicked back one side of the dark waves that fell to her shoulders. "I look strange. But not exactly Middle Eastern, if that's what you're going for."

"No, it's not, but you *do* look very different. The idea is to change your looks. You'll be surprised at how that will automatically alter your behavior, mannerisms, everything. Works wonders," he told her.

"Oh, so now I'll be flighty, disorganized and dumb?" she grumbled. "Tell me, how is this good for the mission?"

He grunted a laugh. "Cute. Now for the makeup." With a deep and audible breath of what sounded like frustration, he withdrew a smaller case out of the large one.

Dawn barely squelched a groan. More touching. Time to call a halt to this torture, or one of them was bound to cave and do something really, really stupid.

She hadn't been this revved up sexually since high-school graduation night when Harry Forsythe seduced her in the back of his parents' van. Her skin tingled like crazy and her pulse must have doubled by now. The sweet memory of old first love Harry vanished completely in light of the hot fantasies this guy stirred up. Thomas or Scott didn't even come to mind long enough to warrant a dismissal.

Then there was the debacle of her trusting Bergen too much. Not that she had ever had any personal attachment to the man, but his overwhelming betrayal had undermined whatever vestige of confidence she had in her dealings with men.

No use making these comparisons. She was not, definitely not and no *way*, about to allow any slap and tickle with beach boy agent, no matter how thoroughly he stirred up her hormones.

There was too much at stake. Her career, to begin with. Her reputation. Her credibility. Engaging in anything like that with him, considering her circumstances, would be disastrous. And there were the other reasons, she reminded herself. Better and more personal reasons than screwing up on the job. She couldn't do the sex thing casually. It just wasn't in her, and she knew it.

It irritated her that she couldn't, because she didn't need or want a commitment at this point in her life, even if the guy was willing to commit. Which Vinland never would be, she firmly reminded herself.

"I can handle the makeup," she declared, snatching the zippered makeup bag out of his hand. "Go do…whatever you need to do to yourself."

She meant for him start on his own disguise, of course, but her guilty glance at his body's reaction to her and his fierce frown told her he had briefly thought she meant something else entirely.

She couldn't help grinning at him.

To her surprise, he didn't shoot back some smart reply. Instead, he took the rest of the kit and stalked into the bathroom, leaving her alone.

Eric had to lean on the sink for a minute to get his equilibrium back. What was the matter with him?

This was one of his specialties. How many female agents had he assisted with disguises during his years with Intel and with Sextant? More than he could count. But this one, even with all her clothes on, did something powerful and unique.

She screwed up his concentration. She overturned his priorities. She aroused him without even being interested.

Generally speaking, he required at least a modicum of interest from the other party. Otherwise what was the point in letting himself get excited?

He had kissed her hand last night, an impulse he had regretted immediately. She'd hurried away the instant he'd let go of her. Maybe she feared sexual harassment on his part, since he was technically running the op and she was the secondary. Still, he didn't have the power to affect her career at NSA since he worked for a different outfit entirely. Surely she knew that.

No, fear wasn't a factor. Dawn wasn't above a little teasing, but he could tell she wasn't up for a tension-relieving tumble. Neither was he, not with a fellow agent. He had rules about that and suspected she did, too.

He looked in the mirror and blinked at his image. Why wasn't she interested? Ordinary-looking guy, he thought. Nothing special, but something about him usually drew women to him, he knew that. They probably sensed his innate love and appreciation of them. He rarely met a woman who didn't have something great to recommend her.

Bev, his friend and sometime lover, once told him that his main attraction was that he truly listened when she talked, that the intensity of his look, the fact that he met her eyes and held them, communicated real regard. Little did she know that he was probing her mind for what she really meant instead of paying attention to the words that came out of her mouth.

He sighed and looked away. If women only knew what a fraud he was, how he played to their own fantasies. That had begun when he was a spindly tenth-grade swimmer instead of the beefy quarterback he had longed to be.

Even though he had never used his mind-reading talent to score with girls, he had used it to insure that they liked and trusted him as a person. Consequently, he felt he had never had a real relationship untainted by his advantage.

Dawn would be the perfect woman to begin one with if he could leave the mind thing alone, abandon all attempts to read her and play it straight. It really bothered him, how much he wanted to do that.

Unfortunately, their present situation made that impossible. He had to keep trying, to somehow get inside her mind and see whether she harbored some little something that might help with this mission.

Not that he believed for a minute that she was holding out details on purpose. It was just that people often knew things they didn't realize they knew. Ferreting those out was what he did best. Usually.

In spite of the necessity and as selfish as it was, Eric almost hoped Dawn would keep blocking him. How much he wanted a chance of something lasting with her surprised and daunted him. The thought, the very idea of that, was premature to say the least. He hardly knew her. And yet he felt he knew Dawn better than other people whose minds were wide open to him. Why was that?

He clearly had the hots for her, but his feelings seemed to go well beyond that even now. His protective instincts had kicked in the second he saw her, even though he knew she had to have been trained to take care of herself.

Something quirky about Dawn had hooked him like a clueless trout and he couldn't for the life of him figure out what it was. Maybe the fact that he couldn't read her mind contributed, but there had been others like that whom he'd shrugged off without a pause. Not her. No shrugging.

No shagging, either, he reminded himself firmly. At least, not while they were working this job.

He turned on the cold water and splashed his face several times, then scrubbed it fiercely with a towel.

"Grow up and quit bellyaching," he muttered to his reflection. "Keep your focus on the game."

Eric reached for the kit on the countertop and set about becoming someone else.

Maybe when he switched identities and cultures, he could temporarily change his attitude toward her while he was at it. If he couldn't, he knew he was in the worst kind of trouble.

Chapter 4

Dawn nearly jumped out of her skin when Eric walked into the den. Until he grinned, she thought a stranger had broken in. Nothing could disguise that grin with its almost-dimples and flash of perfect white teeth, but everything else about him had changed radically.

He had dyed his skin darker than hers and his eyes were so black she couldn't distinguish pupil from iris. Even his eyelashes were inky, their fascinating golden tips a thing of the past. The makeup job was fantastic.

He wore a stark white silk shirt and loose trousers that had to be tailored and looked very expensive. On his head was a linen cloth with a crown of black cord to hold it in place.

His bearing had altered, too. As he walked over to her, she noted how his elbows rested nearer his body, his shoulders were not quite as straight as before and his gait seemed more measured. He gave the impression of being much more self-contained and reserved. If it weren't for that grin.

It vanished abruptly and he regarded her with a serious expression. Now he had become another man entirely. Dawn stared, transfixed and amazed. What a dress rehearsal. She could tell he was enjoying her reaction.

He bowed. "Greetings," he said simply, his voice a caress hot as a desert in July. He added another soft musical phrase, this time in Arabic, lifting the dark eyelashes that had briefly covered his taunting black eyes.

Dawn quirked an eyebrow. "May Allah bless you with many camels. And deliver you from flaky mascara."

He broke up, laughing so hard the ghutra toppled off his head. Still chuckling, he pulled off the embroidered skullcap he had worn beneath it and collapsed on the sofa beside her. "I wonder if anyone would notice duct tape over your mouth under your chador." He ran both hands through his jet-black hair, causing it to stand on end.

"Under my what?"

"Your chador, the traditional veil and robe you'll be wearing." he explained.

She scoffed, crossing her arms over her chest. "I am *not* wearing one of those. I would suffocate or dehydrate from sweating."

Eric sighed. "Your eyes, nose and mouth needn't be covered if you'll remember to keep your head down. Modest western dress is acceptable sometimes, of course, but the chador will be good cover for you, no pun intended."

"So you found out our shooter is headed for Sand Land?"

He sighed, smoothing out the wrinkles on his disguise's headgear and folding it neatly. "No. We don't know yet where the chase will lead, but we do know a buy will go down. It stands to reason there will be a few from that neck of the woods who will want this technology. I plan to be one of them."

"I just don't understand why you are going to these lengths to disguise *me?* I know you think it helps with the personality switch or whatever, but I could act differently than I do without all this. Who's gonna know I'm American?"

"I'm taking every precaution I can think of to prevent anyone finding out. You're supposed to be Andorran, of Spanish birth, but a convert to Islam, therefore not a Western wife. Otherwise, my credibility would be shot with these people. Hell, *I* might be shot if anyone even suspects who you really are. And you surely would be. Or worse."

She picked up the ghutra he had laid aside, giving it a cursory examination as she spoke, studying the intricately braided cord crown that held the linen head-covering in place. "Okay, I can play this part, but even I know enough about customs over there to know I won't be allowed to attend any meetings with you. You can't introduce me or even talk about me to any other men, and I probably won't be able to communicate with any of the women. Why take me along?"

His lips firmed and he shook his head as he smoothed down his spiky hair. "My first thoughts exactly and I told Jack as much, right up front. It was his idea, but I do see his point, despite my objections. You're the only one able to identify the man who killed Bergen and took the information from him."

"What good will that do?"

"Maybe then we could identify some of his associates. Find out where he fits in the scheme of things. I talked to Jack and they've located the car he abandoned at the airport. They lifted a few prints, but none are in our databases, so he hasn't officially made our list yet. We're waiting on Interpol to see what they have."

Dawn shivered every time she thought about who they were after, a soulless criminal who had killed a man in cold blood at close range and dealt with the scum of the world. "Okay, maybe the chador thing's not such a bad idea after all."

"I'll get you one that's top of the line," he said, leaning back and crossing one leg over his knee, tapping the back of the sofa with his fingers. "You know the logic behind making the women wear them?"

She blinked slowly and scoffed. "Oh, there's logic to that, you think?"

"Sure. They say if a man leaves his treasure out in plain view, other men will think it's for the taking. So he must conceal it."

"Then the ridiculous custom should work both ways. How would you men feel if we put sacks over your heads to ward off the competition?" she snapped.

He seemed to consider that for a minute, then shook his head. "Wouldn't work. See, guys will never steal a pig in a poke. They want to see what they're getting for their trouble. But women? They just can't seem to resist uncovering a mystery. Curiosity killed the cat."

"Speaking of animals…" She slammed him with a sofa cushion and got up, crossing her arms, and looking down at him. "You're the pig, Vinland. A truly chauvinistic pig."

"Hold on a minute and don't stomp out on me yet," he said, replacing the cushion and leaning forward. "We need to get a few language lessons going while we wait for our traveling papers. You'll need to know a few phrases in Arabic. It would seem strange if you hadn't picked up any from your husband."

"I know a little. One of my suite mates at college was Jordanian. Her English was good, but I had to help her with colloquialisms. She tried to prep me for a future visit to her part of the world. I think I learned enough to shop and order food."

His newly darkened eyebrows flew up. "Well, hurrah. That's gotta be an omen."

She paused, throwing him a jaded look. "Omen? Don't tell me you're superstitious."

He grinned again. "Sure am. Omens, signs, especially predictions. My grandma, who had the sight, warned me that one day a sharp-spoken woman with red hair would turn my life around. All these years, I thought it was my tenth-grade history teacher who straightened me out by threatening to flunk me. Now I know better." He spread his arms wide. "Just look at how I've changed since I met you."

"I never know when you're serious. This is never gonna work."

"It'll work," he promised, losing the grin. "It has to. I'm deadly serious about this mission, Dawn. There'll be no more joking around once we're on our way."

She nodded, sighed and walked over to the window, looking out again over the quiet neighborhood. The very essence of upper-middle-class America. "I wonder where we will be going," she murmured. "Exactly."

"Doesn't matter as long as it's where he and the stolen information are," he answered, approaching, placing a hand on her shoulder in what seemed a reassuring gesture. She felt the heat of his palm nearly scorch her skin. "For starters, if Allah is with us, we make the deal where it's relatively safe, identify all the parties involved, eliminate the threat and get out before the showdown."

"Are you Muslim?"

"Nope, Methodist. You?"

"Presbyterian." She turned, her face scant inches from his. "And if God's not providing us an easy solution?"

He shrugged. "We go wherever and do whatever it takes."

"Do you know what was stolen and what the outcome

will be if we aren't successful?" Dawn asked, moving away from him so she could concentrate. Lord, he had a force field or something that she knew she needed to avoid. It wasn't that easy when it was drawing her in like heavy-duty gravity.

"Kenro Applications. Ever heard of it?"

"They do atmospheric studies and evaluate ecological conditions here and in space, right?" she guessed.

"Yeah, that's right." He gave her a look of approval and indicated she should sit down again. When she did, he sat opposite her in the chair, leaning forward, elbows resting on his knees. "They're a NASA subcontractor, not a large company, extremely specialized. Some of the stolen data was research they had supplied."

"I'm getting a scary picture here," she muttered.

"You're familiar with Halmann Electronics?"

"Radar." She thought for a minute. "If you're saying Zelcon was working with both, then this has to do with testing a technology that's already developed?"

"Yes," he confirmed. As if only half paying attention to their conversation, he took her chin between his thumb and forefinger and turned her face this way and that. "More kohl on the lower eyelids, I think."

Dawn pulled back absently and pushed his hand away. "So we have specialized atmospheric alterations from this Kenro Apps. And radar from Halmann. The plans must have to do with producing some sort of antiradar thing, maybe a shield of some kind."

"Not producing it. We already have it and it's called AHSADS, an atmospheric dome to prevent any heat-seeking equipment on satellites from pinpointing human activity on the ground. The software for testing it is what they took."

Dawn experienced a chill. She stared into Eric's eyes, seeing her concern mirrored there. "To use over weapons development sites? Training facilities? God, there are any number of uses. Everybody with anything to hide from the world will want that. They can reconstruct it from the testing data, can't they? That would explain exactly how it works, what components are used and so forth?" she asked. "And if they do, it would seriously hamper our efforts to locate terrorist training camps and troop concentrations." She paused, thinking about that. "Anybody's."

He nodded slowly, holding her gaze.

"We have to get it back before they disperse it all over the place," she declared, grabbing his arm. "Our satellites would be useless."

"And seriously impact our intelligence-gathering capabilities." He placed his hand over hers where it clutched his sleeve. "They surely realize that exclusivity of the information will make it much more valuable, so it won't be offered to just anyone. I think there will be a bidding war among several potential customers who would benefit from the technology. They'll be the ones who have big bucks and also the resources to recreate it."

"Bidders like you, in your alternate persona as this Arab?"

"Yes. My job is to outbid the others while taking names. Yours is to see if the seller is the same guy you saw. I'll give you odds he's either the same dude who offed Bergen or a very close associate who'll want to be present when the deal goes down."

"Why would you think so?"

Eric's eyebrows drew together, his face unfamiliar without the light of humor. "Greed. The more partners involved in this, the less hefty the cut."

Dawn rubbed her hands together nervously, then

looked up at him. "How do you find out whom to contact and where?"

"Your None Such Agency, of course," he replied, using the sobriquet some had tacked on to her outfit back in the days when it was not supposed to exist. "Thank goodness your people at the National Security Agency have a finger on the pulse of every transmission worldwide. We'll make use of that. Or rather, *you* will, since we're well aware of what you did for NSA before you switched to fieldwork and started crawling through vents."

She laughed bitterly. "Are you kidding? They won't let me near our electronic brainiacs, not with this cloud of suspicion over my head. No way to hack into their tracking systems, either, trust me on that."

He took her hand, lacing his fingers through hers. "I do trust you, Dawn. So does Jack, or you wouldn't be here listening to all this. And," he added, with a pause for effect, "we wouldn't share the passwords we acquired."

So now he had let the cat out of the bag. She wasn't really a suspect at all. They knew she was innocent, or they'd never allow her in on something as critical as this. Her relief was so enormous, it nearly eclipsed the buzz of tension his nearness caused.

Eric sat quietly and watched while Dawn concentrated, her fingers flying over the computer keys. She had been at it for several hours. She would type like crazy, pause, cuss a little now and then, hum with satisfaction when she met with success, then repeat the process.

At Mercier's suggestion, Eric had brought her to their office in McLean where she could use the secure connections on their top-of-the-line computers in the room they called The Vault. The place always made Eric a little claustrophobic.

The fifteen-by-twenty windowless space was lead-lined and outfitted with every available protection against intrusion, physical or electronic. There was only one seriously fire-walled line leading in and out, a secure connection on which they could access whatever they needed in the way of top-secret sites.

Jack had worked for NSA and the setup here was similar, but on a much smaller scale. His former affiliations served him well in other ways, too. The passwords, however he had obtained them, got Dawn into the bank of sites set up by various terrorist organizations that NSA kept tabs on regularly.

She was searching those that might indicate new technology for sale on the underground market. Word had already gone out to less secure sites that something had recently become available. The timing of that indicated it could be the stolen data.

"Pay dirt!" Dawn whispered with excitement. "Eric, I think this is it. Look." She clicked another page on the benign-looking Web site and moved to one side so he could see. "There it is, the invitation. Arabic, French, Farsi, I think, and English."

Eric slipped on his glasses to cut the screen glare and read what she had found. "This is it! I *knew* you could do it," he said with pride.

He picked up the secure phone to Mercier's office. "Jack? We're ready to RSVP. And we have a name. An alias, of course, but we'll need to run it through Interpol and see if anything kicks out. He signs himself Quince."

"I'll handle that and join you shortly," Mercier said. He hurried into the computer room in less than five minutes.

"Good moves, Moon," he said with a perfunctory nod.

"How do we explain gaining access to their exclusive

client list?" Dawn asked Mercier while Eric e-mailed his acceptance, choosing his words carefully. The characters of the Arabic font strung out across the screen as he typed.

"We don't have to," Eric replied. "I'm attending as Jarad Al-Dayal, oil tycoon and secret leader of a very select Iranian group, ostensibly based in Qatar. Al-Dayal gives no explanations for his actions or how he gleans his information."

"And what if the real Al-Dayal also responds to this?"

He looked up at her as he clicked on Send. "Not a problem."

"Eric *is* Al-Dayal," Jack explained. "He is also the *group*. It has a remarkably deadly reputation in the world community, considering it has done absolutely nothing in the way of terrorist acts."

The computer pinged. In unison, they turned, staring at the message on the screen.

"Bingo. We have a destination," Jack murmured softly, as if the messenger could overhear. "You'll need to get going ASAP."

Dawn's lips rounded in a soundless, "Oh." Then her eyes narrowed. "This says Leros. Isn't that Greek?"

"Leros is in the middle of the Aegean, between Greece and Turkey," Eric announced.

"A Greek Island?"

He nodded. "And a fairly large one with a big tourist population. It's a much better location than I figured we'd draw. My money would have been on Qatar or Jordan, at best. Maybe we can ditch the chador and buy you a swimsuit."

Jack cleared his throat and looked disapproving. "You know that Leros is probably only your first stop. My guess is one of the privately owned islands where it will be next to impossible to get backup to you."

Eric smiled slyly. "I trust you'll *try,* Jack."

Mercier spoke to Dawn, ignoring Eric's aside. "If you would, please back us out of the connection without leaving traces. The plane is waiting. I'll call about the flight plan."

"What about a change of clothes?" she asked, her eyes on the screen as she pecked away at the keyboard. "I am *not* wearing these for the third day in a row."

"Taken care of," Eric said, "Trust me, everything's been ordered and you won't lack for clothes."

He saw her chin come up, a sure sign of rebellion. "I'd rather have picked out my own stuff, thank you very much. And besides that, you could have given me a little more warning that we fly immediately. I might have had things to take care of before we left."

"We've paid your utility bill," he assured her. "And you don't have a cat. The plants can be replaced. Your dieffenbachia is dying, anyway. You overwater."

"Since you've never seen my apartment, I'm not even asking how you know that," she snapped. "We're not flying commercial, I take it."

Eric laughed. "With all my oil money? Are you kidding? Private jet. Straight flight to Athens and a hop from there to Leros."

She gave a mirthless little laugh. He noticed her fingers tremble slightly over the keys when she paused to wait for a prompt. Was she nervous, scared or just eager to get under way?

This mission was unlike anything she had ever been involved with. He wished he could give her a hug right now, take her in his arms and promise her that she would be fine, that he would never take her with him if he didn't believe she could pull it off. There was no point beginning their partnership with a lie, however.

Maybe it would help if he let her know that her personal safety was one of his main concerns. Or maybe it wouldn't help. It could throw her off her game. It could throw him, too. The mission had to take precedence, and they both needed to keep that foremost in their minds.

Mercier was watching them closely, his shrewd gray gaze flicking from one to the other. Eric gave him a thumbs-up and then placed a hand on Dawn's shoulder and squeezed. Her muscles tensed beneath his palm and he could tell what an effort she made to steady her breathing.

Dawn was no novice in this business. He needed to stop worrying about her and coddling her. Nothing would undermine her self-confidence quicker than that.

Eric suddenly experienced a pang of gut-wrenching apprehension, but quickly dismissed it. He couldn't function in this role if he lost his absolute belief in the success of the mission. He also couldn't operate efficiently if he kept allowing that lovely little body of hers to snag his attention and work him into a sweat.

She finished exiting the program, got up from the chair and stretched.

"I'll transmit whatever we can find on this Quince while you're in flight," Mercier said.

Time for a test, one Eric felt extremely reluctant to make, but it had to be done. The removing-glasses trick had not worked with Dawn. He had tried it twice and given up. But Jack was a good subject, one he'd never had problems reading before and usually without even trying.

Eric took off his glasses and looked directly at Jack, fully expecting to glean whether the boss had anything in mind he wasn't saying. Nothing. Not even the white noise that usually accompanied an unsuccessful attempt to read someone. However, the failed attempt didn't worry Eric especially in spite of the surprise it provided. Maybe it was the room itself hampering things. God knows it blocked out everything else.

He slid his glasses back on and shook Jack's hand. They didn't say goodbye. He noted that Dawn followed suit, merely inclining her head to Mercier. Her lips were firm, her stance confident. Together they left silently and hurried down the hallway.

"If you're Al-Dayal, what's my name?" she demanded as he ushered her out to the car. She still wore that obstinate look, one that warned him she might be masking fear with anger.

"Aurora, my second wife. It means Dawn."

"I know that." She frowned up at him as she got into the vehicle. "Give me a break. So where is number one spouse these days?"

He peered down, keeping his expression serious. "No longer with us. She refused to follow orders."

"Okay, hotshot. I get the picture," she snapped as she grabbed the handle and slammed the door, nearly catching his fingers in the process.

He rounded the car and got in. Dawn being a little angry was better than Dawn shaking in her boots, he supposed, but she would have to get over both reactions and do it pretty damn quick. When they arrived at their destination, he needed a calm, subordinate spouse who would stay in the background. Somehow Eric had trouble imagining that.

He sighed and shook his head as he looked over at her and stuck the key in the ignition.

She was probably nervous as hell, but she was concealing it pretty well. Everything about this mission would be as foreign to her as a trip to Mars. He wished she were better equipped, that he could prepare her adequately, but there simply wasn't time for a full indoctrination. He'd just have to help her wing it.

Dawn appeared anything but subservient, and he wasn't altogether sure she could fake that. "Look, you *can* do this, okay?" he said.

She yanked her seat belt across her slender curves, clicked it in place and huffed. "Of course I can do this. I'll just pretend I'm my great-grandmother."

Eric cranked the car and pulled away from the curb, laughing. "Honey, I can't believe the women in your family were servile even that far back."

"Well, she managed up to a point. Until about two years into the marriage, so I was told."

Did he dare ask? "What happened then?"

Dawn smiled, eyes narrowed menacingly. "Granny got fed up and nailed his butt to the wall."

"Figuratively speaking, I hope."

"She shot him in the behind with a load of bird shot. I hear he never walked quite right after that."

Eric winced. "Can you restrain yourself for a week or so, you think?"

Dawn shrugged. "Probably, but just in case, we'd better not drag this out any longer than we have to."

"Ten days, absolute max, I figure."

Eric fully meant to keep to that deadline, but not because he thought for a second she would blow her cool and endanger the mission. Despite her bragging about her granny's dubious antics, Dawn was too much the professional to act out when their very lives depended on it.

If the deal had not gotten under way within a week, Eric knew he would probably be a dead customer and Dawn along with him. It would mean they had been made.

Chapter 5

"How beautiful!" Dawn rarely gushed, but it was hard not to when flying fairly low over the blue Aegean and its green and white dots of paradise. "I'm coming back here for vacation one day."

"Yeah, you should take a yacht tour to Marathi. That's fantastic and fairly inexpensive," Eric advised. "Not too touristy or cluttered."

She turned to smile at him. "I take it you've been here before?"

He nodded and pointed out the window. "That speck off to the right is Horio, I think. Used to be a sponge-harvesting island, but most of that trade moved to Florida when the sponges died out here." He buckled his seat belt.

"Have you spoken with Mercier?" she asked, more interested in the mission now than the sight below.

"While you were sleeping. He ran the name Quince

through all sources and thinks he might have a hit. A Greek by the name of Stefan Cydonia, a mercenary known for his involvement in weapons dealing. He's dealt in uranium and some other components used to make WMDs, too. If it's him, he's an arrogant bastard. Cydonia is Latin for quince."

"So he's suspect because he's a Greek, his name means quince and this meeting is ostensibly set for somewhere in the Greek Isles?" she asked. "Makes sense to me."

"He was involved in an illegal arms deal years ago in Baden-Baden, Germany. We had some pretty good intel on that, but he managed to escape. That's how he got on our 'to watch' list and gained probable credit for some other deals in the same vein."

"I'm impressed. Do we have his address, by any chance?"

Eric shook his head. "No luck there. No usable photos, either. He has managed to stay off the radar for nearly a decade."

"What else do we know about him?" Dawn asked, intrigued and eager to know who they were up against.

"Very little, but Jack's working on that. We'll be landing soon."

No sooner had he said that than their captain announced they were approaching the international airport in Athens.

Two other men accompanied them on the plane, both very large bodyguard types wearing regular business suits and the traditional headpieces of Eric's bogus homeland. One was called Ressam. He was a dour man with darting eyes and quick movements. He reminded her of a ferret.

The other, Eric introduced as Clay Senate, a fellow Sextant agent also in disguise going by the name of Adil. It was impossible to determine what his nationality might be. He stood well over six feet tall, had a light reddish-brown complexion, wise gray-green eyes and faintly oriental features. His formidable height and build were re-assuring, and he was definitely an easy guy to look at. Pity he was so stoic and never smiled. She hoped that was just part of his current disguise and not his real demeanor.

When Eric warned her not to speak with either man except in an emergency because it was forbidden, Dawn knew the ruse had begun in earnest. She was now Aurora, wife of Jarad Al-Dayal, wealthy oil magnate and closet terrorist.

The private jet impressed Dawn, as did the clothing she had been provided. In the smaller piece of her Vuitton luggage that he had told her to open, there were a couple of the traditional robes Eric had warned her she would have to wear, but also included were casual outfits appropriate for a vacation in the warm climes of Greece and the islands.

At Eric's direction, she had napped in the cabin at the back of the plane, which contained a bedroom with a king-size bed sporting satin sheets. She had showered in the fantastic bathroom with its gold fittings and fancy soaps, amazed that the bronze tan he'd sprayed on her didn't seem to fade at all. Then she had applied her makeup—heavy on the kohl shadow, as Eric had suggested—and dressed in lightweight summer slacks and a pink silk tank top. Her strappy little sandals probably cost more than her entire wardrobe back home.

Eric was resplendent, dressed for show as a young oil tycoon from the Middle East. The dark mustache was new and looked perfectly real and at home above his finely sculpted mouth. What a change from the handsome but terse government agent she had first met in that interrogation room. Then later, at his place, he had become that teasing, slightly rowdy blond jock. Was that his natural self, or yet another guise?

She reminded herself once again that she must keep in

mind how easily this guy switched gears. How could any woman ever trust a man like Vinland? She still had no idea who he really was at heart or what the heck he was going to do next. Maybe that was the main part of his charm, that unpredictability.

But for now, Dawn knew she was completely in his hands whether she liked it or not. "Where do we go first?"

"Through security, then customs. Then we reboard for the flight to Leros."

Eric adjusted his ghutra. "Remember you are supposed to be Andorran. When you speak, use English with a Spanish accent. English will be our common language since it's the one I would be most likely to know with my Oxford education. You'll have to suit up before we deplane. Where's your stuff?"

"In the bedroom, laid out on the bed. You'll have to show me what goes where."

He smiled rather evilly, teasing her again. Dawn knew it was his way of trying to put her at ease, so she didn't even pretend to take offense.

"You'd better wear this, too," he said, reaching under his robes to retrieve a small box. In it were a gold band and an enormous diamond solitaire. He slipped both on her finger.

She stretched out her arm to view the rings from a distance. "Tell me this rock is not the real deal."

"Oh yes, darling. Only the most ostentatious for my missus," he assured her. Then he grinned. "On loan with the rest of the bling-bling, so don't lose anything down a drain or you'll be in hock for life."

"The clothes are loaners, too, right?" she asked.

"No, those are yours."

Dawn's eyes widened as she looked at him in wonder. "Really?" She ought to protest, but couldn't bring herself to do it. Though she had seen only a portion of the things someone had packed for her, those she had seen were absolutely fantastic. Expensive. Gorgeous. Made her feel like a million. Looking that way was the whole point, of course.

She chalked it up to a clothing allowance that beat all. Or maybe hazard pay. She'd probably earn the new duds in spades before this was over.

Twenty minutes later, they landed and were greeted by several official-looking men wearing suits.

Covered head to foot in blue, heavily embroidered flowing silk, Dawn kept her gaze lowered. Her face, hands and feet were the only parts of her visible to others. She stayed in Eric's wake while he hammed it up in his new role. He gave the word *pompous* new meaning, but certainly looked grand enough to carry it off with panache.

After they entered the building, she experienced a few minutes of apprehension when they were separated. A female attendant guided her to a private room where Dawn was politely, but very thoroughly, searched. Not a pleasant experience, but tolerable. The wait to get back to Eric and their two bodyguards seemed interminable, but she guessed that was to be expected, too.

She thought she noted a look of relief in his eyes when she rejoined him later. Or maybe he was only squinting from the contacts he was wearing. She missed the glasses.

She blinked and looked down at her hands with their newly tanned skin, natural-colored nails and enormous diamond, and didn't recognize them as her own. This was too weird.

The short flight to the island of Leros and limousine trip to the Milos hotel proved uneventful and was virtually silent. Surprisingly, she missed the easy banter with Eric. But the bodyguards sat across from them, vigilant and fierce-looking as Dobermans. Even though Dawn knew whose side they were on, their somber presence discouraged any conversation.

When she and Eric were alone at last, Dawn quickly removed the confining outer garments and drew in a deep breath. They were staying at a new and very exclusive hotel near the black-sand beach. The place must have been constructed especially for visiting royalty. Though the outside looked relatively modest and in keeping with the simple local architecture, the interior was downright fantastic.

"This place would wow Trump," she muttered.

Eric tossed his head-covering onto the sofa of the sitting room and glared at her. "Silence, woman!" he snapped, then covered her mouth with his hand to keep her from spouting the sharp comeback she had in mind.

Dawn realized at once he thought the place might be wired. He moved his hand and gestured to one of the doors leading off the sitting room. In the bathroom, he turned on the shower and left it running.

Immediately, he moved close to her, embraced her carefully and whispered into her ear, "Wherever we are, assume that everything we say and do is monitored. Especially here. The Milos is the only five-star around and the one in which I, as Al-Dayal, would be most likely to stay. If our rooms aren't bugged, then we're dealing with amateurs."

Dawn nodded, trying to ignore the closeness of his body, his exotic scent and the feel of his palm on her cheek. She could kick herself for not thinking of wires first thing. It was a simple matter for a bribed employee to plant listening devices. That could have been the porter who accompanied them to the room with their luggage, a concierge ordered to dash up to see that all was in order, or whoever had delivered the fresh arrangement of flowers minutes before they arrived.

Eric continued, his voice barely audible, his fake mustache tickling her ear. "Stay in character. *Always,* unless I invite you out of it. I'll decide when it's safe."

She nodded again, not minding his orders in the least. He was running the op and he knew best.

Eric drew back, still holding her, and gave her a tight smile. "All right. Do not forget." Then he drew his bottom lip between his teeth and looked pensive. Tension played between them like a high-voltage current.

Dawn became very aware of his hands on her, the subtle catch in his breathing, the intoxicating sandalwood scent of him this close to her. His gaze prowled over her like a hungry lion.

Suddenly, he released her and left her there alone, quickly closing the door behind him.

Something had happened in that brief span of time and Dawn could not explain it. Sexual attraction peaking big-time, of course, but more than that. It was as if she had felt his thoughts, his worry, even a fear that he was getting too close to her and yet not close enough. Or maybe she was projecting her own thoughts onto him because she was so reluctant to admit they were hers.

She shook her head to clear it and went to the sink to splash cold water on her face. Must be a bizarre case of jet lag, she figured. That man was seriously meddling with her objectivity and professionalism. It had to stop.

Eric felt a little more in control as he set up the laptop he'd brought with him. He sent e-mails to several contacts in Iran, a few to Saudi Arabia and a couple to various places in Europe. The messages were not important, merely for show should anyone tap into what he was doing. Unnecessary detail, maybe, but he liked to be thorough.

Later tonight, he would log on to the address furnished in the message from the seller. Instructions for the next leg of their trip could come through, then. If not, he would know he was being checked out very thoroughly. His identity would be verified with former photos and disinformation Sextant had circulated for this very purpose.

Someone would surely be comparing the fingerprints that were on file as Al-Dayal's with those he had provided on everything he had touched since entering the hotel. Dawn's had been erased from her actual records completely and replanted in all the right places. If the one doing this deal had the resources, this portion of the mission could take several days.

The concierge called and offered to set up a sight-seeing expedition for the Al-Dayals tomorrow. Eric pretended to vacillate. Should he allow his beloved wife the exposure? He even asked how private they would be.

The concierge insisted they would not be troubled by the rabble of tourists or jostled by the locals. In the end, Eric reluctantly agreed to a day of fun, sun and freedom from his spouse's usual confinement. He was the soul of benevolence, the man had told him.

Yeah, right. Eric figured Dawn would kick his butt if he left her in the room while he went out to play sheikh. Besides, this could be the setup for contact with Quince.

"Aurora!" he called to her through her bedroom door. "I have wonderful news. Come here."

She entered, wearing a bright summer shift the color of raspberries. He smiled at her as a fond husband might. "Would you care to go sailing?"

"Oh yes, master," she answered with only the smallest trace of sarcasm.

He shot her a dark look of warning.

She smiled innocently and sat beside him, her hands folded primly on her knees. "Where shall we sail, Jarad?"

"About the islands," he replied. "Perhaps we shall find a secluded beach and go for a nice swim. Would you like that, my heart?"

"Oh, above *all!*" she cried, threw her arms around his neck and kissed him soundly on the mouth.

Eric could have spanked her. Damn, she was overacting. Overacting to a wild and delicious degree, he realized as he abandoned himself and enjoyed her mouth to the fullest. His entire body reacted with a vengeance, blood rushing south from his brain like a tidal wave.

He broke the kiss, then took another angle, pressing his chest to hers until they were nearly reclining on the sofa. Only when he felt the increased pressure of her palms against his chest did he relent.

Damn, she was hot. And he was hotter. Both were hyperventilating.

She laughed as she escaped his clutches and danced back into her bedroom, shaking her finger at him over her shoulder. A quicksilver imp, that girl. And wicked.

For a minute, he was tempted to follow, just to see where things might go. But he knew how out of hand he had gotten with just the kiss, so he stayed put.

No matter how many days it lasted, this was going to be a long, long assignment.

The next morning, in deference to her role, Dawn donned modest white slacks and a loose, flowing shirt that covered her arms. She knotted her hair in a bun at her nape and covered most of it with a floral scarf in soft pastels— colors she could never have worn comfortably as a redhead.

From the jewelry case someone had provided along

with the new wardrobe, she chose gold hoop earrings and numerous bangles for her wrists. She looked prim but fashionable, she thought, as she examined her image in the mirror. Rich, too. The clothes were fantastic, their labels indicating that whoever bought them had pulled no punches where price was concerned. Had Eric chosen these and ordered them? The only opportunity he'd had was when she slept at his house. Maybe Mercier was responsible.

When she emerged from the bedroom, he smiled his approval, slipping a cell phone into his shirt pocket. He had also dressed in white, wearing shorts, a knit shirt and sneakers. It emphasized the darkness of his skin. The man looked scrumptious, but she decided she preferred him blond and without facial hair.

He stood immediately, resting his hands on his hips as he appraised her. "Excellent choice of apparel."

"Gracias. May we go now?" Dawn could not wait to get out of their rooms, or the goldfish bowl, as she was coming to think of it. Having to be seriously conscious of every single move and sound she made was driving her crazy.

He reached for her hand and she gave it. The warmth of his palm and those long, strong fingers laced between hers felt reassuring. Confidence seemed to emanate from his pores and bolster her own. Not that she didn't think she could handle the mission, but she knew she could never have done it on her own. He knew all the ropes. Master, indeed.

Clay Senate, or Adil, as he was to be called, and Ressam joined them at the elevator. Dawn lowered her gaze to the floor, but only after a lightning-quick assessment of the men who would protect them. Ressam had left off his ghutra. Clay kept his. Both men wore slacks with floral cotton shirts worn untucked to hide the weapons she knew they carried. Covered up as she was, she felt naked without hers.

She remained silent while Eric barked a few terse instructions to the men in Farsi. Were there cameras in the elevators, too? she wondered, then decided they were assuming so just in case there were.

Maybe with so many international travelers and no rules governing surveillance, the nooks and crannies of everywhere contained wires and cameras.

God, this was not what she had expected or trained for. Undercover work was not her forté. She much preferred doing sanctioned breaking and entering. Even the official hacking she had done on the computers back at headquarters before being transferred was preferable to this.

Surely on the sailboat it would be safe to be themselves again, at least for the duration of their day trip.

As if he had read her mind, Eric spoke. "Live it, Aurora," he said quietly as they exited the hotel and headed for the car that she supposed would take them to the marina.

Well, that killed that hope, Dawn thought. She had to become Aurora with no hope for a rest until this was over. "Yes, Jarad," she replied softly. "With relish, I promise."

"Good little wife," he replied under his breath. "Allah be praised."

Necessary role-playing aside, Dawn heartily wished she could kick him in the shins.

Chapter 6

"The *Angeline?* What a lovely name for a boat," Dawn said softly as she stepped carefully on board the sailing yacht. "She is very beautiful."

Eric had gone ahead of her. Ladies first did not apply as far as he was concerned. He appeared to be enjoying this charade of theirs to the max.

Dawn had kissed him last night, not just for any cameras that might be running, but also to show him he wasn't calling *all* the shots, at least not between them. The problem was that the kiss had backfired on her and she had almost lost control of it, along with her good sense. The man was no novice when it came to lip-locks, that was for sure.

He grasped her waist and lifted her onto the deck. "A top-of-the-line, forty-two-footer," he replied to her observation about the boat. "Do you know anything of yachts, my sweet?" he asked, steadying her as if she were fragile.

Dawn shook her head. "No, I have never sailed." The absolute truth. All her life, she had hated deep water. It was not a phobia, exactly, and she could swim very well, but all the same she didn't like deep water.

She glanced warily at the man standing several feet away, watching him through squinty eyes. The brown face beneath his captain's cap looked weathered, his body, lean and mean. His khaki shorts and shirt resembled a uniform. The white cap looked too new. She quickly lowered her gaze and covered her mouth with her hand as if automatically attempting to hide her face from him.

"Our captain, Mr. Kerosian," Eric announced, stepping between her and the man. "If you would go below, my dove, we will cast off. You may return to deck in a while when I come for you."

Dawn did as ordered, trying all at once to remain regal while hurrying to obey. She thought she had performed pretty well. Eric should have no reason at all to fuss about her stepping out of character.

Once in the salon, her curiosity got the better of her. She tossed her tote bag onto one of the suede-upholstered lounges, then plundered through every inch of the efficient little kitchen, the head and the two sleeping cabins. It wasn't on the scale of the private jet, but it was very luxurious for a relatively small yacht.

Though this was supposed to be a day trip and they would not be sleeping aboard, Dawn figured she might never get a chance to examine a pleasure yacht like this one again unless she found she loved sailing and then won a lottery. Neither seemed all that likely. The boat was sleek, serene and ultracomfortable.

"Is your stomach surviving, little landlubber?" Eric asked.

"Admirably," she answered, greeting him with a lift

of her chin. "I believe I am a, how would you say it, an old salty."

He laughed and glanced around the salon, taking it all in much more quickly than Dawn had done. "Well done. Come above and we will watch together for dolphins."

Dawn retied the scarf to cover her hair and buttoned her shirt up to her neck. She didn't want to risk sunburn through her artificially darkened skin. And there was her newly acquired modesty to consider.

He took her directly to the bow where they stood against the rail facing forward, Eric's arms braced on either side of her as he held the steel railing. She remained very still when he bent down and placed a kiss on her cheek, then settled his mouth next to her ear. "This is no ordinary sailboat for hire."

"I noticed," she replied, not daring even now to abandon her persona. "You are a very important man who would never settle for the ordinary, even temporarily."

"No one can hear us here. The *Angeline* is custom-made, outfitted for a private and very wealthy owner, not for tourist day trips, even for one such as Jarad Al-Dayal. I want you to be prepared. I'm certain Quince arranged for this. We might be sailing directly to his stronghold now, wherever that is. Unless this trip is simply a diversion to keep us busy until he has verified my identity. I don't believe Captain Kerosian knows which yet until he gets a call."

"I wish I were armed," she said.

One of his hands disappeared from the rail and a second later snaked around her waist to the buttons at the middle of her shirt front. Cold steel and a warm hand slid inside the gap he had unfastened. She sucked in her breath and he tucked a pistol beneath the waistband of her slacks. He smoothed the fabric down over the weapon. Dawn's heart fluttered.

"Your security blanket," he murmured with another kiss near her ear.

Dawn sighed her thanks and rested her head back against his chest, slipping back into her role as Aurora. For a long time they stood there, gazing out over the Aegean.

Suddenly, she saw them. "Look! Dolphins!" she cried, pointing. "Just as you predicted."

"What a sight," he declared as she turned to meet his gaze. "You are almost as beautiful as the moment I first saw you."

"Almost?" she asked, frowning at him.

"But not quite," he answered. "That *is* a sincere compliment, by the way."

"Then I thank you."

Why had he said that? Probably to insure that she didn't screw things up because of her independent nature. And maybe he figured she needed to hold on to her real identity. He must know how much she hated acting subservient.

"You are doing great so far," he said, corroborating her assumption about his praise. Yep, he was pulling strings. Handling her like a pro. What else should she have expected—that he was really interested in her as a woman?

Having him take a serious interest in her was not one of her ambitions, anyway. As it stood now, she had only two goals. She wanted to be known as the best damn intelligence agent in her group, and to help enhance the world's opinion of her profession, specifically female agents. To that end, she used every skill she had learned and threw herself into every mission, regardless of the personal danger. Her second aspiration did deal with men, in a way—she intended to steer clear of them emotionally and restrict her trust, at least in the personal areas of her life.

She seemed to lack the necessary intuition that most women had, and therefore had suffered not one, but two relatively sharp kicks in the teeth. She simply was no good at figuring out men and how they thought, and this particular man gave new meaning to the word *enigmatic*.

She didn't need Vinland's interest or his compliments, only his leadership on this mission and his respect when she did her job as ordered. This was business.

Dawn looked back out to sea where the dolphins leapt in unison and admired their ability to stay in synch. She hoped that she, Eric and the others could perform as precisely as those dolphins did and get this mission completed.

She could stand being Aurora, his compliant little wife, for a little while, but was in serious danger of losing herself in another way if the job with this specific Sextant agent lasted too long.

The day wore on as they tacked around the islands. Dawn tensed a bit when they docked for lunch at a quaint little bay on Kos. She hardly tasted the food that Eric consumed with gusto. However, when they reboarded the *Angeline* a couple of hours later, no one had approached them about a meeting with anyone.

Eric remained on deck and gestured for her to join him. "Shall we go for a swim? The captain says there is a perfect and very private inlet on an uninhabited island he knows about. We're headed there now."

"Your idea?" she asked quietly.

"Yes, but his choice of island," he admitted, letting her know that this could be the rendezvous point with Quince if that was what the captain had been hired to arrange.

"Sounds lovely. Shall I go and change?" At his insistence, she had brought a bathing suit and beach cover in her tote.

"No, we will change after we get out there." He got up and took her hand.

She was getting way too used to holding hands with him, Dawn thought. But to anyone watching, she figured it would seem a natural thing for a recently married couple to do.

Dawn hung back while the captain advised Eric that he would drop anchor just offshore and let the two of them swim to the beach. Damned difficult to do without someone noticing a gun tucked in your swimwear, she thought.

"Impossible!" Eric declared, red in the face and spouting the proper outrage. "I insist you lower the inflatable for us. I will not allow another man's eyes to view my wife uncovered enough to go swimming!"

The captain shrugged as if it didn't matter to him and set about doing as Eric demanded. Ressam gave him a hand with the inflatable, then stood away.

In moments, she and Eric were motoring to the pristine, unspoiled beach that appeared to be shielded completely by rough, rocky cliffs.

He cut the motor and they stepped out into knee-deep surf. She helped him tug the rubber dinghy up onto the shore where it would not be washed back out by the gentle waves.

"So what do we do now?" she asked, her hands propped on her hips.

"Stop looking so saucy and get out of sight behind that outcropping over there while you change." He mugged at her and mouthed the word parabolics.

Was he kidding? Parabolic mikes? Out here? She must have shown her disbelief because he nodded emphatically. Maybe he wasn't paranoid. Or even if he was, who was she to knock that? It would probably be what kept them alive. She obeyed, as usual, and went behind the rocks. But she did not undress right away. What if there were cameras, too?

Nonsense. Parabolic microphones that could aim and

eavesdrop at a distance, she might buy, but video was a reach. Still, she scanned the cliffs very carefully, then looked out to sea. The *Angeline* was the only craft visible.

That was when she saw Eric climbing up the face of one cliff, already about three-quarters of the way up. No rope, no belay pins, nothing but his bare hands and feet.

Dawn covered her mouth to keep from crying out, startling him and causing him to fall. Instead she watched, fascinated by the play of muscles in his calves and forearms as he gripped, reached and gripped again. Terrified for him, she held her breath and prayed for his safety.

The moments crawled by like hours. Finally, he hefted himself up onto the ledge and stood, surveying the portion of the island hidden from her view.

He turned and looked down, waving. She raised her hand tentatively and waved back. Surely he would find an easier way down. Hope fled when he dropped to his stomach, legs hanging over the edge, feet searching for purchase.

"Idiot," she whispered to herself. "What the devil is he thinking?"

Well, whatever that was, she refused to watch any longer. Instead, she whipped off her shirt. Careful to keep the large rock outcroppings between her and those who might view her from the yacht, Dawn had changed and reached the water's edge by the time Eric joined her.

"The place is clear," he assured her. "I could see the entire island from up there and it's uninhabited, only rocks and seabirds. No mikes and no cameras. I believe this is a test and also a diversion to keep us busy until Quince can check us out with his sources."

He zoomed past her and splashed into the water. Dawn followed. When he surfaced next to her after a dive, he said, "Might as well enjoy ourselves while we wait for the real summons. I figure we probably have a couple of days to kill."

She was in over her head in all respects. He looked so damn good with his muscles all wet and shiny, his teeth gleaming when he smiled, his eyes twinkling. She missed the incredible blue of his eyes that was nearly the same color as the azure water in which they swam.

His hands gripped her waist as she treaded water to stay afloat. "Dawn, are you all right? You haven't said a word. No one can hear us here."

She blew out a breath and raked her wet hair off her face. "Shouldn't we be making a plan? Deciding what we should do when we meet with Quince?"

"I told you already before we flew out. I make an offer, buy the gizmo with the information on it and we leave. Someone else will do the actual cleanup. My job is to get in, get the goods and get out. Yours is to identify the shooter if he's there."

She moved her legs, brushing against his, wishing he would turn her loose so she could breathe evenly and get her equilibrium back.

"You stay out of the confrontation so you can maintain this disguise for the next time something like this comes along?" she asked, trying hard to concentrate on aspects of the mission and not the proximity of that heat-seeking missile she felt against her stomach.

He shrugged one shoulder and smiled. "Jarad's persona has come in handy a few times. Hate to ditch a good alternate identity just to collar Quince myself."

"What if he's copied the information? Suppose he intends to sell it more than once?"

"He advertised exclusive use of it when he put out the word. He's gotta know he'd get himself killed for double-dealing. No, all his bidders will be in one place and our people will make sure none of them leave with what they came after. I'll outbid them all, anyway."

It sounded too easy to her. "So we just…buy it and go?"

He smiled, looking straight into her eyes. "*I* buy it and we go. You remain in the background, very low profile. Your only job is to see whether Quince is the one who killed Bergen or if it was a close associate of his who is present when we have the meeting."

She pushed at his hands until he released her. "I'm not in the mood to swim. Let's go."

He turned her around so that she faced the beach. "Stay in front of me till we get behind the rocks. Jarad can't let the others see that lovely bod of yours from the boat."

"They probably saw me get into the water," she reminded him. "Jarad didn't seem to care then."

"Yeah, but that thong is way too enticing to give them a rear view."

"It is *not* a thong!" she argued.

"Close enough. That's the one thing I didn't choose for you. I asked for a modest two-piece swimsuit. Maybe they don't even make those anymore." He sounded so disgruntled.

She half turned to glare at him. "You picked out the clothes? When?"

"While you were sleeping. Now get a wiggle on. We've got to sit behind those rocks long enough for me to have my wicked way with you."

She shrieked in protest when he goosed her waist.

"Not really," he assured her, laughing. "Just for show."

Right. Dawn wished her pulse would quit racing. Her blood just would not behave when he was this close, especially not when he was talking so casually about having sex. Even the pretense of having it.

"I can handle this," she said to herself. "I can."

"Sure you can. Never doubted it for a minute," he said, following close behind her as she waded out of the surf. "Now get your pretty little butt behind that rock. The captain's binoculars are probably glowing red with the heat from his hands."

Dawn laughed with him. "You are impossible!"

"Possible," he argued. "Very possible. Try me."

"Not on a dare," Dawn muttered. Not on a double-dog dare, she added to herself.

They remained behind the rocks for about half an hour. Eric stretched out on the sand, head resting on his hands, and fell sound asleep. Dawn sat there fuming. The least he could have done was talk to her while they knew they had no listeners.

She spent the time brushing off sand and donning her slacks and shirt. When he woke, she was dressed and more than ready to climb into the inflatable and get back to work. Damn the man.

Back in Leros at the hotel, Dawn passed the time watching television she couldn't understand and looking at pamphlets on the local sights and those on the mainland of Greece. The area had never been on her list of places she wanted to visit until now. How beautiful it was, a veritable paradise.

Eric went out periodically and left her alone in the suite. The first time he did, he put on his superprotective husband attitude and gave her a weapon. "If anyone enters, shoot them," he ordered. Dawn's mouth had dropped open in surprise and disbelief that he would say that aloud. "I have left precise instructions that no one is to knock or come into our rooms. If they do so, you are to shoot them, do you understand?"

She already had the pistol he'd given her on the boat tucked away in her purse. This one must be for show, a warning to anyone listening, that she was armed. She held the gun loosely in her hand, as any wife without weapons training would do when handed one. "But why?" she asked meekly.

He glared at her, looking for all the world like the man he was supposed to be. "You must know how vulnerable you are to abduction. I am a wealthy man, Aurora. It would be a simple matter for someone to snatch you away from me and demand a fortune. If that happens, I warn you, I will not submit to it. So protect yourself."

"Very well, Jarad," she said, laying the pistol on the cushions next to her. "But what of you? Have you another one of these?"

"Of course," he replied with a condescending smile. "Not to worry. I shall return in a while. One day before we leave, I will take you around the town so that you might shop. Would that make you happy?"

"Delirious," she cooed, beaming up at him, going for coy. "I shall choose something wildly expensive!"

He laughed, but it sounded forced. "A woman of simple tastes. Silks and diamonds. What was I thinking when I married you?" With that, he leaned down and kissed her briefly on the forehead. "Be good, Aurora."

"As if I have a choice," she murmured under her breath as he left. She heard the click of the automatic lock when he closed the door and felt trapped in a gilded prison. What she wouldn't give to put on shorts and a halter top and stroll the streets of Leros by herself.

A wife such as Aurora Al-Dayal would feel the same if an overbearing and authoritative husband ordered her to stay put while he took in the glorious sights outside. A woman like Aurora might even slip out of the hotel and risk the consequences of her husband's anger if tempted that way. But Dawn knew better than to entertain the thought.

Strange eyes might be watching, ears listening, her every move monitored. Defiance would be highly unprofessional, not to mention possibly fatal. With a sigh, she went back to her magazine with the enticing pictures of all she was missing.

After two full days of seclusion, Dawn's nerves were on edge. When Eric returned that afternoon, Aurora made a few demands of her own. "Take me out as you promised, Jarad. I wish it."

He cocked a dark eyebrow and smiled the patronizing smile she hated. In her mind, she knew it was only part of the role he played, but the entire ruse was becoming somehow real to her. She had begun to feel more like Aurora than the fiercely independent Dawn Moon.

"Now?" he asked idly, strolling over to the window and parting the drapery to look out.

"Yes," she said, almost desperately, almost forgetting her accent. "Today. This moment."

"Put on your chador."

"Must I?" she asked, risking his anger. Rather, Jarad's anger, she reminded herself. Eric would understand.

"Yes, you must," he answered curtly. "This is not Andorra and you are no longer a schoolgirl. There are rules and you agreed to them when we married."

Then he sighed and dropped the curtain back in place, turning to her with outstretched hands. "I know things are changing. Perhaps I cling too fiercely to the old ways." He pondered for a minute, rubbing his chin. "All right, you may leave it off, but only for today."

"Thank you, husband," Dawn murmured, wanting to smack him upside his head. "You are generous to a fault."

She wasted no time getting dressed. Blue raw-silk slacks and a matching shirt looked smart and felt comfortable as well as cool. Instead of a scarf, she tucked her hair beneath a crushable straw hat of bright white that would shade her face. For good measure, she added dark sunglasses and the Beretta to a white crocheted sack purse and went to stand inspection.

"Very cosmopolitan," he commented dryly. "At least you are modest."

Together they went out into the bright afternoon. Dawn wanted to crow with delight. The air didn't get much fresher than this, she thought.

With a spring in her step, she marched along beside Eric as he took her straight to a jeweler and purchased her a bracelet that would wipe out a year's salary if she kept it.

"Image," he whispered, as if he needed to remind her why her wrist was dripping with precious stones. Everything would be returned, of course. She knew that. Even the clothes, no matter what he said or what she wanted. She could not, in good conscience, keep those designer labels bought with government money, no matter how slushy the black op funds might be.

Dawn promptly forgot all of that as Eric drove her around the island in their rented vintage convertible. The two bodyguards rode in back, eyes forever scanning the streets, storefronts and roadsides.

There were people around, ostensibly tourists, who kept turning up at the same sites. They weren't too numerous, but enough so that it was difficult for her to determine whether any of them were actually following to keep up with Eric's little sightseeing expedition.

They climbed to the castle built by the fourteenth-century Knights of St. John as a defense against invaders. "It's so huge! And so old," she whispered. "Awe-inspiring."

"At night they light it. Glows like something you would imagine in a fairy tale," Eric told her. "Can you fathom the difficulty in constructing something like this here on such a small island over five hundred years ago? Think of the manpower and engineering it would have taken."

They did not enter the church built within the castle. Though she truly wanted to see inside it, she did not ask. They were supposed to be of the Islamic faith, not Christian. To enter there would be forbidden. Later she would come back, Dawn promised herself.

Together they visited several of the inlets on the island with their picturesque villages of white houses trimmed in blue. Hand in hand, she and Eric strolled along the beaches barefoot while their well-armed shadows followed, ever vigilant for a threat of any kind.

When dusk came, they headed back toward the hotel, tired and hungry. Eric stopped at a small restaurant in a village that was inland, well back from the coast. "I'm famished," he announced. He ushered her out of the car and into the humble structure. Clay and Ressam remained outside.

"We need to talk," he told her when they were seated. "Here we won't be overheard."

"You're sure?" she asked, looking around them. One old man wearing an apron scurried toward them. The only other customers sat well across the room out of earshot, a couple who were obviously enthralled with each other and had been for a while.

"Certain." Eric greeted their server and ordered.

This was the first meal she had consumed in public since they had arrived four days ago. Already she had her favorites among the local dishes, thanks to room service.

"Tonight, something new," Eric told her. "You must try the tzatziki."

"Not snails, is it?" she asked, wrinkling her nose.

"Yogurt and cucumber dip. With pickled octopus, of course."

She grimaced again. "You said that with a straight face. You really eat that stuff?"

"You can't live on salad alone. We're having moussaka, too. You'll like that."

She recognized the eggplant-and-meat dish she had grown quite fond of. "Wish I could try the ouzo since I've heard so much about it."

"No booze. Sorry. But I promise no more goat's milk. I ordered tea."

When his hand moved over hers, she didn't pull away. At this point, she needed a human touch more than she needed food. He had not really touched her, except inadvertently, in a couple of days now.

If someone were watching them every minute at the hotel, wouldn't they find that odd? She couldn't ask him that, however. If she did, he might think she was suggesting they actually do something married people would do.

His fingers played with hers as their eyes met over the small table. "How are you holding up?"

"Going bonkers with the waiting. Will this show ever get on the road?"

"Soon. We're leaving for Kos tomorrow."

She sat up straight and gripped his hand. "You heard from him?"

Eric nodded. "He called this morning and left a message at the desk. The instructions were very precise. We're to go on the *Angeline*."

Dawn considered that. "So you were right. Our sail was a test."

"I think we've passed on all counts. The invitation indicates that. Or else he has us pegged and intends to kill us. You ready to rock and roll?" He grinned and wriggled his eyebrows, letting her see the old Eric behind the usually stern, brown-eyed mask of Jarad Al-Dayal. The sight was disconcerting, to say the least. It also proved to be comforting.

Dawn ate with relish when the meal arrived, fueling up for the action. Adrenaline would probably keep her from sleeping a wink tonight.

Clay was gone when they exited the restaurant. Dawn didn't ask where he was and Ressam didn't say. He never said anything. Eric did not appear to be concerned. The ride back to their hotel was short and uneventful.

When they reached their floor and got off the elevator, Clay was waiting. He spoke with Eric for a minute, his voice so low she couldn't hear a thing he said. Then he accompanied Ressam down the hallway, leaving her and Eric alone to enter the suite.

"You have what you wanted. Go to bed now," he ordered, fully into Jarad mode. However, when she obeyed without question, he soon followed her into her bedroom and shut the door.

Dawn looked the question she wanted to ask, but didn't speak. "We can talk freely in here," he told her. "Clay swept the rooms. There are no cameras, except outside by the elevator to keep tabs on everyone's comings and goings. He left two mikes working in the sitting lounge and my room and deactivated the one in here. I thought you might rest better and you *will* need a good night's sleep."

"Won't whoever is listening in suspect something's up?"

Eric made himself at home by flopping down on her bed, his head resting on his hands. "If Clay had done this to begin with, they probably would. Now they'll think it's an equipment malfunction since it's only the one mike he tampered with. He's very good at what he does."

Dawn sat down on the edge of the bed and kicked off her sandals. "It was a lovely afternoon and evening. Thank you for that." His smile drew her like a warm caress.

No sooner had she thought that than he reached out and touched her arm, his palm and fingers hot against her skin. "You needed it. You were wound tight as a top string."

This was only her third mission in the field and on the other two, her life was never at risk. She had barely gotten started in fieldwork. Dawn felt justified in being a little nervous about it.

"I know this kind of thing is new to you," he said, "but you were trained well and you're doing fine."

"For someone inexperienced?"

"For anyone. You're a good actress. You won't slip up. I know it. Your record with NSA is excellent."

"That's hardly fair. They should have let me read yours."

He rolled over on his side so that his stomach rested lightly against her lower back and propped his head on one hand. She felt the hand that had caressed her arm come to rest between her shoulder blades, rubbing lightly. "This is not a come-on, by the way," he said seriously.

She turned a little and faced him, feeling bold as she looked into his eyes. "Why not?"

His smile was wry and a little regretful. "I think you know why not."

Dawn felt such an affinity for this man. Such a connection. And such an overpowering need to get closer. She figured that this tension between them was as wicked a distraction as anything. Relieving it could only help, she rationalized. Once they put out the fire, maybe she could think straight. On impulse, she leaned down and met his lips with hers, then drew back to look at him again. "That *was* a come-on, by the way."

"I know," he whispered, still stroking her back. "This is a distraction we can't afford, Dawn," he warned, but his expression displayed another message entirely.

"I can," she told him, feeling bold and incredibly turned on. Oddly enough, she felt she could say anything, no matter how outrageous, to him. Caution flew right out the window, just like that.

Chapter 7

Eric stifled a groan of frustration. The point was to do the right thing here. The thing he had intended when he had instructed Clay to find any listening or surveillance devices in the room. If he'd had any sense, he would have begun doing that the moment he closed the door instead of taking a while to get her comfortable and reassure her.

She wanted him. God knows he wanted her more every second he spent with her and that wasn't going away, no matter how hard he tried to deny it. But Dawn didn't really know him, couldn't even guess what he was capable of. But she needed to.

She only saw the chameleon. That had sparked some interest, maybe. Could be that she saw him as a sort of mentor, too. He had been doing undercover work for quite a while now. This was not only Dawn's first mission outside the scope of her regular security duties, but also her first international assignment. That made her dependent on his expertise.

The real truth about him would probably scare her or at least put her off. He doubted she would believe him at first, but he could convince her. She deserved to know the truth before they went into the final phase of this mission. It could save her life, or his. And she certainly should know what she was up against on a personal front. That was only fair.

Resolved, Eric sat up and took her by the shoulders and looked into her eyes. "There's something I have to tell you, Dawn."

She blinked and looked away. "I knew it. You're already involved. Or married?"

"No way, not even close. I would have told you that in the beginning." He took a deep breath and went for it. "You have to know what I'm about to tell you because it's who I am. If you don't know it, then you don't know me."

"So let's have it. What are you?" she asked, tracing his chin with her finger. "A vampire or something?"

He shook his head. "I'm able to *see* certain things normal people can't."

One corner of her lips rose in a very wry half smile. "Oh, fascinating. You see dead people? Find missing objects? What?"

Eric released her and pushed himself back against the headboard, crossing his arms over his chest. "Both, if conditions are right. I'm a telepath and a clairvoyant."

She rolled her eyes and laughed. "This is absolutely the worst line I have *ever* heard for sidestepping an unwanted advance. Stop it."

"This has nothing to do with sidestepping anything. I'm telling you that I'm a psychic, Dawn."

Tongue in cheek, she regarded him closely. "All right, Kreskin. Then tell me what I'm thinking right now."

"You'd like to strangle me with my own tie?"

"You aren't wearing a tie," she reminded him, leaning back on her arms, kicking one foot idly, or maybe nervously, against the bottom edge of the bed. "But that would be a natural reaction to a man explaining to me why he's unavailable, wouldn't you say? Especially when the reason he gives is so weird. No special skills needed to figure that out."

Again he sighed, and nodded. "Yeah, I guess it would be. See, what I would like to do with you is not possible, at least not right now."

Her gaze narrowed. "Try not *ever*. This is so lame it's funny. All you had to say was no. I'm not so dense that I need some fairy tale excuse for a turndown."

"If I'm freaking you out with this, I'm sorry, but it is true."

Her lips firmed, then relaxed as she spoke and cast him a sidewise look. "Speaking of mental vibes, you've been sending me signals since the minute I first met you, Eric. All those little touches, looks that could scorch, kissing me back the way you did. Tell me I read all that wrong."

"You didn't." He ignored her rising anger and continued explaining. "I want you, Dawn, make no mistake about that. But if you and I get too into each other, it could really interfere with my perceptions of other people, like Quince."

She got up and walked over to the bathroom, turning, with one hand on the door frame. "Tell you what, just in case your wavelengths are not fully operational at the moment. You go to your room and mind-meld with anybody you damn well please while I take a shower. Then I'm going to sleep and forget you exist, okay?"

"Wait, Dawn. This has to do with our mission, too. You need to let me finish."

"You *are* finished. Seems like you would have divined that already since you claim to be so *perceptive*."

"It's why I'm in Sextant," he added anyway. "All of us have some form of special powers, even if it's just lucky hunches that always play out. My particular aptitude exceeds that. I—"

"So go bend a spoon!" she snapped, then whisked into the bathroom and slammed the door.

Eric stared at the barrier between them and exhaled the breath he'd caught and held at the exceptional sight of Dawn in full-blown fury.

"That went well," he muttered to himself and got up off her bed where he had no business being in the first place.

An hour later in his own room, he closed his laptop. The coded message he had sent Mercier and the answer to it had done nothing to further the mission.

Quince remained a mystery. No one knew where he was. No objects were available that he might have touched that could conduct the necessary energy for Eric to locate him. Until they actually met, Eric had no way to get inside the man's mind and determine the extent of his plans.

He realized he could think of no way to prove to Dawn that he had the capability to do that. Eric had never been able to read her at all unless what she was feeling appeared on that lovely face of hers for anyone to see. Maybe he could fake it that way.

Somehow, he needed to get past Dawn's defenses and make her believe him. The more he thought about what had happened between them, the worse he felt.

Hell truly had no fury like a woman scorned, and that was what Dawn felt he had done, scorned her. However, if he had made love to her the way they both wanted and she found out what he was like later, she would probably hate him. And as he had told her, there was a distinct possibility that it might skew any readings he got from anyone else if his mind was preoccupied with her.

It bothered him that he'd had no luck reading the concierge or the captain of the *Angeline*. Clay was usually a snap. Ressam was sometimes a little difficult, but not impossible. Eric hadn't fully tested his ability on them, not since he had met Dawn. Suppose it didn't work? What would he do when he needed to read Quince or others who were critical to the mission's success?

What if his only hope of getting his powers back was to break down Dawn's defenses? Could he make himself do that? Was he even able to? If he did, how could they hope to have anything approaching a normal relationship? He would have too much of an advantage and she'd soon come to resent that, not to mention how she'd hate the invasion of privacy it involved.

However, her safety, maybe even her survival, might depend on their being able to communicate, and he couldn't ignore that. Tomorrow was D-day and he suspected he had left giving her this information until it was too late. They would not be able to deviate from their new personas once she came out of her bedroom tomorrow morning. If he was to have any success in letting her know how he intended to work this op and what his real mission was, it had to be tonight.

He tugged on his robe and headed back to her bedroom. The door was locked, but he had expected that. He slipped the credit card he'd tucked in his pocket between the door and frame and entered. The lights were off, the curtains drawn, the room black as pitch.

"Dawn?" he said softly.

"Good way to get yourself shot," she replied out loud as she punched the light switch, nearly blinding him.

Eric blinked and turned. She stood behind him, weapon in hand, wearing the slinky little slip thing he had ordered for her travel wardrobe. It was teal, setting off her fake tan and dark hair to perfection. In his mind, he pictured how much better it would complement her fairer complexion and red hair once she could abandon her disguise. But the pistol she held intruded on that thought. He could be entertaining a bullet if she hadn't hesitated.

"Get out," she advised him. Her tone sounded soft, but deadly. "Now, Vinland."

"Unless you plan to shoot, put that thing away. I have to talk to you, and this is no time for either of us to let personal feelings intrude. That's an order."

She lowered the gun and shrugged. "Official and offensive. Try to stay that way."

"Sit down and listen to me, Dawn," he demanded.

"Make sense and I will," she replied, in full command of her emotions, by the look of her.

They marched to the sitting area of her room, two comfy chairs flanking a round, skirted table. Eric waited until she sat, then joined her.

He clasped his hands together, resting his elbows on his knees as he leaned forward. "Look, I know how far out this sounds to you if you've had no prior experience with paranormal events, but I swear I'm being straight with you."

Dawn studied his face carefully, examining his every feature. He could feel her disdain like a pinch. She inhaled, then released it. "I'm aware that the intel agencies have done some studies in that area. I'll give you the benefit of the doubt here. But if I find out you're putting me on about this, Vinland, you're in deep trouble."

"No. I do read thoughts," Eric said seriously. "That is no joke. I'm for real."

She shifted in the chair, crossing her legs, apparently not in the least concerned about how seductive she appeared wearing that little confection she had on. He looked away, trying not to get any more distracted than he already was.

Obviously she planned to use that old trick of making him want to fill the silence, so he went ahead and bit. "I understand that you're a skeptic. That's okay. I've lived with this all my life and sometimes I forget how difficult it is for some people to buy into it if they've never encountered anything like it before. You haven't, have you?"

"I guessed the number of marbles in a jar once. That's as close as I've come, so don't expect much."

He nodded. "Okay. I am able—sometimes, most of the time, actually—to connect to people as they're thinking. If they think in words, I hear them. If not, then I get their general mood, hints of their intentions, specific feelings."

"Like mine?" she asked wryly. "Are you getting my general mood?"

He nodded. "Yes, anyone could see you're still mad as hell. I don't have to be psychic to know I blew it. But I can't read your mind and never could."

"Why not?"

He shrugged. "You have a natural block, I guess, or really good defenses. Some people do."

"Whew, what a relief," she said, sounding bored. "But I suppose you'll have no problem with Quince? Is he an open book, too?"

"I don't know yet. I won't until I meet him."

"So, tell me, what other tricks do you do?" she asked with a mirthless smile.

Eric decided to lay it all out there and see if she would buy any part of it. Maybe in the meantime, he could figure some way to demonstrate his abilities so she would drop the sarcasm and patent disbelief. "Remote viewing, are you familiar with that?"

"Oh yes, from television. You see things that happen, a little videotape in your mind. Flashing and in fragments, of course, like the results of bad camera work. It's a great hook in the world of fiction."

"That's pretty close to how it works. Don't smirk. I can sometimes see hidden objects or even people if I can touch the place where they lay or clothing they wore before they went missing."

She got up and began to pace. "Sometimes? Not an exact science, then. Pity. It would sure make our life simpler if you could have touched that computer and pinpointed the location of that gadget with the information on it, wouldn't it? Wow, think of the manpower and money that could be saved if your little talents were consistent."

"Stop it. You know paranormal phenomena exist, Dawn. You admitted yourself that the government has been studying this. They have, in all its forms, for decades. I am a telepath, more consistent than most."

She stopped pacing and faced him with her hands on her hips, her jaw set. "I don't believe you. Is that clear enough?" She flung out her hands. "It's hooey. So go to bed. I promise you there's no need for you to worry. What I felt was a momentary jolt of lust. You're a good-looking guy, Eric, and it has been a while since I've been alone in a bedroom with one, but I'm not quite desperate enough to jump you in your sleep, okay?"

He was already on his feet and unable to stop himself. He grabbed her and kissed her before she knew what was happening. For a second, she froze. Then she relaxed into the kiss for all she was worth.

The next thing he knew, he was flat on his back on the floor, Dawn straddling his waist with her sharp fingernails biting into his neck. "You move one inch and I'll open your jugular and laugh while you bleed out. Got that?"

Eric knew better than to smile. "Got it."

She didn't budge. "Now you listen to me, Vinland. I've about had it with you. You have one chance to make this right. When I release you, get up slowly. Walk directly out of this room and when I see you first thing in the morning, this night never happened. I don't want to hear any more about how you *see things*. Not one more word. And you will never—I repeat, never—kiss me again."

Eric, perfectly relaxed, grabbed the hand that gripped his neck, flipped her easily and reversed their positions. "You want to do this the hard way, okay. No, nothing sexual and no more kisses tonight, but you will listen to me and you will believe what I say."

But for the life of him, he couldn't think of a single thing he could do that would convince her he was telling the truth.

For a long moment, they glared at one another, breathing hard with exertion and bold remnants of unwanted lust. Then she spoke.

"I read once that some prominent scientist has a standing offer of one million dollars to anyone who can prove this exists. Why haven't you collected if you're for real?"

"Maybe I already have a million dollars."

"Let's say you do. Then tell me where I lost my grandmother's ring," she challenged. "It was on my ring finger, right hand, for years. Where is it now?"

Eric slid his hand from her wrist up to her fourth finger and touched the place, closing his eyes. It came to him as easily as anything ever had.

"There's a pool. The ring… It's in the drain. It's in the drain of that pool."

He opened his eyes and smiled down at her, still full of the delight she had experienced in that long-ago moment. "It's a very small size. You were a kid when you lost it, right?"

The look of shock on her face was priceless.

"Oblong, diamond-shaped. It has one stone surrounded by chips," Eric told her.

Her gaze narrowed with suspicion. "How do you know that? How could you possibly know?"

He released her other wrist and sat up, moving off of her. "I saw it."

"So where's the pool with the ring?" she challenged.

Eric reached down to give her a hand getting up. "I have no clue, but surely you can remember the day and where you went swimming."

It wasn't telepathy. He considered it little more than a parlor trick. Still, it had come in handy in a lot of instances. Inanimate objects were usually a piece of cake, the more insignificant, the easier they were to locate. Still, this little success gave him a swell of relief. He hadn't completely lost his powers.

Her body relaxed beneath him. "Leave me alone until the morning, will you?" she asked quietly. "This is a lot to digest and I'm still not sure I trust what you're telling me. If you can do all this, why are we here? Why don't you just zone in or whatever it is you do, and send in a contingent of special ops to grab Quince and the others?"

"Would that it worked that way," Eric admitted, shaking his head. "I need to explain a little more about the specifics of what I plan to do and how it might affect you, okay? Then I'll go."

She nodded wordlessly, looking at him with suspicion.

"The idea is to glean whatever I can from Quince about his intentions for the stolen information and whether he's made copies of it. If so, where he has those stashed. Anything I can get. I'll try to pick up on any names associated with the theft and how he chose these particular bidders to deal with."

Dawn had no expression whatsoever on her face. She did not believe him. At least not now.

He continued. "I'll transmit this information to you, so that one of us has it in case the other can't make it off the island for some reason."

"Say what you mean. One of us could die."

"Yes. But if we play out our roles, we should be safe enough. Quince is no fool. His intention is to sell what he's got. If he behaves himself, he can deal again next time. Only we won't give him that chance, of course."

"What if…"

"What?" Eric prompted.

"Suppose this Quince is similarly talented and figures out what you're doing? What if he reads you better than you read him?"

Eric sighed. "Then kick off your high heels and swim like hell because we won't stand a bloody chance."

"Go to bed, Eric," she said with a shake of her head.

He left the room and closed the door.

"Now *that* went well," he said to himself, strolling casually into his bedroom, almost satisfied. Not physically, of course. He was trying to ignore his heightened state of arousal.

He couldn't have her and he knew that. A little corner of his brain wouldn't quite accept it, though. That part kept urging that after this was all over, then maybe…

* * *

Dawn did not argue when Eric advised her to don the chador the next morning before leaving the hotel. Beneath it she wore a white sleeveless cotton top and slacks. Her shoes were leather with intricate embroidery on the toes that matched the blue color of her robe.

Together they preceded the porter who pushed the brass trolley holding their luggage. Clay and Ressam followed the porter. Their bags would be delivered to the *Angeline* in time for them to sail at noon.

She remained as unobtrusive as possible when they boarded the boat, going directly to the deserted salon without a word from Eric. He wore the role of the haughty Jarad Al-Dayal as if born to that name and station. She attempted to match his effort with the same ease.

One hour into the trip, he beckoned to her from the steps leading up from the salon to the deck. She rose obediently and joined him.

"Dolphins again. I thought you would enjoy them."

Dawn nodded and walked with him to the rail. She noted the captain ducking into the cabin. "Making a call?" she asked Eric.

"Looks like it. Are you all right?"

"Of course. Are you? How's the old gray matter receiving today?"

He didn't answer directly. "I think the captain will troll us around until dark, then disorient us with a few wide turns before making landfall."

Dawn could figure that much without the benefit of telepathy. It's what she would do if she were the captain delivering them to some secret destination. "So we keep an eye on the stars to determine where we are, right?"

"Clouds expected and probably a storm. That's why

this is happening now. Good news, though. That means Quince still plans to let us go later or he wouldn't bother trying to conceal his whereabouts."

"How will our guys find out where he is if they don't know where we went for the meeting? Unless this Quince is an idiot, he won't allow you to bring your laptop or cell phone."

Eric smiled a cat's smile. "Under the skin on my left shoulder is an implant that gives off intermittent signals. They can follow wherever I go. Soon as we are ready for it to happen, they'll strike."

"And how will they know that we are ready?"

"I'll contact them, don't worry."

"How? With a mind link?" she asked, not bothering to mask her skepticism.

"Hey, we have running conversations sometimes. Better than a telephone." Now he was joking, she could tell by his grin.

"Excuse me if I prefer Ma Bell."

"*Shhh,* captain's coming back. Ooh and ahh at the dolphins a little, then go below. I need my mind on what I'm doing and you look entirely too fetching in that table-cloth. Blows my concentration."

Dawn did as he asked, then spun neatly out of his grasp, actually enjoying the swirl of the robe around her ankles.

Could he actually do what he claimed? She had never met anyone who claimed to possess psychic abilities. He wouldn't be that confident if he wasn't sure his worked, would he? Would she actually find that ring he told her about? Dawn knew she would have to try, just to see if it was where he said it was.

She exhaled sharply and headed for the salon to pour herself a cup of coffee. Maybe he was delusional and they would both die as a result. How had she gotten herself into this mess?

She passed near Clay as she reached the door to the cabin. "Open your mind," he said emphatically in a deep, but nearly inaudible voice, the first words she had ever heard him speak. "Trust him."

Before she could respond by gesture or word, he hurried away. A servant realizing he had passed too close to the *mamsahib,* or whatever the boss's wife was called.

Okay, she decided. She would make herself trust. As if she had any options. Maybe a little meditation would calm her.

A good old Presbyterian prayer might not hurt, either, she thought with a heavy sigh.

Chapter 8

They sailed all afternoon and on into the night. The reason for that was a given. The location of the island was to remain a secret. That indicated it might be Quince's permanent home, or at least his usual base of operations.

The captain looked mighty smug and had an evil glint in his eye. He was probably making plans to get rid of the "bodyguards" Al-Dayal had brought along.

Dawn should be safe enough, though. How much trouble could a woman be anyway, the captain would figure, especially one as meek as Al-Dayal's wife? Eric almost laughed out loud. She had played her part so perfectly that no one could see her as a threat.

"We'll anchor here for the night," the captain said as he approached Eric. "If you and your men could give me some assistance."

They must be close to the rendezvous. Eric nodded and beckoned to Ressam and Clay.

Once the sails were furled and the anchor dropped, the captain bade them good-night, informing Eric that he would remain topside while Eric and the others were to use the cabins fore and aft.

"You are too kind," Eric said, shared a meaningful look with his men, and went below as the captain suggested.

Dawn was already in the forward cabin, reclining on the bed with a book. She glanced up as he entered. Since he had only a couple of feet of floor space, he kicked off his deck shoes and crawled onto the king-size bunk beside her.

"Are we there yet?" she asked with a saucy smile, turning down the page to mark her place and then tossing the novel aside.

Eric glanced at the author's name. Ian Fleming. "We will go ashore in the morning, I expect. So you are a James Bond fan?"

"Not really. I found it in the salon."

He laughed. "Decadent western novels, scorning your protective attire and taking the tone of a liberated woman. What are you coming to, Aurora? Will I have to take you in hand?"

"Have you the time for that before we disembark?" she asked playfully, all the while glancing curiously around the cabin and pointing to her ear.

"It's okay," he told her. "Clay swept the place. There are mikes hidden in the salon and in certain locations topside, but the cabins aren't bugged."

She grimaced. "Then why are you being such a jerk when you don't have to?"

He grinned. "Sorry, just yanking your chain. Are you ready for tomorrow?"

"Absolutely," she declared. "All this lounging around is boring as hell."

He lay back, linking his hands behind his head. "There'll be more of that once we get there, at least for you. But we could have some fireworks tonight if the captain tries to unload Ressam and Clay. No doubt Quince ordered him to."

"How do you know that?"

He quirked an eyebrow. "Wouldn't you if you were him?"

Dawn grabbed his arm and leaned close. "You think he means to kill them in their sleep?"

Eric grinned up at her. "The day they can't handle one spindly-legged, fifty-year-old wannabe pirate, they'll deserve what they get."

"We should keep watch or something in case they need our help."

"Relax. They'll be fine." He loved the feel of her hand on his arm, the concern he felt emanating from her in waves. She had a good heart and was a fine agent. Even though she barely knew Clay and Ressam, she would go to the mat to save them.

Though he sensed her goodness and her worry, it was not extrasensory perception at work, only normal observation. *Normal.* Dawn made him feel that way, and he couldn't help but love it. She saw him as a man, not some strange, inexplicable phenomenon. Maybe that was the reason he wanted her so much. But was that the only reason? Somehow, he didn't think so.

At a very young age, he had learned to brush off the awe people sometimes felt at what he could do. He did it with humor, merciless teasing and, if that didn't work, outright avoidance. Not many bothered to get to know the real Eric Vinland. He wasn't even certain he knew himself as well as he should.

His life had been mostly smoke and mirrors, a series of acts to either use or to cover his powers, depending on the situation. With Dawn, he felt he could be himself, providing he could figure out just who that was.

"I have you all figured out," she said, jerking him to attention with her words. God, was she reading *him* and not realizing it? "You observe body language and expressions really well," she continued. "Then you combine that with things you learn from your sources. For instance, you made a good guess that I lost my ring in a pool somewhere. How could I ever prove or disprove that?"

"Find the ring, maybe?"

She scoffed. "The pool is probably no longer there."

"Ah. So I'm like the fakers who wow folks at carnivals, huh? Or maybe a con artist on the psychic hotlines?"

She shrugged.

"I get that you don't believe me," he said.

Her expression was kind. "I believe that *you* believe it, like celebrities who begin to believe their own press. It could be dangerous, this overestimating what you can do, Eric."

"Thanks, I'll keep that in mind," he said dryly, now a little miffed that she thought he was so self-delusional that he would risk their lives.

"Hey, don't be mad. I'm trying to help."

Eric rolled over, giving her his back. "Okay, thanks. Get some sleep. Tomorrow's gonna be a big day for both of us."

"C'mon," she urged. "Don't pout. You're ruining your image. Or have you suddenly run out of jokes?" Her hand closed over his shoulder.

It was too much. Entirely too much to tolerate when he was already hyped up to kiss her. One kiss. That's all he'd do, to shut that smart little mouth of hers.

He rolled back to her and sealed his lips to hers. Only

hers were open in surprise, giving him full access, tempting him to explore her fully while teaching her a lesson in tact.

Tact went right out the window, along with any subtle punishment he'd intended. How sweet she was, and how perfectly fitted to him. He embraced her full length, planning to enjoy every second until she cried wolf.

But Dawn didn't cry wolf. She didn't push back, and she didn't protest in any other way. Instead, she shifted against him, stoking his need even higher and harder. Damn, he wished she would hurry up and learn her lesson, give him a hard smack on the head or something, because he couldn't seem to stop himself as long as she was cooperating.

The little groan she made reverberated through him like a plucked string. An electric, erotic note, one that played over and over in his head, drumming out coherence, vibrating, sending all the blood in his brain to parts of him that never thought for themselves.

Her hands grasped his shoulders, slid down his back, firmly gripped his butt and urged him closer. She wants this. She really, really wants this, cried that devil fighting his conscience. And he wanted it even more than she did, too keenly to resist.

He slid a hand beneath her blouse and found bare skin, firm and welcoming, burning with the same fever that gripped him. He felt the budding of her nipples, caressed them with eager fingers and both heard and felt his reward in her response.

She was so damned responsive it blew him away. He had to taste her, touch her everywhere, inhale her, be a part of her in every way possible. This intense need for total possession shocked him. He had never wanted to *own* a partner before, but Dawn was not just a partner. This was not just sex. This was everything at the moment, everything he had ever wanted or would ever want. No, he knew it was not a momentary thing at all. He might never recover and be what he had been, but he didn't care.

Dawn filled him up somehow, occupied all those vacant places he never realized existed in him. This phenomenon had been at work for days now, about to culminate in this unstoppable act. The sheer power of his feelings and this new vulnerability scared the hell out of him, but he knew he had no defense. Didn't even want one. He only wanted *her*.

"Mine now," he murmured against her mouth.

Hardly breaking the kiss, they tore off clothes and came together in a rush of heat. No way to stop, no way. Fractured thoughts tried to intrude, but he drowned them out with a growl of pleasure so intense it nearly hurt. She met his every move, urging him on, banishing any coherent thought he had left.

Her soft exclamation rushed out against his neck when he thrust inside her and took her with all the finesse of a novice.

Regret wouldn't register. He didn't care about technique, about anything but becoming one with Dawn, living, breathing, being a part of her. And he was. For a few minutes, it seemed as if her every feeling rushed into him and expanded his own.

Faster and higher, keener and sharper, the ecstasy mounted until they exploded together in a cry of completion.

But once he withdrew, Eric realized he was no longer complete. Something would always be missing unless he held her as close as could be, unless he was part of her and she a part of him.

Breathless and confused, he couldn't seem to let her go, to give her space to recover. Instead, he pressed her closer and buried his face in her neck, reluctant to discuss what had happened.

"Now I can sleep," she murmured, placing a soft kiss on his temple. "Don't talk."

Well, damn. What kind of woman was she that she didn't want to dissect what had happened and ruin the magic?

Eric smiled and caressed her naked back with his hand, letting go just a little, certain that he could get the magic back again once they had rested. Dawn amazed him. She just amazed the hell out of him.

Drifting into oblivion was the last thing he wanted to do. She had gone there before him, her breathing already becoming even and her heartbeat calm. His one thought was of how happy he was. For the first time in memory, truly happy. How rare was that, to experience it and know it as it was happening?

Happiness made little sense, knowing what they might face in the morning, how they might not survive if Stefan Cydonia, the indomitable Quince, guessed who they really were. Eric could die a happy man if he expired right now, but he wasn't ready to go just yet. And he could never let any harm come to Dawn.

Things had to go perfectly. Had he considered and prepared for every eventuality, every contingency? God, he hoped so. He prayed so.

In the aftermath of their lovemaking, Dawn feigned sleep. It was too soon to talk about what had happened between them. Maybe she wouldn't discuss it at all. If she could pass it off as an impulse, that would be best. People in dangerous situations often did reckless things they wouldn't ordinarily do. But if she were completely honest with herself, Dawn had to admit she might have done it under any circumstances.

She couldn't bring herself to regret it, not when her body still glowed with pleasure. There was another feeling as well, the sublime comfort of truly connecting with another person.

She and Eric were special together, even though she knew in her heart that it was only temporary. Eric Vinland wasn't the type for a girl to pin any long-term hopes on, but that was all right with her. Nope, no regrets at all, she decided.

What if they had never found another chance? They certainly wouldn't on that island, where they would surely be under constant surveillance. And after the mission was over, assuming they survived it, they would go back to their respective jobs and probably never see each other again.

He was not the marrying kind, and Dawn knew it. Not that she had even entertained the thought of that. Not seriously, anyway. It was just that she had experienced something, however brief, with him that she never expected. That feeling of belonging, of being part of another.

She sighed and snuggled against him, still pretending to be asleep. Maybe it was only great sex that made her feel this way. That was something she hadn't experienced before, either. All her adult life, she had wondered what the fuss was all about. Well, now she knew.

For the rest of tonight, she planned to luxuriate in the pleasure of being her own well-satisfied self, lying beside her evanescent lover and partner. Tomorrow, she must become Aurora again, a completely cloaked shadow in the wake of the great Jarad Al-Dayal.

Eric sat straight up out of a sound sleep. Whether a sound or a premonition had awakened him, he couldn't tell. He placed a hand on Dawn's shoulder and gave her a gentle shake. "Wake up. Something's going down."

He hurriedly yanked on his loose trousers and crept barefoot through the salon, sensing Dawn right behind him. He hurried across the salon to the other sleeping quarters.

The aft cabin door stood open. Clay rushed out, glanced around the salon, then pointed to the deck. When they were topside, Clay leaned close and spoke. "I killed the captain. I couldn't avoid it."

"What happened?" Dawn asked.

"Ressam, since he's smaller, hid in the salon. We figured the captain would come after us, so we made a plan. Ressam would grab him from behind when he started for our cabin. I'd be inside, ready to assist. But the door opened and I saw a blade coming at me. I kicked him in the chest. Then he just fell across the bunk, dead to the world. No pulse."

"You tried to revive him?"

Clay nodded. "The kick must have stopped his heart and I couldn't start him up again. We need to find Ressam."

The clouds had passed and the moon beamed down on them, throwing an eerie blue cast over everything on the deck. The scene looked surreal.

The three of them searched. Ressam was missing, but there was blood on the deck, a trail of it leading to the side of the deck. Eric looked down into the water. Though there was nothing to see but black waves calmly sloshing against the side of the *Angeline,* he knew. "Ressam's dead."

"The phone in the salon's ringing," Dawn said.

Eric strode past her and went inside. Dawn and Clay remained on deck.

He picked up the receiver and listened. "Kerosian?" a low-pitched voice asked. "Are you there?"

Eric took a deep breath. "This is Jarad Al-Dayal. Are you Quince?"

"Put Kerosian on."

"He is no longer with us," Eric admitted. "The poor fellow suffered heart failure and expired despite our attempts at resuscitation."

A long silence ensued before the voice spoke again. "Then you must complete his task."

"I am no sailor and have no idea where we are at the moment. I was seriously contemplating ringing up the authorities to come and rescue us."

Bitter laughter sounded on the other end.

"Unless you have a better suggestion," Eric said, using his most condescending tone.

"You can guess what must be done, so do the deed yourself, Al-Dayal. No one else must be privy to this arrangement. Dispose of your remaining watchdog. After you are finished, weight the body down and put it over the side. I have infrared and will be observing. And listening."

Eric pretended to consider it. "And if I refuse? He is a loyal retainer and can be trusted."

"Not by me. I shall terminate the plans for your visit and you will have no need of sailing experience when you depart. And with regard to your wife…"

"She knows nothing," Eric assured him, "and will do as I command."

"Your Aurora is of little consequence other than as a beautiful asset, I know. But I would like her involved in this bit of business on the yacht. If she could be implicated in getting rid of your bodyguard, then she is less likely to report the tale to anyone later, wouldn't you agree?"

"Leave her out of this. What can a mere woman do anyway?"

"As you said, whatever you order her to. I will ring you again when I see you have done as instructed. You and the woman will take the inflatable and come ashore. If there is evidence of life on board the *Angeline* after you leave it, you will never return to it or to the mainland. Are we understood?"

Eric hesitated a minute for effect, then agreed. "It shall be done."

He replaced the receiver and went topside to rejoin Dawn and Clay. "Adil, prepare the inflatable for us and load our bags into it," he ordered Clay. "We are to go ashore soon."

Dawn looked at him curiously. He wished he had time to tell her what was to happen, but maybe her natural reaction to it would satisfy Quince. Then Eric wondered if he would actually get the response from her that a woman such as Aurora might give.

To insure that, he muttered to her as he passed her on deck. "Trust what I'm about to do. He has a night scope trained on our every move. Act appropriately."

Eric stood idly by and watched as Clay prepared the small boat as ordered. Then his friend retrieved their bags from their cabin and put them aboard. "Ready to go," Clay told him.

Eric beckoned him back on board, then glanced out over the water to the blue-gray island, now barely visible on the horizon. He pulled the nine millimeter out of his belt and aimed.

Clay nodded once, holding up his hands as if pleading for his life. Eric fired, one miss, one hit.

Dawn screamed. "What have you done?" She ran toward the fallen body.

Eric grabbed her arm. "Get something heavy to weight him down!" he shouted.

"No!" she screamed, batting at him with her hands and arms.

Eric shook her and pretended a slap. She recoiled, went

reeling like a practiced stunt woman and screamed again. That one would surely reach the mikes, Eric figured. It probably reached the mainland without a microphone. His ears certainly were ringing.

He leaned forward to help her to her feet and murmured low, as his head neared hers, "Scuba gear's in that hold over there." He guided her with a look. "Go in and grab a bedsheet first to disguise the tank. Put on your garb while you're in there."

She nodded, then scurried back inside.

Meanwhile, Eric had noted that Clay was not moving. He rushed over to make sure the bullet hadn't penetrated the vest Clay always wore. "You okay?"

Clay cursed, still not moving. "I *hate* this job."

Eric snickered, keeping his voice low. "Quit belly-aching, you're on vacation in Greece, dude. How's your Houdini act?"

"Rusty. Don't do the knots too tight or you'll damn well be on your own."

"You aren't bleeding anywhere, are you? Hate to give the sharks a snack."

"Had to mention them, didn't you?"

"Hang on to the inflatable and we'll tow you as far as we can. I'll veer right as a signal for you to let go. Sun's about to come up. Great timing. Quince's infrared will be practically useless in this much light, but it's still dark enough that a telescope won't show details. Let's get you outfitted."

Dawn returned, properly covered in a dark blue robe and matching head-covering. She deposited the air tank nearby and began to help Eric buckle Clay's motionless body into it. He was well over six feet tall and as heavy as lead. Eric wondered how the two of them would heft him over the side.

"Catch you later," Eric said as they managed to drag Clay upright and bend him forward over the rail. Then Eric stepped back and motioned imperiously for Dawn to tip up Clay's legs and send him into the drink. She grunted with the effort, but performed admirably, he thought.

With a satisfied nod, he guided her down into the inflatable Zodiac. Three bumps on the rubber side of the boat and the appearance of air bubbles told him Clay was good to go. "Let's do this," he snapped, and they were off for the island.

Several hundred yards offshore, Eric turned right, ostensibly to approach a better section of the small beach. Less drag on the boat told him Clay was now operating on his own.

The craggy section of rock to the left would provide perfect cover for Clay's secret insertion. The waves dashing against the rocks worried Eric, but Clay Senate was the ultimate warrior, an excellent swimmer. Now was not the time for a mind link, but Eric gave it a shot. All he picked up was solid determination mixed with a smidgen of annoyance. Or maybe those were his own feelings.

Reluctantly, Eric deliberately quit trying to connect with Clay and concentrated on their own landing.

The welcoming party was well armed with automatics. Eric approached as far up on the beach as possible. Two of the four men slung their weapons' straps over their shoulders and waded out to meet them. Eric climbed out first, ignoring their greeters. Then he caught Dawn up in his arms to carry her ashore.

"Here goes nothin'!" he muttered in her ear.

"Eric, about what happened between us…" she began. "It was just…"

"Fantastic, I know. Now hold that thought until we get off this island," he ordered.

She pinched his neck. "I was going to say it was a freak mistake and we ought to put it out of our minds."

"Okay, go ahead. I can if you can," he replied without a touch of bitterness.

"Sometimes I could just shoot you, Vinland," she huffed.

"Yeah, well, you might have to get in line behind those oafs with the Uzis. Now morph into meek mode, will you? We've got a job to do here."

Chapter 9

There were steps carved in the sloped crags that surrounded the crescent section of beach. Eric deposited Dawn on her feet and left her to follow him. He briefly noted that the men who had dragged the Zodiac ashore were now collecting the bags out of it. The two remaining kept their weapons trained on him. The swish of wet fabric behind him assured him that Dawn was keeping up with his long stride.

He allowed one of the men to run a metal-detecting wand up and down the length of their bodies without actually touching them. It was to be expected. They had left their weapons aboard the *Angeline* since the hardware would have been confiscated anyway.

At the top of the steps, he paused. What a layout Quince had here. A virtual castle of natural stone blended beautifully with the island's natural vegetation. From the air, it would probably go unnoticed. Up close, the attention to detail was impressive.

The care with which the surroundings were culti-vated proved Quince had good maintenance help. That probably meant a large staff beyond these guards he had sent to meet them.

"This way," one of the men instructed in Greek, stepping around Eric and pointing to the right.

Eric followed, listening for Dawn's footsteps on the flagstone path behind him.

When they neared the double doors of the entrance, one panel opened, then the other. A white-coated servant gestured them inside and led the way to the curved stair-case. The majordomo, Eric supposed.

The older man smiled. "Madame is to go to her rooms with the baggage, sir. If you will come with me?"

"I will see her to our room. *Then* I will come with you," Eric announced, at his most imperious.

"As you will, sir. This way."

The rooms proved to be more than adequate. They were adjoining, large and airy, containing identical king-size beds draped in white gauze. The rest of the furnishings looked antique and very expensive. "This will do," he said, deliberately exhibiting impatience.

He watched the hirelings deposit their bags. One disap-peared with the case containing Eric's laptop, an expected act.

Then he addressed Dawn, not bothering to lower his voice. "Remain here. Lock the door.

"Out," he ordered the others and waited until they left. He stopped outside in the hallway and listened for the snick of the lock. With a satisfied nod, he followed the servant who had requested he do so.

A feeling of excitement pervaded his every nerve. Now

he would meet this Quince and see what they were up against. Dawn was probably seething at being excluded from this first meeting, but Eric felt a little relieved that he could scope out the situation first. Then again, he didn't much like leaving her alone in the event Quince was on to them. Not that he thought Dawn was helpless, but she might be if caught unawares.

Worrying about her could be deadly in itself, preventing him from doing what he came to do. He had to stop that now before he met Quince.

"Here we are, sir," the servant murmured as he tapped twice on the highly polished door and then opened it. "Mr. Jarad Al-Dayal," he announced.

Distinguished was the word Quince brought to mind. He reminded Eric of a silver-haired actor he had once seen in the vintage movies he loved to watch. Stewart something-or-other. Piercing gray eyes that held a coldness. Dark, expressive eyebrows, one now quirked as he examined his guest.

He rose slowly from the luxurious leather chair and extended a long-fingered, well-manicured hand. "Greetings," he said softly. "Won't you sit down?" He gestured to the matching chair facing the one in which he'd been sitting.

Eric swept his robe back and sat stiffly, regarding Quince with his most imperious glare. "Shall we get to the business at hand?"

Quince smiled. "Patience, my friend. I have always heard that men of your persuasion preferred a bit of social discourse before discussing weighty matters. We have the entire weekend for business. And longer if we need it. Would you care for a drink?" He inclined his head toward the elaborate wet bar that filled one corner of the study.

Eric narrowed his eyes. "You must know that *men of my persuasion,* as you so delicately put it, avoid alcohol."

"Perhaps a coffee, then?" Quince suggested, oozing hospitality, charm and sophistication.

Eric sat back, tapping his fingers on the arms of the chair. "Orange juice."

Quince smiled and sat down as he spoke to the servant. "Two juices, Conroy."

They waited, observing each other without any subterfuge until they had been served. Then Quince said, "We will breakfast in the dining room in a quarter hour, Conroy. Inform the lady and have her join us."

"She will not," Eric informed him. He sipped the fruit juice from the expensive crystal.

"Why not relax the rules for the duration of your visit, Al-Dayal? This is a new world, and too much adherence to tradition impedes progress. Come now, I insist. Your wife will be perfectly safe." His smile was almost a smirk.

Eric returned it in kind. "I meant that she will not come if I do not order it personally. Unless you intend to use force upon her, which I would not advise you to do."

Quince laughed. "Is that a warning against the lady herself or repercussions from you?"

"Both," Eric stated without pause.

"Then please, go with Conroy and fetch her. If you do not trust me to share a simple meal with your wife, how am I to believe you would trust me in any important transaction?"

Was that an implied threat? Eric studied the man's beatific expression but could not see behind it. However, Quince was providing the perfect opportunity to introduce Dawn to him so that Eric could add her reactions to his own. Dispensing with Dawn's isolation would be convenient. The question was, how would it benefit Quince?

Eric shrugged and took his time finishing his juice.

"Very well," he agreed. "It is no great concession. My wife was born in the West and is familiar with your customs."

"Excellent," Quince said smoothly. "I am happy to see that you yourself are adaptable to Western customs when the need arises, Jarad. I may call you that?"

"Of course, Quince. Or have you a *Christian* name you would like me to employ?" Eric asked with no small amount of sarcasm.

"Quince will suffice."

Eric left the study, carefully concealing a frown of consternation. Their adversary was Greek, as the identity Interpol had for him indicated. He had learned his English in England, perhaps attended school there. He was absolutely fluent and well-spoken. That didn't gibe with other indications of his social status, however. Middle- to lower-class Greeks didn't usually have access to a public school education abroad.

Maybe Quince had not been born to wealth, but he possessed it now, that was for sure. This place had cost several fortunes. Quince worked hard at giving the appearance of old money, but little things gave him away. A few statues that were too Romanesque to mix well with classic Greek. Furnishings that were not quite eclectic enough to have been gathered at leisure over decades. This place had been thrown up all at once, accessories bought in bulk and the entire estate done up for show. Like Quince himself, whose sophisticated exterior sported a few telltale cracks in the facade. He was an actor who had done exhaustive research for the role but neglected to immerse himself in it or, perhaps, didn't quite know how.

While observations might be helpful, Eric regretted he had not penetrated a single thought of Quince's the entire time he was with the man. Not even when they had shaken hands.

First, Dawn had blocked him without even trying and now Quince seemed to possess a solid mental barrier. Eric found he couldn't even read old Conroy's thoughts. The servant was most likely cursing the need to climb the stairs again. His arthritis was giving him fits. But it was not from the man's thoughts that Eric divined that information.

Maybe the problem lay in trying too hard, Eric decided. He was too uptight. That had to be it. Dawn's fault, of course, though he could hardly blame her. She hadn't asked him to obsess over her the way he was doing.

He shook his head and tried to clear it, but it seemed too filled with thoughts of her and whether she would be as relieved to see him as he would her in a few seconds.

What a helluva time for him to fall like a third-act curtain. The play had barely begun.

Dawn dressed casually for breakfast. She wore a white long-sleeved blouse, embroidered about the neck with a red Greek key design, and a calf-length flowing skirt cinched with an intricately woven belt of red cord. Dainty red sandals completed her ensemble. She quickly fastened her hair in a knot at her nape and went to present herself to Eric for his approval.

He frowned up at her when she entered his room. "For the length of this visit only, I shall allow you to revert to your European customs because our host expects this. Do not make me regret it, Aurora."

Of course, he was performing for any audio or video surveillance installed in their rooms. But even knowing that, it amazed Dawn how that tone of his ruffled her feathers. The man was entirely too good at acting the chauvinist.

She granted him a tight little smile. "Whatever you desire, of course, Jarad."

"Come." He led the way out of the room, then held the

door for her. The old servant was waiting for them in the corridor. Silently they followed him back down the stairs to the dining room.

When they entered Dawn had her first glimpse of their adversary. Her breath caught in her throat. She had fully expected to see the man who had committed murder right before her eyes. The one who stole the information. It definitely was not him. But surely this guy must have hired someone to have it done.

Quince rose and smiled at her. He was an incredibly handsome man, tanned and fit, impeccably dressed in a pale blue cashmere pullover, gray pleated slacks and sandals.

"Welcome to the island, Mrs. Al-Dayal. Would you mind if I call you Aurora?"

Dawn shot Eric a questioning look, as if asking his permission, and watched him nod once, his imperious frown darker than ever.

She turned back to Quince. "Yes, of course. Thank you, Señor Quince," she said, employing her Spanish accent.

"Just Quince will do." His smile widened as he gestured to the table. "Please, join me, both of you. The others will arrive momentarily, and in the meantime, we will have coffee."

Others? Dawn resisted voicing the question, but she was eager to see who else and how many had come to the island to bid on the information.

There were only six chairs at the table, though it could comfortably seat fourteen. Was that significant?

Their host sat at the head of the table, Eric to his right, she to his left.

Dawn stirred cream into her coffee and kept her eyes averted from Quince, as was proper. His deep voice rambled on about the weather.

In less than five minutes, two men and a woman arrived. Quince greeted them as cordially as he had Eric and Dawn, then proceeded to make introductions. "Carlotta Vasquez from Colombia," he said, bowing to the tall, sultry woman whose sharp brown eyes raked Dawn with blatant curiosity. "You and Aurora should get on remarkably well since you share a common language. She is originally from Andorra," Quince continued.

Dawn nodded shyly and murmured a short, formal greeting in Spanish, which gained her no response at all.

Quince turned then to a man who was extremely dark and sinister looking. "Obaya Minos from Tanzania."

That one said nothing, merely kept his thick lips pressed firmly together, his hands clenched by his side and appeared to be holding his breath. A portly man with a cleanly shaved head, Minos had elected to dress formally in a suit and a tie that must be choking his thick neck. Obviously, he did not like the atmosphere of bonhomie their host was attempting to instill.

"Last, but certainly not least, we have Sean McCoy from Dublin."

The Irishman nodded and pulled out a chair for Carlotta, who pierced him with a disdainful glare over her shoulder. Whether that stemmed from the fact that Carlotta liked to do things for herself or because McCoy looked like an unmade bed was anybody's guess. The man had a certain wild charm, Dawn guessed, if you liked spiky hair, thrift-store apparel and a probable connection to the extremist element of the IRA.

"Jarad Al-Dayal and his lovely Aurora complete our party, my friends. Please, feel free to chat and get to know one another. We are a select group, all in the same line of work, as it were, though I do not like discussing business matters until the time is right."

Silence ensued as a white-coated servant poured more coffee and another began serving. The plates of fruit were fresh and beautifully presented with sprigs of mint and candied violets. Pastries gleamed with their golden crusts and sweet glazes.

Dawn's mouth watered as she kept her hands in her lap and waited for Quince to begin.

Tension grew as thick as the honey Quince started spooning on his croissant. Everyone at the table must be wondering the same thing, of course.

Sean McCoy took a deep breath and treated them to a crooked grin before addressing Quince. "I'll ask for us all, then. Why would you be revealing our names?"

"Insurance," Quince replied evenly, taking a bite.

"I don't understand." Eric leaned back his head and stared down his nose at Quince. "We are competitors, at least in this transaction."

"But you need not be," their host said smoothly, lifting his cup. "Have your coffee, eat. There is a method to my madness, as you shall see later. For now, enjoy the meal."

The African stood abruptly. "I shall *not* make this pretense. Summon me when you are prepared to do business."

Quince stood, too, splaying his fingertips on the table-top. "Sit *down,* Minos. Now!" His curt command left no room for quibbling.

Minos paused only two seconds, glaring, then dropped his gaze and resumed his seat.

So did Quince. "Thank you. Now eat. There are activities planned for today that you will not wish to miss."

"Ridiculous farce," muttered the exotic Carlotta. "And dangerous." She poked at her fruit with her fork, speared a ball of cantaloupe and chewed it viciously.

Eric shrugged and began shifting the strawberries on

his plate to one side as if they were slugs. His eyes met Dawn's, a brief connection offering reassurance he didn't try to conceal. His little know-nothing wife should be wondering what the hell was going on, Dawn figured. After all, she was the only one at the table not directly involved in the imminent bidding war.

Never one to pass up a chance to fortify her strength, she dug into the luscious fare Quince had provided and satisfied her hunger.

Might as well seize the moment. It was rapidly becoming the creed she lived by. She had certainly done that with her partner in the early hours of this morning. There would be no further assuaging of that particular hunger any time soon.

She should kick herself for it, but she wouldn't. The slip-up had hurt no one. Not yet, anyway.

Their meal concluded with Quince's announcement. With a clap of his hands, he stood. "I have a fishing expedition planned for the morning. We will hike to an inlet where my thirty-two-footer is docked and—" he leaned forward eagerly as he spoke "—hopefully bring in a noteworthy marlin."

Everyone glared at him except Dawn. She had no problem looking puzzled. It was Sean McCoy who protested. "A waste of time, Quince. What are you tryin' to do here, make us all mates or somethin'?"

"I did not travel halfway around the world to fish," Carlotta snapped. "This is absurd."

Minos remained silent. So did Eric. Dawn looked to him for direction, as a wife should, but he was studying Quince intently. Could he divine what the man had in mind here? No, she still didn't quite believe Eric could do that.

They could be in big trouble if Eric was relying on that

dubious ability to get what he needed from Quince. Not to mention what a problem it could be if he intended to use whatever mind-melding talents he thought he possessed to call in the cavalry if things got hot.

Quince must be playing for time, delaying the bidding for some reason. But what could that be?

Suddenly Eric stood. "The sooner we leave, the sooner we can return. I am ready."

"Wonderful!" Quince crowed. "Aurora? Have you ever fished before?"

She ducked her head shyly, then shook it to indicate she had not.

"Fine. It's an uplifting experience, I can tell you. Nothing like a day in the good salt air to boost spirits."

Carlotta huffed audibly. "I am not dressed for this…fishing," she complained. It was true. Her shirt and pants were silk and she wore three-inch heels.

"Go and change, anyone who needs to," Quince said. "The rest of us will wait in the courtyard. But hurry. It will be an eventful trip, I promise."

None of them dared miss the outing, of course, even though nobody wanted to fish. Who knew what business would take place on Quince's yacht? Anyone left behind could be at a disadvantage if he decided to conduct the bidding there.

She needed to let Eric know Quince was not the one who had killed Bergen after he stole the information on the radar shield. That fact meant there was another man involved in all this, perhaps even on this island, keeping out of sight. Maybe with plans to eliminate all the disgruntled bidders after the deal went through.

As Quince led them down to the courtyard to wait for Carlotta and Minos, she addressed Eric. "I had so hoped we would see our friend again while we were on vacation. Odd how he's disappeared when we expected to see him."

Eric cleared his throat and glanced at Quince who was busy chatting with Sean McCoy about fishing in Ireland. "He will probably appear again before we return home."

"You think he will surprise us?" she asked with a sigh.

Eric's lips quirked in a half smile and he reached for her hand as they walked. "No doubt. I'll have another friend try to find him."

Dawn squeezed his hand. "Good. I would feel much better if we knew what happened to him." And infinitely better if he didn't pop up somewhere with a weapon trained on them.

"So you have never fished?" Eric asked.

"Doesn't one use worms for this?"

He threw back his head and laughed heartily, attracting Quince's and McCoy's attention. "No, my dear. I promise we will use no worms today."

The other men joined the laughter at her naiveté. All except Minos, who remained grim. Dawn blushed appropriately and ducked her head again, biting her lip to keep from laughing, too.

God grant her a chance to hold that fishing rod and she would show these yo-yos how to land the big one. Gramps hadn't dragged her down to the coast every summer for nothing.

Eric, however, had seen the gleam in her eye and issued a wordless warning by pursing his lips and giving an infinitesimal shake of his head.

Dawn sighed, shrugged and looked out across the placid and incredibly blue waters. How could evil exist in such a beautiful haven? Why would anyone desire any more wealth than a place like this island, especially if it meant conspiring with terrorists to create more havoc in the world?

* * *

The afternoon proved pleasant, considering the circumstances. No one other than Quince seemed to know exactly what those circumstances were. What was his plan?

Dawn noticed that the *Angeline* was nowhere in sight as they left the island. There were eight in all aboard the *Diana,* including Eric, herself, Quince, Carlotta, Sean, Minos, the Greek captain Helos at the wheel and a young fellow called Paulo who remained below unless he was serving drinks. Everyone else lounged topside.

Dawn relaxed in the sun beneath a wide-brimmed hat Quince had offered her from the salon below. They sped out across the Aegean, ventured very near the coast of Turkey and then trolled the deeper waters for the marlin Quince said they were after.

Carlotta grumbled periodically, her voice nearly as harsh as the prominent bones of her face and the slicked-back hairstyle that made her ebony hair shine with cold blue light.

Minos remained silent and avoided the others as much as possible, biding his time until the expedition was over, Dawn supposed.

Sean McCoy, on the other hand, threw himself into the expedition with gusto. But it was Eric who snagged the fish.

They were off then, giving the marlin its head while Eric's rod bent under pressure and the tendons in his bared forearms accepted the strain. His delighted grin looked genuine, his euphoria was contagious.

Dawn felt mesmerized by the sight of him locked in an elemental struggle with a creature easily triple his size and weight.

Quince hovered, offering sage advice, his gaze never leaving the prey. Periodically it would jump clear of the water, writhing with strength and grace, then splash down again and tear forward, still firmly hooked. It seemed a shame to catch and kill this beautiful denizen of the deep, but Dawn felt the excitement anyway. A paradox, for sure.

When the fish tired, Quince shouted for the others to come and help bring it aboard. Carlotta approached, wearing a cat's smile as if she planned to devour the thing then and there. Sean hopped around like a seasoned deck hand used to such chores. Minos was conspicuously absent.

As soon as they had secured the fish and everyone remarked on its size and power, Eric glanced around the deck. "Where is the African?"

Quince shrugged. "Probably below with Paulo."

But he was not. Paulo appeared with cold drinks and declared he had not seen Minos. A search of the entire boat turned up no sign of the big man from Tanzania. As the old gangsters used to say about their victims who were disposed of in the water, Dawn would bet he was *sleeping with the fishes*.

"Perhaps he fell overboard! We should go back for him!" Dawn said, stating the obvious to see what sort of reaction she'd get. They all looked at her as if she were the token imbecile.

"Back *where* precisely?" Carlotta asked wryly. "I say good riddance."

Sean's quick gaze glanced off each of them, but he said nothing.

"Shouldn't you call for a search?" Dawn asked Quince, wide-eyed.

Eric's arm slid around her and drew her close. "This is not for you to worry about, Aurora. Be silent now."

Though his voice sounded gentle, the command was firm. Dawn dropped her gaze to the deck and sniffled for effect while her mind raced, trying to recall where everyone had been during the last hour or so.

Unfortunately, her attention had been so locked on Eric's battle with the fish, she had not thought about keeping track of the other members of the party.

Quince had remained beside Eric, of that she was certain. The captain had been occupied at the wheel. And if Paulo had come on deck, she would have noticed. Wouldn't she?

It was a cinch Minos hadn't taken a dive over the side of the boat on his own. Either Carlotta or Sean must have given him some help.

Surely no one, with the possible exception of Quince and the captain, was armed, but she would bet her last nickel they were all trained to disable or kill bare-handed.

She should have been watching them all. But who would expect anyone to disappear off a boat?

Quince had expected it, though, she thought suddenly. He didn't look at all surprised when they noticed Minos was missing. Now she realized what he must be doing. He was giving them the opportunity to eliminate the competition.

Was this a game for his amusement or simply a business decision? All Quince had to do was issue the invitation to bid, see who responded, run financial checks of their organizations and determine which one was likely to pay the most for what he had to sell. Then he could give that one the best opportunities to kill off the competition.

If they were all dead but the buyer, Quince would remain safe on his uncharted island, his whereabouts unknown. It would be much easier to transport the lone survivor, the one who actually bought the information, back to the mainland without revealing the location of this place than to arrange for all of them to return. Less chance of betrayal that way, too.

Those who were not successful at getting what they had come for might want a little retribution. Or their respective organizations might.

Captain Kerosian, who had brought Eric and her here, had probably been the one to transport the others to the island. Now he was dead. Would Helos be next? As far as Quince knew, Eric's two bodyguards were out of the picture. The other bidders seemed to have none accompanying them, either.

"How unfortunate we are in no position to call for help," Quince said without conviction. "We will naturally return to the island by the same route we traveled, but I seriously doubt there is much hope of locating him now. Captain Helos? Set the appropriate course."

And the captain would, Dawn thought. They would return with all the many twists, turns and diversions that brought them to the spot where the marlin were plentiful. Who but someone tracking it on the charts would know if it was the same?

The fishing expedition was over and the bidders reduced to three, plus one unnecessary and highly expendable wife. She looked up at Eric, then at the others. They had figured that out, too. Who would be next?

Chapter 10

Eric marveled at Quince's ingenious plan. It was dastardly, yes, but you could hardly expect more from one who made his living off terrorists.

Quince had to be aware of the financial standing of the groups represented in the bidding war or they wouldn't have been invited here. When each of the losers returned unsuccessful, there could be repercussions. If they didn't return at all, that might also be the case, but by then he would bet that Quince would be impossible to find.

Dawn looked worried, as she should. Quince had noticed her consternation. Some of that worry was real, Eric knew, and at least a part of it was for him personally, not just the outcome of the mission. Though there was still no direct mental communication between them, he felt very strongly that she cared. If not romantically, then surely the way she would in covering a partner's back.

They were guided below where they lounged in the cabin with cold drinks. With the sun directly overhead, it would be impossible for anyone to gauge their direction on the return trip even if they remained on deck.

Quince had choreographed everything. How he had gotten the marlin to cooperate was anyone's guess, but it had gone down like clockwork, Eric had to give the man that much. Or maybe Quince was just lucky things were working out as he'd planned.

He sipped his soft drink and placed a protective arm around Dawn. As little Aurora, she performed beautifully, looking up at him with those soulful doe eyes, letting her sensitive lips tremble just a little.

God, he would have given his eyeteeth to kiss her, but an open display would be totally out of character for Al-Dayal. Instead, he squeezed her shoulder and released it. "Get me another pillow. My shoulders ache from all that exercise."

She hesitated only a second, then obeyed. Eric noted Quince's gaze flick from him to Dawn and back again. Then he smiled. "You are a very lucky man, Jarad."

Eric frowned, then folded his hands across his stomach. "So it is said. Perhaps a man makes his own luck."

Quince shrugged. "Some think that's true and in the event of good luck, it might be. I've found that bad luck, however, usually takes us totally unaware."

"It is how one reacts to any luck that determines his ultimate fortune," Eric replied evenly, adjusting the cushion Dawn placed behind his neck. She sat down beside him again, ever the dutiful wife.

"Enough stupid philosophy," Carlotta snapped, addressing Quince. "I need to have done with this now and fly home. Why can we not present our bids now and have you drop us on the mainland?"

She clunked her glass down on the table and stood, rubbing her upper arms with her palms as if she were cold. Or frightened.

"Patience, my dear," Quince said with a toothy smile. "All in good time."

He reached behind him and hit a switch. Music flooded the cabin. "*Rebetika*," he explained. "Sad, isn't it? For a time, this music was outlawed by the government because it so often deals with poverty and suffering, but now it is becoming prevalent again."

He listened to the plaintive, haunting strains for a time, then added, "Governments come and go, but the people themselves will prevail eventually."

"Now there's a freakin' message to live by," McCoy agreed, his voice rife with feeling.

Eric felt, aside from his and Dawn's reasons, that the Irishman was probably the only bidder present whose motives for acquiring the radar-shield plans were in any way connected to patriotism. However extremist their views were, the members in Sean's sort of group almost always possessed passion and dedication. He would die for his cause, but he would rather kill for it.

Carlotta rolled her eyes at Sean's comment and sat down again, resigned to endure whatever Quince arranged. She had little choice. Her motive was power. She got off on control, too, and now she had none. He didn't need her thoughts to know this woman was determined and deadly.

He wished he hadn't been forced to bring Dawn along on the mission. Though he wouldn't have had the chance to know her if he hadn't. Her presence put her at tremendous risk, and seriously hampered his goals.

Eric was unused to fear while on the job. Only a fool was never afraid, but he had never let it become a problem for him. Mostly he ignored it, but now he couldn't. He was afraid for Dawn.

Sure, she was good at testing security. Her record showed she was great at hand-to-hand and an expert shot, but he knew she had never come up against these sorts of international hard-asses before.

If McCoy or Carlotta managed to take him out first, she would be left a lamb among wolves. She had no weapons except her wits. He prayed those were as sharp as they appeared to be. Maybe he should plan to strike first and eliminate the risk of leaving her vulnerable.

Eric tried again to read Quince, hoping for some indication of what was on the agenda when they reached the island. He drew a blank. Quince merely smiled at him, nodding in time with the sorrowful strings of the bouzouki.

Neither could he read the others. Maybe Quince's block had shaken his confidence in that regard. Maybe Dawn had. Maybe he had simply lost the ability. He could function without it, he assured himself. Somehow.

A little over an hour later, they were back at Quince's estate having a light luncheon on the terrace. No one ate at first. They didn't touch a dish at all until Quince himself had eaten some of it.

Eric and Dawn were no exception, though Eric was doubtful Quince intended to do away with any of the bidders himself. No, he apparently planned to let them take care of each other. The man was enjoying himself, that was plain to see.

Carlotta kept casting sly looks in McCoy's direction. Maybe she planned to join forces with him if she could arrange it. Two of them working together could dispatch ol' Al-Dayal in a heartbeat. Even now, she was most likely thinking about the cold-blooded seduction she had planned for the Irishman tonight after everyone else had gone to bed. Eric switched his attention to McCoy and figured that Sean would be wise to such tricks. Had he decided what he would do about it?

Eric concentrated on the excellent souvlaki. Greece was famous for the skewered meat, grilled and sliced thinly, then tucked inside pita bread. He absolutely loved the stuff Dawn had jokingly called goat burgers. She was daintily wolfing hers down now, obviously famished after their morning outing.

"Why not go for a swim after lunch, eh?" Quince suggested. "There are suits in the cabana that should fit everyone."

The pool looked inviting and the heat had become almost oppressive. The high walls that surrounded the terrace, pool and gardens blocked the sea breeze that might have cooled it a bit. The fans only stirred the hot air.

"I'm for it," Sean announced, tossing down his napkin. He chucked Carlotta under her stubborn chin. "If the little chili pepper here promises not to try to drown me."

She jerked away from his touch and gave him a haughty glare. "Go straight to hell, McCoy."

He laughed merrily and sauntered off to change. Moments later, they watched his expert dive into the pool. "Water's fine," he crowed, daring Carlotta with a look. "Cool," he added provocatively, drawing out the word.

She tossed her braid over her shoulder and went to change into a suit.

Quince raised a brow. "Jarad? Do you not swim?"

Eric pretended resignation. "If you insist. Aurora, you will remain here where I can see you."

It went without saying that Al-Dayal would never allow his wife to swim in the company of other men.

Even Quince did not bother to suggest that. Instead, he offered to keep her company. "I promise to be a perfect gentleman, Jarad. Go have your swim. You have nothing to worry about."

With a warning glower, Eric went to the cabana, reluctantly leaving Dawn alone with their host. He trusted she could handle herself in broad daylight with him less than fifty feet away. Maybe she could get something out of Quince about what he had arranged for the evening.

Dawn watched Eric's controlled laps as Sean and Carlotta splashed around like dolphins. She ignored Quince, even though she could feel his cold gaze fastened on her.

"You would like to swim, too, wouldn't you, my dear?" he asked, all tea and sympathy. "What a pity Jarad is so mired in the old ways."

She shrugged and continued observing the pool.

"You strike me as an independent woman at heart, Aurora," Quince announced, his voice low and persuasive. "I'd wager you didn't know what you were getting into when you married him, did you?"

"I knew he was a Muslim."

"But not that he would stifle your every impulse and thought. That has to become tiring after a while."

"I am a faithful wife, Señor Quince. And a faithful Muslim since I converted."

"Ah, and a retired Catholic, if there is such a thing," he said, nodding. "So you love the man that much, eh?"

Dawn cleared her throat and looked away, out at the controlled riot of flowers, the elegant frangipani trees and the sweep of manicured lawn. "Of course."

He laughed. "Of course *not,*" he corrected. "If you want out, I am the way."

She turned to look directly at him and hesitated a couple of seconds for effect. "What do you mean…out?"

"Of the marriage. I could help you escape him. You must know what he is…what he *does*."

"He is in the oil business. And he *does* very little," she replied.

Quince's eyebrows drew together, and he sighed loud and long. "My dear, he is a terrorist, a leader in a movement that is bent upon destroying Western civilization as we know it. Surely you've become aware of that during your time together."

Dawn swallowed hard and ducked her head as if in shame.

"I will give you the means to end your servitude to this arrogant man permanently if you say the word."

For a long time, Dawn continued to watch the swimmers. Then she turned and asked in a whisper, "What word?"

Quince smiled. "Patience, little one. As I said to Carlotta, all in good time."

Lord have mercy, Dawn thought, carefully schooling her expression of awe, Quince meant for *her* to kill Eric, or at least his alter ego, Jarad.

"If you tell him of this conversation," Quince warned, "he will never trust you again. Always, he will be expecting you to act on my suggestion. I advise you to keep this to yourself for your own good. If he asks, we have been discussing the garden and grounds."

"Yes," she agreed. "The fragrance of the frangipani and the recipe for controlling snails."

"That would be beer?" he asked, smiling sweetly.

"And salt. Now we need not lie about the subject of our talk. At least not entirely."

"I like you, little one," he said gently. "And I want you

to leave this island in a better spirit than how you arrived. You deserve that."

"Thank you," she murmured, wondering whether Quince meant *spirit* as in frame of mind, or *spirit* as in ghost.

As it happened, Eric, Carlotta and Sean survived their swim and soon were back at the table.

Dawn could hardly keep her eyes off the expanse of smooth brown skin exposed in the brief suit Eric was wearing. The ruddy-faced Sean McCoy was pale all over, fairly buff, but, she would guess from his muscles, not as efficiently trained as Eric. Also, he lacked the tensile, athletic grace Eric possessed.

Carlotta's bikini left little to the imagination, though Sean kept eyeing her as if his might be working overtime. She was stacked, to put it mildly. Her body was long-limbed, and she moved as fluidly as a jungle cat, with muscles concealed under a slick, firm exterior. Dawn thanked her stars she hadn't had to don a swimsuit and compete with that body today. That would have been enough to give a girl a complex.

Relief poured over her when Quince finally suggested they retire to their respective rooms for a siesta, or whatever the Greek equivalent of that might be called.

Quince reminded them for the third time that dinner was at eight and there would be entertainment. Then he walked on ahead of them to speak with his man, Conroy, who waited just inside the open doors.

"Probably planning a public execution or something," Dawn muttered under her breath as they crossed the terrace to the French doors leading in. "He virtually offered to help me kill you."

"Shh," Eric warned. "Play along with whatever he suggests."

Dawn wondered if that included taking a knife to his jugular while he slept.

Eric clasped her hand in his and began questioning her loudly about her short visit with Quince. She dutifully told him about snails, unfamiliar perennials and tamarind trees, noting the satisfied gleam in Quince's eyes when he glanced over his shoulder at them.

When they reached their rooms, Dawn headed to the bathroom where she systematically searched for any concealed mikes. It was the smallest room and would be the most difficult to wire. But it was wired, of that she was certain. Anybody with any half sense would go in here and turn on the water to conceal any conversation. That was basic stuff. She had the water on now, to hide any rustling sounds she made.

There was no camera. She had looked for that first. Either Quince had a jot of decency left in him or hadn't been able to figure out how to hide one in the john.

She discovered the mike, minuscule and sophisticated, top of the line. It wouldn't do to deactivate it right now. She only needed to know where it was.

She continued probing every possible spot where she might find another. Bingo. On the frame of the mirror above the sink, away from any noisy jets of water, and at mouth level with anyone standing nearby.

Okay. Threats identified. Just to be sure, she completed her organized search of the entire room until she was satisfied there were only two microphones. Realizing she'd have to wait to tell Eric about her conversation with Quince, Dawn gave way to mental exhaustion and slept like the dead.

She knew Eric would be keeping watch. A few hours later, she woke and took her turn while he caught a few winks. Who knew what the evening would bring?

Dawn donned one of the beautiful gowns that had been packed for her. The pale green satin flowed like soft liquid against her skin, revealing her arms and shoulders, swirling about her ankles and tickling the tops of her matching pumps. If their ruse were real, a gown such as this would be worn in private for her husband's eyes only. Dawn wondered what Eric's true reaction to it would be. Feeling pretty sexy, she swept her hair up into a twist, secured it and added a small spray of diamonds to cover the pins.

Eric looked elegant in his dinner jacket and black slacks. The snowy white shirt complemented his fake tan to perfection. His teeth gleamed when he smiled. With panache, he produced a delicate diamond bracelet and fastened it on her wrist. "For my precious gem," he crooned in Al-Dayal's possessive manner.

Dawn sighed, wishing for a second that he was simply Eric, clipping a rhinestone bauble on her just because he liked her. She examined the stones and nodded. "Thank you, Jarad."

"You are most welcome, my dove. Tonight I must share your loveliness with others and I hate the very thought. When this business is finished, I shall have you all to myself again. Only then will I be content."

How could he look so sincere and say things like that? Dawn almost laughed to think any female would treasure such a possessive relationship. And yet, she had to admit there might be a certain comfort in knowing a man would go to such lengths to protect his woman from the leers of other men.

There had actually been times she wished she were wearing the concealing robe and veil. At least when she had it on, she didn't have to worry about schooling her reactions. In spite of what most people thought, it did give a woman a kind of freedom from pretense.

At precisely eight o'clock, they went downstairs, arm in arm, to join the motley crew that made up Quince's house party. Conroy met them at the bottom of the staircase and directed them to the lounge, as he called it.

It was the living room, of course, beautifully decorated in a Tuscan style with tones of amber and gold. The glow of candles lent an old-world charm, though the furnishings looked rather new to Dawn. The others were already there, standing around with drinks in hand.

Sean had cleaned up nicely, but hadn't completely ditched his rough-edged appearance. His spiky blond hair stood on end, probably without the benefit of gel. He had shaved, but not closely, leaving a slight stubble.

McCoy's lively green eyes danced when he assessed her and his lips quirked appreciatively, drawing a warning growl from her *husband*.

Carlotta wore a crimson chiffon wrap that bared the top half of her generous breasts and one long leg, emphasizing her height. Her hair fell straight and thick, caught behind one ear with a matching silk flower.

Dawn suddenly felt totally eclipsed. She shouldn't have minded, ought to have felt relieved, but she couldn't help but wonder how her own appearance held up in comparison, at least in Eric's estimation.

For the first time, she was playing in the big leagues and wanted to measure up. Little Dawnie Moon from Middlesex, New Jersey, recently inducted into the world of espionage, wanted to be a Bond Girl.

The thought made her wince. What was wrong with her? Did she really want to be like Miss Galore over there?

At least her boobs were as big as Carlotta's. That was something. However, her genes dictated her legs were several inches shorter than the long-stemmed Latin beauty's. That was okay, Dawn decided. She visualized her precious marksmanship medals and the days in training when she had taken down male agents who were twice her size. Yep, she could hold her own where it counted, she was sure of it.

At that moment, Eric squeezed her hand and beamed down at her, ignoring the woman who shone like a red neon sign advertising sex for sale. His regard made Dawn feel better. But then again, he *was* pretending at everything else. She shook off the thought.

Quince approached from the mirrored bar with two glasses. "Nonalcoholic wine, especially for you two," he announced.

They accepted the drinks without tasting them. Poison was a distinct possibility, Dawn realized. But then, Quince could simply shoot them, or have them shot, and bury them on the island if he wanted them dead right now. No, he wanted to watch them all match wits, she figured.

"Since it's quite impossible to import any talent to the island for the purpose, I've decided that we will entertain ourselves tonight after dinner," Quince announced. "Sean here is an accomplished tenor."

Sean's smile vanished and he set his drink down on a marble-topped table.

"Surely you realized that I would delve into your pasts extensively," Quince said with a clever grin. "Can't have strangers hanging about when the stakes are this high."

"I won't sing," Sean said.

Quince's grin disappeared in the instant. "I encourage you to humor me, my boy. If you refuse, or if you haven't a tenor voice that rings true to form, I will have to wonder whether someone has seen fit to replace the real Sean McCoy with an imposter."

"That's absurd," Sean remarked, shaking his head.

Quince pursed his lips and shrugged. "Surely you understand that it pays to be thorough in these matters. Let's call tonight's event a verification of sorts."

Sean threw up his hands and surrendered. "Aye, I'll sing, then, if it'll make you happy."

Carlotta laughed. "What do you sing, McCoy? Sad Irish laments?"

He forced a grin. "'Danny Boy', wouldn't you know?" he replied. "A favorite of yours, Lottie?"

She tossed back the remainder of her drink. "Oh please, spare me. Or at least pour me another scotch first."

Quince turned to her. "And you are an incredible dancer, so I am told."

Carlotta inclined her head in a pretense of modesty. "I do try." She raised a jet-black brow at Eric. "And what does our esteemed sheikh do, I wonder? Camel calls?"

Eric shot her a nasty look that included Quince. "I do not perform," he stated categorically. "Ever."

"But you have," Quince argued. "When you attended Oxford, you were known as an excellent pianist." He gestured to the baby grand that occupied one corner of the room. "We would be honored if you would play for us." He paused, then added to all of them, "As I said to Sean, this would certainly establish your backgrounds as genuine."

"Come now, Jarad," Carlotta said provocatively. "If I dance, then you must play. What else is there to do in this godforsaken place?" She cast a dismissive look at Quince. "Until our erstwhile host decides to end our captivity and allow us to get on with our lives?"

Then she seemed to remember Dawn. "What about her?" She flicked a red-tipped finger in Dawn's direction.

"Oh, Aurora sings, too," Quince said. "At the École de Fleur in Nice, she sang with the choir. I'm quite sure she would be happy to grace us with a song. Perhaps Jarad will accompany her on the piano?"

Dawn's heart plunged to the pit of her stomach, but she retained her placid expression. Someone in charge of their cover identities had invented a persona for Aurora that listed *choir,* of all things?

She hadn't sung a note since high school when she entered the contest for sweetheart of the FFA. Even the Future Farmers of America had been discriminating enough to recognize a shower singer when they heard her. She had lost to Susan Zimmerman, who wasn't very good herself.

Quince didn't quite trust that they were who they said they were. Okay. She could do this if it came down to the wire. What could she sing? Her old rendition of "America the Beautiful" was definitely out.

Something easy, then, that didn't require much range. Nothing recently popular in the West. An old song that had probably made it to Europe. Peggy Lee's "Fever"? She glanced surreptitiously at Eric. Okay, maybe not "Fever." *Jarad* would have a fit.

With a shy smile, she looked to Eric for help. "Is this allowed?"

She noted the surprise he instantly masked with disdain. "Nothing of a religious nature," he warned, referring to the fictional Aurora's Catholic school education in France.

"Secular, of course," she replied. "Perhaps something French? 'La Vie En Rose'? Do you know it?"

"Edith Piaf?"

"She is a favorite of mine," Dawn answered. "You have

heard it, then?" She injected a saucy note into her question that drew a reprimanding frown and a reluctant nod.

"Excellent!" Quince said, clapping his hands. "Off to dinner, now. I see Conroy is about to announce it. Come along, all of you. Aren't we famished?"

He herded them to the dining room where they were expected to enjoy the fruits of his chef's labors. Dawn tried to relax. Her nerves were strung so tightly, she was afraid she couldn't eat a bite. However, everyone's mood seemed to have lightened and hers did, too, eventually. Even the dinner conversation exceeded her expectations.

All the while, Dawn wondered just how Quince had managed to get them psyched up to show off abilities beyond their regular occupations.

Carlotta was bragging about the places she had danced when she was a girl. Sean kept trying to top her stories with anecdotes about the clubs in which he had sung.

Egos were odd things and reared up at the strangest of times. She was actually looking forward to trying her hand at being Edith Piaf and leaning on the piano while Eric played.

Jeez, she *hoped* he could play, and if he could, he was probably hoping just as fervently that she could sing.

As distractions went, the imminent program of entertainment served admirably. She could almost forget for whole minutes that one or more of the group might not survive the night.

Chapter 11

God help her, she was next. Following Carlotta's erotic heel-clicking routine that had shown off so much prominent bosom and leg wouldn't be easy. The girl had some great moves, Dawn had to give her that. The flashy red dress hadn't hurt the performance a bit. Had to make you wonder if she knew ahead of time she'd be cutting a rug.

Poor old Sean had to reel in his tongue when she stopped. Eric had applauded, too, surprising them all. His appreciation apparently whetted Carlotta's ham factor and caused an immediate encore. Now a thin sheen of sweat coated Carlotta and she'd had enough adulation to do her a while, Dawn guessed.

Quince was fiddling with the stereo system that had provided the rousing bambuca music.

Eric rose and offered his hand to Dawn. "Shall we?"

She stood and trailed him across the room to the piano.

"What key?" he asked under his breath as they approached it.

"You choose," she whispered, now terrified and trying hard to mask it. She didn't even read music, much less know what key she sang in, but she couldn't admit that in front of Quince. She was supposed to have been in a choir.

"You begin and I'll follow. Whatever key is comfortable for you." He squeezed her hand. "Relax, Aurora. I'm certain you will be fine."

Dawn swallowed hard, blew out a breath and sucked in another. "I was never a soloist," she admitted to Quince, "but I shall do my best."

She had been running over the words in her mind. Her French was fair and she did love the song. She had heard a scratchy recording of Piaf singing it on television.

All eyes were on her now—Carlotta's mocking, Sean's curious and Quince's ready to assess. She looked at Eric for reassurance, and his smile did the trick. He hit several chords, pausing between each, then waited for her to begin.

She closed her eyes and leaned against the piano, feeling the smooth hard surface beneath her forearm.

You're in the shower. All alone. Doors locked. No one to hear but you. Dawn imagined the water pulsing down on her, soothing, warm, relaxing.

She began with a breathy talking of the first line of lyrics, then found her way into it, raising her voice as she let loose. The vibrations from the instrument's strings reverberated through her, giving her confidence.

Words poured out almost without effort and before she knew it, she reached the last note and held it, knowing it sounded sweet. She was a chanteuse!

When Eric's music trailed away to nothing, she heard only dead silence.

Oh God, she had blown it. Dread held her immobile as she forced her eyes to open.

Sean stood and began to clap, his face rapt and his smile wide. Quince followed suit, grinning from guest to guest. Carlotta merely rolled her eyes and gulped her scotch and water.

Unable to help herself, Dawn turned to Eric. He smiled, too, plunked a resounding chord and added a trill of notes. "Very nice, Aurora," he said almost inaudibly.

Quince sat down again and waved an autocratic hand at Sean. "Top *that,* I dare you!" he said with a gruff laugh.

Dawn's knees were absolutely too weak to walk back to her chair. Eric seemed to realize it and got up to escort her, his strong forearm and hand supporting hers. She would have killed for the remainder of Carlotta's scotch and she didn't even like the stuff.

Eric returned to the piano to accompany Sean on the ballad. He did "Danny Boy," probably to annoy Carlotta, Dawn thought. His voice was clear and sweet, reaching notes that sent goose bumps chasing up and down her arms. The boy had missed his calling. What a waste of talent. Or maybe he had talents on the terrorist front that surpassed his music. God only knew.

Eric remained seated after Sean's offering and gave them a small taste of Beethoven. Just a dash of culture that supposedly wasn't his but had been necessary to acquire while he had been a foreign student.

Dawn smiled with true satisfaction. He played both the piano and the audience to perfection, she thought.

Everyone had convinced Quince they were who they proclaimed to be, that was obvious. He looked very pleased with himself and with their efforts as he got up from his chair and suggested drinks on the terrace.

The whole evening seemed surreal.

Dawn grasped Eric's hand in a death grip as they climbed the steps that led up the high wall that surrounded the terrace. The scent of the blooms below swept up and enveloped them in a swirl of heady perfume tinged with salt air. Wind off the sea tossed her hair in every direction, all but blinding her.

He stopped and sat down a few steps from the top where they had an excellent view of both seascape and the terrace where the others were sitting with drinks.

"Let's play newlyweds," he suggested quietly, turning her so that she lay back against his chest with his arms around her to ward off the night's chill. He placed his lips near her ear. "Keep your voice low and no one can possibly hear us up here if you have anything you want to say."

"Parabolics?" she asked, reminding him of the possibility.

"They'd be useless with this wind, but there won't be any set up out here anyway. The house isn't even properly bugged." He hugged her. "It's okay."

"I hate having to interact with them," Dawn whispered, eager to share her thoughts. "In some respects they seem almost normal at times." She turned her head so that she could see his expression as they talked.

"Yeah, we'd rather think of them as monsters without conscience, things with no feelings or emotions. But they are people, too, you know," Eric said with a sigh. He smoothed down the sides of the fake mustache and regarded McCoy, who was laughing merrily at something Carlotta had said. "You know as well as I do that people are seldom all bad or all good."

"You believe that?" Dawn had known people who were definitely all bad. And her grandmother had been good clear down to the marrow of her bones. "One of them is a killer."

"And definitely more bad than good," Eric admitted with a grimace. He lifted his chin in McCoy's direction. "Take Sean there. Given his behavior toward you and Carlotta, I'd be willing to bet he was always kind to his mother. Loved her. But he was raised in a society filled with hatred for the opposition, and war has always been a way of life for him. He thinks he's honoring his family with what he does and they may think so, too. No doubt he's loyal to the death when it comes to his cause and his comrades. Likable fellow under the right circumstances."

"These are not those," Dawn muttered darkly. "I suppose you see redeeming qualities in Carlotta, too."

He chuckled and took her hand, teasing her fingers with his lips. "The girl can dance, you gotta give her that."

"Big deal. And Quince, what about him? I swear I can't get a handle on that guy. Why is he playing at this and dragging it out this way? You'd think he'd be anxious to be done with it."

Eric seemed to be assessing their host as she spoke. For a long time, he said nothing, then shook his head. "Something's not right about him. Have you noticed how tentative he seems at times? He'll be totally in command, marching all of us around like chess pieces and then you see this hesitation, like he's not quite sure what to do next."

Dawn nodded. "Exactly. I think he's the front man. Somebody else is running the show, someone who doesn't want anyone to see his face." She sighed. "Anyway, that's my take on it."

"Astute. I get the same impression."

She leaned even closer. "Impression? What happened to your mind-reading talent? Can't you delve into the old gent's thoughts, or won't he cooperate?"

He didn't want to answer, she could tell. After a long moment of silence, he replied. "I can't do it anymore."

"C'mon," she teased, certain now that he had been feeding her a line of bull about it from the beginning. "Not at all?"

"No. I could before and now I can't, except when…" His voice trailed off as if he'd said more than he meant to say.

"Okay, except when?" she prompted, sure it was a game.

"When we made love. I could see right into your soul," he told her. He looked so deadly serious, he had to be joking.

Dawn laughed. "Wow. Good one. Was it a pretty sight or did you have to wrangle with my dark side?"

He grasped her chin and kissed her thoroughly, erasing every thought she had except how much she wanted him. And he didn't stop. Her body hummed, shot through with a current of longing so intense it scared her.

Before she knew it, he had twisted her around so that they embraced fully. If not for the fact that they were outside, balanced on a steep stone stairway with terrorists looking up at them, Dawn knew they would have made love then and there.

When he finally relented, she had trouble catching her breath and recalling what had prompted him to kiss her in the first place. "Wow," she said on a protracted exhale.

"Yeah," he agreed. "Wow."

"You're angry?" she asked, smoothing her palm down the front of his shirt.

He caught her hand in his and squeezed. "Not with you. Let's get down from here and cut this out before I lose what's left of my control."

On the way down, he preceded her so that she was about

level with his ear as she whispered, "Could you read my mind when you kissed me?" Teasing him seemed to be the only way she might coax him into a better mood.

"Silence," he snapped, his voice gruff and definitely Jarad Al-Dayal's.

Dawn made a face at the back of his head, drawing a hoot of laughter from Carlotta, who was watching them.

He turned quickly, his dark eyebrows drawn together in a warning frown. Dawn gave him a bland look of pure innocence and Carlotta laughed again.

"Perhaps we should say good-night now," Quince announced as she and Eric reached the terrace. "We have a big day tomorrow."

Carlotta stood. "Wait a minute. How long is this going to continue, Quince? You asked us here to bid on the damned plans. I can't speak for the rest, but I have other commitments. Could we finish this tonight?"

"No," he said simply. "If you no longer wish to participate, I will arrange for you to leave."

That shut her up. Her lips firmed, probably to hold in an epithet.

"Well?" he asked, one dark eyebrow raised in question.

"I will stay," she declared with a huff of frustration. "You know how important this is to me."

He nodded, and left them without another word.

Sean went to the bar and poured himself another drink, then relaxed back against it and held up his glass. "Well then. Here's to us and those like us. Damn few, and they are all dead." With a snap of his head, he downed the whiskey and plunked down his empty glass.

"A stupid toast," Carlotta remarked. "What does it mean?"

Sean grinned. "You have to be Irish to understand it."

"Thank God I'm in the dark, then," she replied.

"Speaking of a beckoning darkness, would you care to take a stroll in the gardens before bed?"

She hesitated only a moment, then pasted on a patently fake smile. "I would like nothing better."

They left without saying good-night.

"Interesting evening," Dawn commented when they were alone. Not really alone, she remembered. Almost certainly there were ears listening and probably hidden cameras watching.

She wanted to ask Eric whether he thought it would be Carlotta or Sean who would return from that walk, but she didn't dare. After listening to them banter and watching them perform, they had become individuals to her, real people, not simply faceless terrorists. She had to make herself remember who they really were and what they did for a living. One of them had killed Minos on the boat today while everyone else's attention was on Eric landing that fish. She was sure of it.

Eric frowned at the couple disappearing down the path. "You should go to bed now."

Yeah, right. As if she would sleep a wink wondering what was going on in that garden. Would one of them have disappeared by breakfast? Or would Carlotta and Sean join forces to try to get rid of Eric?

"You will come with me?" she asked. More of a demand, really.

"Not yet. I plan to take a walk myself."

Dawn grasped his arm and shot him a warning look. "I don't like to be alone, Jarad. I'll come, too."

"No." He smiled down at her and pulled away from her grip as he stood. "Don't worry. I will return before you know it." He glanced at the open door to the hallway. "Go up to our rooms. I'll watch from the hall until you are safely inside. Remember to lock the door."

With one further plea in her eyes, Dawn realized she had no way to keep him from going out there and that he wouldn't let her come with him, no matter what she said.

When she reached their quarters, she set the lock and leaned back against the heavy portal, praying he would stay safe. He would try to prevent whatever Sean or Carlotta were planning to do, whether to each other or to him. Hopefully, his friend was out there somewhere keeping watch. If Clay had made it safely ashore. Eric had not seemed too concerned about that, so maybe he knew something she didn't.

She pushed away from the door and started across the sitting room to her bedroom.

"You shouldn't worry about him, you know," a deep voice said, scaring her out of ten years' growth. She whirled around to find Quince standing in the room with her. Where the devil had he come from?

He gestured to the panel behind him that appeared to be part of the wall when closed, answering her unspoken question. "Forgive me for intruding, but I thought we needed to talk."

She pressed a palm firmly against her midsection. "Jarad will kill me if he finds you here," she whispered.

He chuckled and sauntered over to the formal sofa that sat in the middle of the room. He took a seat and patted the cushion beside him. "No doubt he would. This husband of yours is a violent man, Aurora. And so suspicious! You must know it's only a matter of time before he gets rid of you. All it will take is his meeting another who intrigues him more than you do. Any trumped-up charge against you would vindicate him in the eyes of his law. He'll either divorce you or find a more permanent solution. Why not arrange a preemptive strike? I'll help."

She widened her eyes and touched trembling fingers to her lips. "You want me to…do something to him first?"

Quince clicked his tongue. "Makes sense, wouldn't you say? Here is the perfect place to do it. There are no authorities to call his disappearance into question."

She pretended to digest the thought and come to terms with it. "How?" she asked, her voice still a whisper.

He got up then and headed back to the panel which opened as if by magic. Or perhaps a remote he carried in the pocket where his hand had disappeared. "I will work that out for you if the others are not successful."

"The others? You mean Carlotta and Sean?"

"Of course. If he returns, try to act normal so you won't give yourself away. Remember," he said seriously, dropping the attitude of amusement, "if he suspects you plan to betray him, he might kill you before you have a chance to act. If that happens, there is no one here who would even think about bringing him to justice. Even *I* wouldn't, so be warned."

"But why do you want this? His death, I mean? I thought you wished Jarad or one of the others to buy something from you, to pay you a fortune for whatever they came here after."

"I will be compensated," he assured her.

"What of me, Quince? When you are finished with your games?"

He shrugged. "You are an innocent, caught up in a web not of your making. If I can, I mean to save you." Then he smiled at her, not a baring of teeth, not taunting, either. A real smile that looked sincere.

Dawn watched him leave. The panel slid soundlessly back into place and the wall looked as solid and impenetrable as the rest. She sank down onto the sofa and sighed loud and long, not caring who heard or observed.

What had he meant, *he would be compensated?* Was someone paying Quince to get rid of the bidders? If so, why not just kill them all and be done with it? Or at least kill them all but the one lucky winner who got to buy the plans from him?

But maybe he wasn't selling the plans after all. It sounded more and more to her as if he had set a trap with the offer just to get them to the island.

She needed to discuss this with Eric and get his thoughts on it, but there was no way they could speak openly. It wasn't safe to talk. She wished he really did have that handy mind link thing going on.

So here they were, acting up a storm, while everybody tried to murder everybody else. Except for Quince. It seemed he intended to keep his hands clean and let the others—and her, of course—do his dirty work for him.

Eric stood in the shadows near the pool, observing Quince, who strolled the terrace while smoking a cigar. Try as he might, Eric could not tell what the man was thinking. What an enigma.

He was just about to reveal himself and see whether he could get anything from Quince with a one-on-one conversation, when Conroy appeared.

"Have the new bidders arrived on the mainland?" Quince asked quietly.

"Yes, just this afternoon. They should be arriving here the day after tomorrow if that is still your wish, sir."

"Fine. This group should be out of the way by then. If not, we will combine them and see what happens. Carry on, my friend."

Conroy nodded and went back into the house.

There were others coming? What was going on here?

Eric had followed Carlotta and Sean, knowing that Carlotta was planning to seduce the Irishman into helping her get rid of the competition, namely himself.

But Sean had other ideas. Eric listened as they had a heated argument. Sean said he hated all she represented. The organized manufacturing and marketing of drugs worldwide was anathema to him. Her blatant sex appeal and the way she used it went hand in hand with the seductive powers of her product, as far as Sean was concerned. McCoy was an idealist at heart.

When the two had separated, Eric had returned to the terrace. Somewhere out there in the darkness, one of them would probably die. Eric hoped Clay would be able to prevent it. If he could secure one or both, they could be taken into custody for questioning later when the Sextant team arrived.

However, now there would be others arriving soon. It made no sense, unless Quince was systematically getting rid of terrorist representatives, or at least arranging it so they could conveniently knock off one another.

Where was the profit for him in that? What was his game? Maybe Quince saw himself as one of the good guys. Eric walked out of the trees onto the terrace.

"Come join me, Jarad," Quince said, a smile in his voice. He puffed on his cigar and blew a stream of smoke upward, watching it dissipate into the humid night air. "Smoke?"

"No," Eric answered, sauntering over to take one of the cushioned lounges. He sat down on the edge of it, leaned forward and clasped his hands. "What are you planning, Quince?"

"Why, nothing," he replied. "There is very little more to offer here on the island in the way of entertainment that we haven't already done. Brilliant fishing today, by the way."

"One of them killed Minos and you know it," Eric stated.

Quince nodded. "It is a cruel world, Jarad. In your line of work, you come to expect death to rear its ugly head fairly often, as do I. In my opinion, Minos is no great loss."

"His people might disagree, and they knew he was coming to you for this deal."

Quince smiled. "I expect and hope for a response to his death when they learn of it. The same with the woman and the Irishman." He grinned and pointed at Eric with his cigar. "And you, too, of course, if you are a victim."

Eric laughed, a bitter sound. "You plan to kill me, too?"

Quince affected a wounded expression. "But I have killed no one, Jarad. Each of your organizations will be informed of how their delegate met his or her end. The repercussions will fall on other heads, you see."

"Ingenious, but not too lucrative," Eric remarked, pushing back on the lounge, linking his hands behind his head. "Why the advance warning? You have put me on guard against the one who returns tonight."

"And you will prevail, I'm certain," Quince agreed. "Maybe you will survive to make me a fabulous offer and then go home with what you came here for."

Eric knew that was not in his plans. Quince thought he had a deal with Dawn, as the unhappy Aurora, to get rid of the offending husband. The bidders would all be dead if he had his way.

The new group coming in would probably repeat the scenario. How long did Quince plan to keep this up? And had he been at it a while already, changing the bait as necessary?

Eric got up and leisurely headed for the French doors. "Good night, Quince."

"Good night, Jarad. Sleep well." A chuckle accompanied the suggestion.

Had Quince already provided Dawn the means to take him out? She must be jumping up and down to share what had happened in Eric's absence, but there was no way they could talk about it.

The microphones in the suite would be of the best quality, able to detect the slightest whisper. Quince had a fortune at his disposal for such things. He would employ them, too, to stay aware of any side deals made by his guests.

Whatever was going on with Sean and Carlotta would probably be caught on audio if not on tape. How else would Quince convince their respective organizations that he wasn't the one who had gotten rid of their valuable representatives? No, he was pitting not only the buyers he had invited to the island against one another, he was extending the battle to their respective fraternities.

The chaos created by that could only benefit mankind in the long run, Eric thought to himself. But it was still vigilante justice anyway you looked at it. If, indeed, providing a little justice was Quince's intent. God, he wished he knew the man's mind.

Chapter 12

"Aurora?"

Eric was back at last, thank God. She hurried out to the sitting room and walked into his waiting arms just like a good little wife should. Dawn had to admit she didn't mind this part of the charade at all. Eric didn't seem to, either.

"I was afraid for you, Jarad," she said, laying her head on his shoulder.

He caressed her hair, smoothing it, soothing her. "No problems. After you left us I saw no one out there but our host. You should be in bed." He smiled down at her, his eyes gleaming as he eyed the pale yellow satin nightgown she'd donned and plucked away the clip she had used to pin up her hair. "You smell of jasmine."

"I am just out of the bath," she explained.

"I should have returned a bit sooner. I could have joined

you." He bent to nuzzle her neck. His lips sent delicious shivers down her spine.

She pulled away. "Have your bath now. I'll assist you." She took him by the hand and led him to the bathroom, allowing herself to frown after she turned away from him, in case Quince was watching them.

Once they were in the bathroom, she turned and mouthed the words, "There are no cameras here. Two mikes," she said, pointing to the locations.

He smiled and nodded his approval. "I hope the water is hot. My legs ache from the long walk. Perhaps you could help relieve that."

She turned on the water in the tub, then faced him again. He was scanning the room, probably wondering how thorough her search for cameras had been.

"I'm very good at it," she assured him, following the path of his scan with one of her own.

"I know," he replied, and began shucking his clothes, apparently trusting that she was talking about the physical security of the room, not her leg-rubbing skills.

But how could they communicate unless she deactivated the mikes? She really needed to talk to him.

Suddenly she had an idea. Hadn't he mentioned being a Scout? She knew they had the finger-spelling alphabet in the Boy Scout manual. Her cousin, who was deaf, had proudly pointed it out to her once. But then, Jim was older than Eric. Maybe it wasn't in the handbooks Eric had used. Still, it was worth a try.

It was a long shot, she knew, but Eric was supposed to be very proficient in a number of other languages. Dawn had learned to sign as a child in order to communicate with Jim. Maybe Eric had been as fascinated with the language as she had been. "Do you understand the alphabet for the deaf?" she spelled out slowly.

Eric looked surprised, then smiled and gave her the sign for *yes*. He finger-spelled the word *genius* and pointed to her. Then he proceeded to tell her, in ASL, the American Sign Language, that they should have thought of this sooner.

Dawn, stared, openmouthed, while he then removed the rest of his clothes and got into the tub.

She caught herself ogling and turned away slightly, but continued to steal glances at him. It was impossible to ignore his nudity, and he obviously thought it funny that she would try.

They had been intimate the night before, but somehow this seemed even more so. His muscles rippled as he began to soap himself, watching her all the while as if daring her to join him. She forced her gaze to remain on his face.

Dawn was sorely tempted, but knew exactly how that would end. They would make love in that enormous tub. Enticing as that was—as *he* was—at the moment, she knew they needed to talk. Besides, she didn't exactly relish having a listener or listeners at tubside while they frolicked in the suds.

Signing comfortably, she told him of Quince's visit to her room through the concealed doorway and explained what he wanted her to do.

Eric revealed what Quince had admitted to him, and the possibilities that brought up. Quince would have to silence her, too, eventually. They agreed on that.

Even if the man's motives were lofty and he let her live, she would never be allowed to leave the island if he succeeded in what he was doing. Their mission had to succeed and the team would have to arrive soon to accomplish that.

Eric's command of the language was imperfect, interspersed with many more spelled-out words than she used, but it proved fully understandable.

Every now and then, he would speak out loud as Jarad, ordering her around, sounding suggestive and teasing. Finally, downright provocative. Dawn got the feeling that he meant at least half of it.

She watched his hand rise and approach her breast. With one wet finger, he touched her through the gown and smiled into her eyes. His lips formed the words, "I want you" while he made the sign for it.

Her heartbeat raced even faster. What would it be like to take his dare, to slip off the satin and slide into the warm water beside him? Her imagination ran wild. She knew exactly what it would feel like. Dawn needed to be held. And he wanted to hold her, that was very clear.

Their gazes locked. What was left of her resolve melted. She stood, peeled off her peignoir and gown and stepped into the huge marble tub. He reached over and pushed the button to turn on the jets of water, surrounding them with warm, powerful streams that seemed to force their bodies closer.

Not that she needed a push. His hot slick skin slid against hers when he embraced her, firing her to fever pitch as his lips met hers in a devouring kiss. Damn the mikes, she couldn't contain the groan that rose from her throat, merging with his.

He lifted her slightly and entered her without breaking the kiss. *Complete,* she thought. *I feel complete.* Nothing mattered but this, this incredible oneness.

He felt the same and she knew it somehow, sensed that he had abandoned all caution, all thought of self-preservation, all pretense. This was as real as it got. And as profound a feeling as she had ever experienced. Nothing compared.

Dawn moved sinuously, grasping for more, winding her arms around his neck, sliding her fingers through his hair and holding on for dear life. The sensations bombarding her stole what breath she had left. Strong pulsating jets pummeled the base of her spine and the middle of her back. Powerful legs entwined with hers.

The scent of him, earthy, exotic, mingled with the sandalwood soap that half coated his body. His growl of pleasure reverberated through her while his hands glided over her, now gripping firmly, then searching madly.

Higher and higher she flew until he splayed one hand against her lower back and pressed her to him for a final, shuddering thrust. She must have cried out. His mouth covered hers and took them under the water for a second. That did anything but douse the pure glee that welled up inside her.

They surfaced, sputtering and laughing, bodies still joined. His expression grew tender as he brushed the wet hair from her eyes and looked into them, the sign for *I love you* on the hand he used for the caress.

Did he realize that? It was a fairly common position for a hand to take, thumb and fingers extended except for the middle and ring fingers, which were folded down.

This was no time to think about love. She was lying in a bathtub wired for sound, glowing in the aftermath of the greatest sex she'd ever had, and in the greatest danger she'd ever encountered in her life.

Slowly he lifted her off of him and sat up. "Later, then," he muttered, sounding very sure of himself.

His on-the-mark comment shocked her a little. No, he couldn't be reading her mind, but he sure wanted her to think he was. What she was thinking was probably written all over her face with her defenses down the way they were.

Dawn scrambled out of the tub as gracefully as she could and grabbed a towel. She tossed him one, too. Hit him in the face with it and grimaced when he raised both eyebrows and offered her a satisfied grin.

"I hate you!" she signed with fake vehemence.

He laughed soundlessly and began to dry off.

Dawn had a feeling she wasn't going to get out of this with her heart intact even if she did survive the mission. If she had any sense, she would rebuild her barriers even higher and denser than before. She did not need to fall in love with Eric Vinland. She *wouldn't*.

Eric's certainty about Dawn's feelings began to fade as soon as she left the bathroom. He wrapped the towel around his waist and watched her march across the sitting room and enter her bedroom. She didn't slam the door, but she closed it firmly, letting him know she wanted to be alone.

He wasn't used to this. Oh, he occasionally ticked women off, sure, and most of the time it was on purpose when they got too involved. But he knew Dawn wasn't really angry with him. Embarrassed, maybe, or upset that she had sort of lost control. Hell, he had, too.

He shouldn't have seduced her in there, not with microphones stuck all over the place. He hadn't intended to carry through and actually have sex with her, but things had gotten out of hand in a hurry. Not that they had made much noise.

She probably wondered if he had done it on purpose, staking his claim so Quince would know they were being intimate. To tell the truth, he hadn't so much as thought about their host or hidden mikes or anything else once he had begun to kiss her. There could have been cameras running and he wouldn't have cared.

Well, he would have *cared,* of course, but probably after

the fact. He gave a mirthless little chuckle. So much for professionalism. Damn, the woman had him off center. She had wrecked his confidence in his psychic abilities. Or destroyed them. He wasn't even picking up any thoughts when he tuned in on the others, only reading their body language and expressions as anyone might do.

As a quick check, he tried to connect with Clay who was somewhere out there lurking in the trees and rocks.

Nothing. No matter how hard he concentrated. Not one damn thought. Of course, Clay could be asleep. Eric tried to visualize. Most of the time he could do that, get a brief glimpse of a person's surroundings in real time. *Nothing.*

He had picked up a brief warning out there in the dark when he was on his walk. *Go back to the house.* However, that could have been his own alarm system kicking in and not anyone else's thoughts at all. Dawn had been alone with Quince, and he hadn't liked leaving her.

Everything always came back to Dawn. She was his primary concern and that shouldn't be the case. The mission was the all-important thing here. He needed to remember that.

He thought about linking with Mercier, sending a concentration of energy that would serve as a green light to ending all this. But there was a new group of bidders arriving tomorrow. Better that they were already on the island with less chance to escape capture. No, he couldn't endanger the mission merely to test his powers.

He cursed under his breath and went to his own room to put on some clothes. And he was *keeping* his clothes on until this thing was over and they were back on the mainland, he firmly promised himself.

Damn Dawn's pretty little hide, she had probably ruined him for this kind of work. He might wind up teaching languages at Podunk University one of these days instead of what he was doing now, but he couldn't for a second regret what he felt for her, despite that. She was worth any price he had to pay if she loved him, too.

He had been so sure she did in those intimate moments. It was as if he could reach clear into her soul and experience every nuance of her feelings right along with her, a sharing such as he had never known before. Now he wondered if maybe he had been indulging in a fantasy.

The time had come to get his act together and put his personal life on hold, or he and Dawn might not have lives to straighten out later. Whatever Quince's objective was, he meant business.

Breakfast was at nine on the terrace. Eric and Dawn were seated having coffee when Quince arrived, for once unsmiling. He sat down, leaned forward and clasped his long, slender hands on the tabletop, looking from one to the other. "Carlotta and Sean are gone. No one can find them."

Eric heard Dawn's gasp and wondered if it was real or for effect. He wasn't all that surprised and she shouldn't be. Quince didn't exactly look broken up by the news, but there was a shade of worry in his eyes.

"Maybe they found a way off the island," Eric suggested.

"No," Quince assured him. "Carlotta did not leave. Not the way you mean."

The minute Carlotta and Sean left for their *walk,* everyone figured that one of them would not be coming back.

"Then what do you think has happened to her?" Dawn asked.

Quince shrugged and sat back, allowing Conroy to pour his coffee. "It appears that she fell from one of the rock faces. There were signs of a struggle. One of her shoes was found on a ledge ten feet down. There are jagged rocks lining the shore at the bottom of that cliff. She probably fell and was washed out to sea."

"And Sean?" Dawn asked.

"Missing," Quince admitted, biting off the word as he raised his cup to his lips.

"Not for long, I'm certain," Eric commented. "I shouldn't think there are many places to conceal oneself on an island of this size. Besides, he will return in order to make his bid."

Quince said nothing further as they finished their morning repast of delicious pastries and fruit. Then he excused himself and left the house.

Dawn quickly slid out of her chair. "I think I will go upstairs and read for a while."

"I'll come with you."

When they got upstairs, they headed straight for the bathroom. She whirled around and signed to him. "We should find out whether this group arriving today will really be the last."

Eric agreed. "We need the list. There's a computer in Quince's study where I was taken when we arrived. If we could somehow bypass the cameras, maybe we could get into his files. He will delete everything if our people lose the element of surprise when they come in."

She nodded and sat down on the edge of the platform around the tub to think. "There has to be a base of operations somewhere in the house. The trick is finding it without being seen." She brightened, making the sign for *idea.* "The secret door Quince used to come in here! Maybe the corridor inside the walls leads to the control room."

Eric picked up his shaving cream container and went back to the sitting room. Casually moving a chair to the outermost wall near the window, he climbed up and squirted a little glob of foam into the hole that was the size of a quarter. That was the only camera in the room and by staying near the wall, took advantage of its limited scope. "There," he signed.

Dawn gave him a thumbs-up and began searching for the release mechanism where Quince's hidden door was located. But it was nowhere to be found. She and Eric punched and prodded every possible location and nothing happened. "Remote control," she mouthed and then shrugged.

Well, it had been a great idea as far as it went, Eric thought, disappointed. He would just have to get into the control room another way.

Someone rapped on the door to the hallway. Eric went to answer. It was Conroy. "More guests have arrived, sir. You and the lady are requested to attend Mr. Quince in the lounge."

Eric nodded and beckoned to Dawn. They followed the butler down the stairs. Seated in the room with Quince were three men in business suits.

Quince stood. The others remained seated. "Ah, Jarad. Come and meet Cal Markham. He has come all the way from the States. He runs an organization that plans to better the fate of Americans." Then he slid his jaw to one side in a wry look. "*Selected* Americans, of course."

Markham shot Quince a killing look. Their host ignored it and proceeded to introduce another of the men. "And here we have Boris Korkova, who intends to reorganize the Kremlin." Quince issued a little chuckle. "And finally Ali Mohandra. He hails from the Sudan. Allah only knows what he's up to because he insists on secrecy. But we can guess, can we not?"

"Damn you, Quince!" the man shouted as he leapt to his feet. The two armed guards raised their weapons.

Quince lifted his eyebrows and smiled. "Please resume your seat, Ali." He then turned to Eric and Dawn. "I would like you all to meet the esteemed Jarad Al-Dayal and his lovely wife, Aurora." He made a slight bow in Dawn's direction. "Jarad is well-known for his unorthodox methods of warfare against the Western powers that be. I hope no one here takes offense at that." He looked pointedly at Markham, who was grinding his teeth. "After all, Cal, he is abetting your contretemps with your American government."

Boris rose slowly from his chair. "Now that you have done your social duties, Quince, I see no reason to delay. Let us get on with the bidding."

"Not today," Quince replied, strolling over to take Dawn's arm. "I don't like skipping the amenities. First, we shall take a tour of my home so you will all feel comfortable. Then we will take a turn around the island."

"Now see here…" Cal began to protest.

"Come along," Quince advised, pointedly gesturing to the two armed guards. "Now."

With Quince and Dawn in the lead and the others in tow, the guards brought up the rear as they wound through the downstairs rooms, suffering Quince's running dialogue as he admired his own art objects and antiques, inviting comments.

No one provided them but Dawn, who said all the right things and kept her arm linked with Quince's.

Eric trusted Dawn would keep the man's attention off him while he tried to figure out where Quince's control room was located.

He also noted the position of the cameras. No way those could be avoided in an out-and-out search of the place. They had to find out how to get into that hidden passageway. He wondered if anyone had noted yet that the camera in the main room of their suite was no longer operational.

When they toured upstairs, he saw a jog in the wall of the hallway that shouldn't be there, according to the shape of the rooms they were allowed to view. That must be Control.

Dawn turned slightly and met his gaze. She had figured it out, too. Even that feat didn't account for the smug little upturn of her lips. What was she up to now?

He begged off the tour of the island, which he and Dawn had already been through the day before. To his surprise, Quince allowed it.

Who would be missing on their return? Eric wondered. Not that he cared. Dump *all* these guys off a cliff and no one would be the worse for the loss.

As soon as they were alone again, seated in the lounge with a glass of juice, Dawn toyed with the scarf she wore around her neck, surreptitiously finger-spelling the word *remote*. Then she patted the pocket of her skirt and winked.

Damn! She had lifted the remote control right out of Quince's pocket! Eric suggested they retire to their rooms immediately.

"What a cream-fed expression you wear, little cat," he said as he escorted her up the stairs. "It makes a man wonder what you have in mind."

She wisely didn't reply, but flashed him a droll look as they reached the door to their suite. He hoped anyone watching them would think they had come upstairs with sex in mind and would leave them alone for an hour or so. He also hoped that if anyone was minding the cameras, they didn't intend to stick around for the show.

Chapter 13

As soon as they reached their rooms, Dawn systematically found and disabled the two mikes she knew were in the sitting room. They were exactly where any novice would have planted them, which sent up red flags in her mind. Quince was no beginner at this. She kept searching, as did Eric.

When Eric grunted with satisfaction, she turned to see him taking care of another that had been placed in the side hem of one of the drapes. He gave her a nod. "That's all."

She smiled and pulled the remote out of her pocket, waggling it in front of him.

"Dangerous," he commented, but she could see he was impressed with her pickpocketing ability.

Hopefully Quince wouldn't miss the thing until he got back to the house. By that time, she hoped to have placed it somewhere that he might have inadvertently lost it.

"Stay here," she whispered. "Make some noise in the

bathroom so they'll think we're in there. If anyone's listening, I'll need them distracted." She kicked off her shoes so she could move soundlessly.

"Don't worry. I know what I'm doing." With a flourish, she pointed the remote at the wall and pushed the button. A panel slid back, just as it had when Quince was there.

"Be careful," he warned. "Leave that door open and yell if you run into trouble."

She blew Eric a kiss and stepped into the narrow corridor to explore.

The passageway, less than two feet wide, had not been finished on the inside and she had to take care not to snag her dress on the rough timbers.

If she went right, she knew it would lead to the quarters of the other guests. Since their rooms were closest to the irregular wall they had seen, she went left. She tried to visualize where it was leading her, though she knew roughly where the control room must be from her earlier observations. It couldn't be very large, possibly only six by nine feet. Close quarters for a confrontation if anyone was in there.

She crept forward as quickly as she could, running out of light from the open door after she turned the corner. Feeling her way along, measuring the distance by the protrusion of the studs placed at four-foot intervals. Suddenly, the floor seemed to fall away, but her foot caught on a step as she grabbed one of the timbers. There were stairs! Quince's control room wasn't on this floor after all.

Cautiously she descended, the darkness total now, and came to a closed door at the bottom. Dawn felt carefully for a knob or handle. There was none. She took a deep breath, almost coughing at the stuffiness of the air. Then she fished the remote out of her pocket, backed up a few steps and pushed the button. The light almost blinded her.

She bent double and head-butted the figure that had stood to greet her. A loud *oof* resulted. Without a pause, she fell back and kicked upward, catching him just beneath the chin.

Thank God he wasn't one of the beefy armed guards Quince employed. A computer geek, she guessed, not trained in hand-to-hand.

Before he could recover, she popped his ears with the flat of her palms, then chopped the back of his neck like a cinder block in karate class. He fell and lay motionless at her feet.

The first thing Dawn did was find his weapon, an automatic pistol, loaded. It was cheaply made and showed signs of neglect, but she immediately felt less vulnerable. Next, she felt for a pulse and found one, then looked around the room for something to tie him with. Nothing but computer cords.

Well, she'd just have to hurry and finish before he came to. Then she would have to hide him somewhere until Sextant sent the team in. Or kill him outright, which she wasn't entirely sure she could do. Defending herself was one thing, but the man was out cold.

All the while, she had been scanning the bank of computer screens set up around the room. There were only eight, which meant there weren't as many cameras as she had figured. One showed the terrace to keep track of the comings and goings in and out of the house. One pictured the cove where they had landed. The other six were set up in the guest rooms. No movement anywhere at the moment except from the one guard watching the beach.

Dawn systematically disabled all the surveillance equipment.

She noted another door and headed directly for it. *Pay dirt.* This was Quince's study, lined with bookcases and outfitted with expensive mahogany and what appeared to be a sophisticated computer system. She hurried to the keyboard, tapped it and watched the screen saver disappear. The idiot! He had files on his desktop.

She clicked the one that announced *Waste*. A list popped up with Jarad Al-Dayal's name second, beneath Carlotta's. There were ten names on his guest list, with only the first six recognizable to her. Her name was not included. Neither was Sean McCoy's.

What did those exclusions mean? She quickly committed the names to memory, closed the file and checked several others. Maintenance stuff. Frantic to finish her search, she checked the desk drawers.

Only one was locked. She forced it with a letter opener. Lo and behold, all by its lonesome, there lay a slender attaché, the portable flash drive, the same size and shape as a disposable cigarette lighter.

Hopefully this was the same thing she had seen stolen by Bergen at the Zelcon lab. No time to check it out. She stuck it in her pocket with the pistol, straightened everything else she had touched and got out of the room, closing the door behind her.

Quince's man lay where she had left him. Dawn unfastened the tightly woven cord from the attaché and used it to bind his hands behind him. He wasn't much bigger than she was, but no way could she drag him up those stairs. What could she do with him?

"I'll take him," Eric said from the stairway door.

"What are you doing here? You were supposed to—"

"You were gone too long. I was worried, okay?" he snapped.

Thank God he had followed. "Where will we put him?"

"The bathroom for the time being," he answered. He shouldered the body as if it were a sack of feathers.

It would be a tight squeeze getting back through the passageway carrying the computer tech, but they had little choice.

She closed the doors behind them with the remote and followed Eric's slow but steady progress back to their rooms.

With the man securely bound and gagged in the enormous marble tub, she and Eric collapsed in the sitting room to rest. No one was monitoring them now. She had fixed that for sure. "It's safe. No ears, no eyes," she reported.

"Good girl," Eric said.

"My boy, you have no idea *how* good," she replied. For the first time, Dawn allowed herself a self-satisfied grin. "I have the list of names." She paused to watch his surprise, then presented her next feat, adding, "and a gun, of course."

He nodded, pulling a face. "Of course."

She put the pistol away. "And the plans, I think." She drew the little flash drive out of her pocket and dangled it between her thumb and forefinger.

He laughed. "I'll be damned. You really think that's it?"

"It stands to reason. The one thing in the only locked drawer." At that moment, Dawn wanted to rush into his arms and do a little victory dance. She could see he felt the same way.

His excitement dimmed a little as she watched. "Now how do we keep Quince in the dark about your discovery until I can get the team in here to clean up?"

"Better call them in now. According to the list, there are only four who haven't arrived yet. Maybe they can be picked up on the mainland."

He rubbed his brow, frowning now. "If we can take them here, it would be better." He looked up at her. "Want to risk another day or two?"

Dawn shrugged. "I'm game, but Quince is gonna know

something's up. His guy is missing from the control room and somebody sabotaged his surveillance toys."

"We play dumb. Maybe Sean will take the heat for that since he's still out there running around," Eric reminded her.

Suddenly Dawn remembered. "Hey, I'd better get rid of this remote before Quince gets back. We can't lay *that* on McCoy."

"Downstairs," Eric suggested, getting up. "You can stick it between the cushions where he was sitting before we went on the house tour."

They hurried down to the lounge. Voices wafted up, alerting them that Quince and his other guests had already returned.

Eric stopped her on the stairs, tousled her hair and kissed her soundly on the mouth, smearing her lipstick. He grinned playfully when she tried to wipe it off and catch her breath at the same time. "We've been busy in bed, okay?"

"Don't you wish," she murmured.

"Absolutely, even if it is almost as nerve-racking as what we were really up to," he replied under his breath.

"Nerve-racking?" She couldn't help but smile.

Quince raised his eyebrows when they came in. "I trust you two have been entertaining yourselves while we were out."

Eric marched across the room to the bar without answering and helped himself to a glass of juice. "I tire of this incessant touring of yours, Quince. Shoot me if you will, but cease pretending this is some…" he windmilled one hand and scoffed "…house party."

"Ah, but that's precisely what it is, my friend," Quince said, turning away from Dawn, who moved surreptitiously toward the chair where she intended to drop the remote.

"Where is the American?" Eric demanded, looking around as if Cal Markham might appear out of nowhere.

"What do you have there, woman?" Boris demanded as soon as Dawn drew the remote from her pocket.

Dawn froze as all eyes turned to her, Eric's question about Cal Markham's absence forgotten.

She raised her chin and pinned the Russian with a haughty look. "You think I have a weapon?" She laughed mirthlessly. "I merely intend to watch television while you men argue." She pointed the remote at the big-screen TV housed in the entertainment center. "I will place it on mute."

"Wait!" Quince moved hurriedly and snatched the remote from her hand. "Where did you get this?"

Dawn pointed to the chair. "There."

"No television," he barked. "All of you, retire to your rooms immediately." He was suddenly sweating profusely.

He gave no explanation for his dismissal, nor did he have to. No one in residence was under the impression that they really were Quince's guests. They were captive here until he decided to hold the auction of the information and allowed them to leave.

The armed guards were just outside the door. As for Dawn and Eric, they both knew why Quince wanted everyone out of his way. He was going to check out his control room.

"Now you have angered our host, Aurora!" Eric accused Dawn as they marched up the stairs with the others. "I shall have to punish you."

Dawn hung her head, as if shamed and afraid. Boris grunted his approval and the African laughed. Men of a feather, she thought to herself, glad Eric didn't really fit that mold. If Quince wasn't careful, these jerks might actually bond into a new group instead of offing each other the way he planned.

She wondered where the other guy was. How would a

big, bad white supremacist have reacted to a Muslim man berating an uppity wife?

Eric herded her straight into the bathroom as soon as they reached their quarters. The computer weenie they had tied up in the bathtub was still there, wriggling uncomfortably, still secure. Dawn ignored him and addressed Eric. "What now?"

He was ripping off his shirt. "I need to contact Mercier. We can't wait. It's time for the showdown."

"For that you need to be naked? Somehow I expected you to close your eyes, go all woo-woo for a minute and that'd be it."

His lips quirked in a mirthless smile. "Better use something more concrete than a mind link. I don't seem to be functioning too well in that capacity, thanks to you."

"Me! What do I have to do with it?"

"Inadvertent interference. Not your fault." He tossed his shirt aside and reached for the back of his left shoulder with his right hand, feeling the skin there as if looking for something.

"What *are* you doing?" she demanded, moving around to see what was wrong with his shoulder.

"Get something sharp and remove this, will you?"

Dawn squinted at the mosquito bite he was touching with his forefinger. "What is it? Oh, the transmitter you mentioned?"

"It will be when I get it out and activate it. Right now, it's only emitting an infrequent pulse to give our location. Quince's scanner would have picked it up when he searched me if it emitted constantly. Not squeamish, are you?"

"No." She shrugged and went to search her makeup bag. She came up with a pair of nail scissors. "These should do."

He patiently sat on the lid of the commode while she

performed minor surgery, quickly slitting the skin that covered the tiny device. She noted the scattering of tiny freckles that lay beneath his fake tan, readily visible to anyone who looked closely. They reminded her how vulnerable he was, disguised this way. With one slipup, she could have punctured his plan as neatly as she had his skin and gotten them both killed. And yet, he had trusted her to become Aurora, who was the total opposite of her real self. How did anyone come by such trust, especially in someone they knew so little about?

"There," she muttered, handing him the instrument that proved to be about the size of a hearing-aid battery. She pressed a folded wad of toilet tissue over the incision and bore down on it to halt the bleeding.

He rolled off more tissue, cleaned the transmitter and took the nail scissors to it. She watched him poke it, then tap it lightly, using what was obviously a code. Not Morse, she realized. He repeated a pattern five times, then stopped. "That should do it."

"Are they near? Sextant, I mean?"

He nodded. "They should be just beyond the horizon, waiting for the signal."

Dawn bit her lips together, then suggested, "Could you maybe try that other method of contact, too, just to be on the safe side?"

He grinned up at her. "But you don't really buy into that. You said so."

She backed up a step, placing her free hand on her hips. "Any minute now, Quince is likely to come storming in here demanding what I took from his office. He has that bevy of trigger-happy guards with him and all we've got is a cheap pistol with four rounds in it. Anything you can do to hurry our backup along, I really want you to try." She frowned at the tiny transmitter. "That thing could be gunked up or something."

"All right. Then go in the other room. You distract me," he ordered.

"I want to watch," she argued.

His look turned serious as he placed a hand on her arm and squeezed it reassuringly. "Please."

She took his hand and placed it over the makeshift bandage. "Well, hold this while you *communicate* so you won't bleed to death."

"Thanks," he replied simply, then added, "I mean it. You've done a great job here, Dawn, however the mission ends. You remember that."

Dawn didn't reply. She might have asked him what he expected to go down now, why he looked so worried. He might have told her that their chances of surviving this had dropped to near zero because she had gotten caught with that remote control. The less said, the better, she guessed.

Eric was getting nothing back from Mercier. No confirming vibrations from the transmitter, none mindwise, either. Nada.

Okay, they would have to play this out as if backup was stuck out there with no wind for the sails. He checked the pistol again, as if that would help. Four rounds, not enough to take out the guards, much less the two terrorists left and Quince himself. Then there was the wild card, Sean McCoy.

Eric had tried to summon Clay. No response there, either. Maybe he was dead.

Dawn's yelp from the next room catapulted him into action. He cast a warning look at the man in the bathtub, then burst into the sitting room ready to fire.

Quince held up one hand. "Wait!"

Eric held his stance, the gun aimed directly at Quince's head. "I should shoot you," he rasped. "You came in here thinking my wife was alone."

"Not at all," Quince argued, sounding less than his debonair self. "I was...looking for someone...else." His eyes narrowed. "Where did you get that weapon?"

Eric didn't hesitate, banking on the hope that Quince was only searching for his missing computer tech. "Off the little man who was searching our room when we arrived."

"Where is he now?" Quince demanded, his fear obviously lessening with each second Eric allowed him to live.

Eric nodded toward the window. "He escaped. An eel, that one. If I see him again, he is dead."

Quince's jaw slid sideways in an expression of doubt. "It is three floors down to the terrace. Are you saying he survived such a drop and ran away?"

"Frankly, I don't care." Eric lowered the weapon marginally. "Should I assume his search was unauthorized? You should know by now that Aurora and I have nothing to hide from you."

"So I do," Quince agreed. "No, I gave no one permission to search these rooms or to be here for any other purpose. Now if you wish to stay in my good graces, Jarad, please give me the gun."

Eric laughed. "Be satisfied that I have not used it." He glanced again at the window and added, "Yet."

He added a smug chuckle. "I won't kill you, Quince. You have something I want and there is no way to get it if you're dead. However, I make no promises as to the others."

Quince stared at him for several seconds, then shrugged. "Very well. Keep it." With that, he turned and left the room by the hall door.

Dawn waited until Quince was gone, then turned to Eric. "He doesn't know we found the control room."

Eric agreed. He hurried her back into the bathroom. "We have a problem," he confessed.

She sighed. "They seem to be stacking up on us. What now?"

"I can't connect with Mercier," he admitted. "Or anyone else on the team. Looks like we'll have to wing it."

"You know what'll hit the fan when Quince discovers that flash drive is missing." She looked at their captive. "And if he finds Bozo over there and learns what happened, the jig's up. He'll kill us both."

"We could toss him out the window now," Eric suggested.

The man's eyebrows shot up and he began making whining noises.

Dawn caught on. She stood over the guy with her hands on her hips. "He's okay where he is *if* he'll stay quiet," she said pointedly. The whining stopped abruptly. "Better." She granted the man a smile. "Remain our little secret and you'll live. Understand?"

He nodded frantically.

Eric loosened the gag and removed it. "We need some answers. Help us and we'll help you. Who are you and where are you from?"

"Niko. From Ankros on the mainland. All I know is how to wire things. This is all I do. And listen and watch. This is my job."

"Stop hyperventilating, Niko," Eric advised. "Take a deep breath." He waited until the guy calmed down. "Now then. Tell me about the cameras located around the island and who else is watching the footage."

"Only I was to do that," Niko insisted. "The feed goes directly to the control room from all of them. I ate and slept there, only I was not to sleep except during specified hours of the early morning. If things of interest happened, I was to buzz Mr. Quince and advise him immediately. Everything is taped by day and to be saved."

"Why only you?" Eric asked, though he already knew. The questions were calming Niko, and they needed him to be calm.

"Because there are so few of us, and it is what he hired me to do. The others have their own tasks."

"When did he hire you, Niko? And for how long?"

"Six days ago. For two weeks, he said. No more and maybe less. A house party, he said, with guests he must watch closely. I think then that he intends blackmail and tell him no, but he promised me it was no such thing, only for his own protection."

"Were the others here when you arrived? The guards?"

"No. We came out together. Six guards, the butler, two servants and the chef. Quince brought us."

"Not the captain, but Quince," Eric stated, nodding. "Thank you, Niko. I'm going to replace your gag now. Don't be afraid. I promise we will not harm you unless you make noise. This will all be over soon and you'll go free, back home to your family in Ankros."

Dawn looked confused. "Six days ago? We were already on Leros then."

"Maybe that accounts for our delay there. Had to get things set up. But why issue the invitation before everything was ready to go?" He glanced around. "This place was already here, obviously, but is it Quince's usual lair or a recent buy?"

She sat down on the edge of the tub, her hands clasped in her lap. "Odd. What do you think it means?"

"That Quince is running with a skeleton crew that

probably knows nothing about what he's doing. Something's off about this. Way off."

Eric considered how the game had run this far. "It's almost as if he doesn't know what to do next and he's just hoping we'll bump one another off so he won't have to complete the deal." He scoffed. "He even let me keep the gun."

"Oh, he's saving you for me," Dawn said with a smirk. "He's sure I'm the bullied little wife who'll be damned glad to get rid of the big, bad overbearing husband. Probably means to slip me a ring full of poison for you or something like that."

"Exactly. He wants me to finish off the others, then you get to take care of me. But, the question is, how does he think he would profit by all that?"

"Maybe he plans to have another auction."

Eric shook his head. "But why? *We* are the primary buyers. The big money. If he eliminates all of us, he goes with the second-string. Plus, he's got all the big boys mad as hell because their prize negotiators are missing and presumed dead."

"Not a bad presumption in some cases. So what do we do now?"

"Find Clay and get him to call in the cavalry with his transmitter. We've done about all we can do here."

A shot rang out somewhere below. Eric rushed out into the hallway and headed for the stairs. "Something's going down now! C'mon!"

"What do you think…" She was almost running to keep up with his long strides, but he couldn't afford to slow down if they wanted Quince alive later to give them some answers.

Eric handed her the pistol. "Here, take this."

She huffed, speeding up as he did. "And what will you do, point your finger and go *bang?* Keep the damned gun."

"Won't need it," he assured her. "Wait here."

"Like hell," she muttered, staying right behind him as he pushed into Quince's study.

Chapter 14

Mohandra had the guard's automatic to Quince's head, apparently demanding access to the information they had come to bid on. Eric merely granted him an impatient look and marched directly over to Quince's desk and began opening drawers.

It had the desired effect. Mohandra redirected his weapon immediately, pointing it at Eric. "What are you doing?" he demanded in Arabic.

"What do you think? Ah, and here it is!" He lifted a disk out of the lower right-hand drawer and plunked it down on the desk. It was labeled a list of artworks, probably for insurance purposes. "You want to bid on it, Ali? Or will you simply take it and run? And if you run, where will you go to avoid my wrath? Kill me and even Bin Laden's best caves will not be deep enough in the ground to hide you. My people are everywhere and you know it. Put down that weapon and let us conduct business."

"I think not," Ali growled, shoving Quince away from him and approaching the desk.

Eric kept his gaze trained on the Arab, his peripheral vision noting Dawn's quiet moves. She was directly behind Ali now, her weapon drawn, almost touching the back of his head.

Could she fire? Eric knew she had never killed before. Shooting man-shaped targets was one thing; taking a life was quite another. He couldn't afford to doubt her now.

"Put down the weapon," she demanded, touching Ali's neck with the barrel. Surprised, he whirled, but she was faster, ducking the spray of bullets that took out several glass shelves lining the wall above her head. Eric leapt on him from the rear, pinching the nerve in Ali's wrist that controlled his gun hand. The weapon hit the floor and bounced. Dawn scooped it up and backed away.

But Ali didn't go down easily. Eric took a sharp blow to the ribs and a fist in the face before he clipped the Arab with a right cross that ended it all.

"Kill him!" Quince ordered in a near scream, pointing frantically at the unconscious man.

"No," Eric replied, catching his breath. "He will go home in disgrace. It is enough."

"No, no, it's not enough. He…he would have killed me!"

Eric turned on him. "Did that possibility never occur to you when you brought us here? That some might not hold to your fancy rules of etiquette?"

"But…but I have what all of you need and if you kill me you can never have it!"

"You are not dealing with mere greed here, Quince. Ali fights a holy war and you are his enemy. He takes what he wants. It's his way."

"And yours as well?" Quince asked, straightening his tie, brushing back his hair and recovering a little of his equilibrium.

"Mine as well," Eric agreed. "But I am a shade more civilized and a good deal more intelligent."

Heavy booted footsteps thundered down the corridor and two of the guards burst in. "Secure this man and confine him," Quince ordered.

Dawn had sunk into a crouch in the corner of the room, the two weapons on the floor behind her and out of sight. Eric stood and backed away while the two bound Ali and hauled him away. Odd, that Quince had not ordered *them* to kill the Arab, Eric thought.

Quince left soon after the guards, citing his need for a drink.

"Are you all right?" Eric asked Dawn.

"Fine," she said, getting up from her crouch and handing him the Uzi. She tucked the pistol back into her pocket. "We're building a little arsenal here and no one seems to care."

"You should have shot him," Eric said firmly. "You can't afford to hesitate."

She frowned and propped her free hand on her hip. "I didn't hesitate. I opted to take him alive."

Eric laughed at that. "He could have killed you with that volley. Or Quince. Or me, for that matter."

She worried her bottom lip with her teeth for a second, then admitted. "I couldn't shoot a man in the back of the head with no warning."

Eric blew out a frustrated breath. "Fair enough. You did fine." That's when he noticed her hands shaking, only a slight tremor. "Come here," he said softly and opened his arms.

She stepped into them and put her head on his shoulder. He caressed her hair and rested his hand on her neck, massaging it gently. "Will you be all right here if I go out for an hour?" he whispered.

She nodded. "I've got the pistol."

"Next time, don't think. Just shoot, okay?"

"A thousand pardons, *Jarad,*" she said with a wry twist of her lips. "Be careful yourself."

"Stay out of everyone's way until I get back." Eric didn't like leaving her, but he needed to locate Clay and get the team in here. Things were falling apart fast and would collapse with a bang once Quince found out his prize was missing, but he was so shaken up right now, he'd be busy hitting the bottle. God only knew where the Russian or Cal Markham were, but they had no reason to bother Dawn.

Staying out of the way sounded good to Dawn. She'd had about all the excitement she could stand for the day. If she wasn't supposed to be converted, she'd be joining Quince in the lounge for a good stiff drink. Having your hair parted with a few Uzi rounds tended to make a girl pretty thirsty. Maybe she would go anyway and have a glass of juice or something and keep an eye on Quince.

She patted the pistol in her pocket and tried to walk without a betraying wobble in her knees.

Quince greeted her with more aplomb than she expected. Great recovery time, she had to give him that much. "Would you care for a brandy?" he asked, sipping his own.

She made a face. "I don't dare, but thank you for thinking of me." With a sigh, she helped herself to a bottled fruit juice from the small refrigerator behind the bar.

"Where is Jarad?" he asked. "And how is it he trusts you to wander around alone all of a sudden?"

Dawn took a deep draught of the juice and swallowed before answering. "He was upset and went out for a walk to cool his temper. He does that."

Quince nodded knowingly, his lips pinched in thought. Then he pointed to her with his snifter. "You handled yourself better than most women would under fire. How do you explain that?"

Dawn shrugged. "Jarad's training."

"I'm not certain I buy that explanation, Aurora," Quince told her frankly. "What you did seemed too…professional." He sighed, his gaze never leaving hers. "Perhaps you are not his wife at all."

Dawn laughed bitterly. "Believe it. He gives me lessons in self-defense. He's paranoid about some man accosting me and dishonoring him, you know that. Do you think for a moment Jarad would hire a *woman* to watch his back? Besides, if I were here for that, he would have me out there with him now." For a minute, Dawn was afraid she had overexplained, protested too much.

Quince shrugged. "Quite right." He smiled, toying with his drink, looking into its depths. "So, have you given any more thought to our plan to free you?"

"What do you have in mind?" Dawn decided to stop playing it coy. He had seen her in action and knew she was no shrinking violet. "It appears you are systematically eliminating all of those you asked to come here. One has to wonder why and whether *any* of us will be allowed to leave. Why should I trust you?"

He rolled the snifter between his palms. "I have eliminated no one."

"Then, let us say you have encouraged their elimination at every opportunity. Share with me why that is, and I might be inclined to trust you further."

He leaned forward then in an attitude of strict confidence. Dawn held her breath, certain he was about to give her his reasons. "These men, your husband included, represent the most evil elements of human society, Aurora. Whatever their reasoning, based on ideology or hunger for power, they are terrorists, bent on destruction. Why should you care—"

She interrupted. "And if I am not misinformed, you are providing them a means to do more of it," she reminded him, "for which you will be amply rewarded. Tell me I am wrong in this."

He assumed a wounded expression that looked sincere. "Rest assured, my motive is not fueled by greed. Look around you, woman! I have *enough*."

"Then why did you ask them here? Why would you offer them whatever it is they are so eager to get? I know it is something to further their respective causes, something valuable and secret."

"Something they must never put to use," he added succinctly, reaching across to take her hand in his. "Help me."

She tried to pull away, but he held her fingers fast in his. "This was a trap? You brought them here to kill them?"

Gunshots popped outside and the window of the lounge shattered. Dawn dived for the carpet, seeking shelter between their chairs. Quince fell on top of her, shielding her body with his.

"Let me up!" she cried, struggling to reach her pocket where she had hidden the pistol. But Quince held her immobile. Heavy as he was, she couldn't dislodge him. "Get off!"

He scrambled to one side and yanked her by her arm. "Stay on the floor. Crawl behind the bar!" he ordered. More shots rang out.

No fool, Dawn did as he suggested. The heavy mahogany structure offered the safest haven in the room. By the time they reached it, she had the pistol out and the safety off.

Had Eric's team arrived? She hoped to God that was the case and that this wasn't some other force attempting to take over the island. Especially since the thing everyone would be after was securely tucked between her breasts inside her lacy underwire bra. That gave a whole new meaning to Victoria's Secret.

The click of footsteps sounded on the tiles of the foyer, then on the stairs. No way could they exit the lounge without being seen by whoever was on the way up. Were there others waiting? She and Quince were trapped behind the bar with nowhere to run and only four rounds for defense. "Do you have another weapon?" she whispered.

"Not in here," he admitted. "You'd better give me that," he said, reaching for the gun. Dawn batted away his well-manicured hand and leaned to peek around the lower edge of the bar.

He tugged at her shoulder. "I said—"

"Shut up, Quince!" she snapped, her patience thin and her nerves on edge.

Eric had guessed right; Quince didn't know what to do next. He had gotten in over his head. How could that be? Given the rep Interpol credited him with, she didn't know. He was supposed to be the big deal maker, the mercenary even the baddest boys in the business bowed to. He had talked a good game up to a point, but she sensed he was shaking in his Italian leather mocs right now, too frightened to take the little peashooter away from a girl half his size.

"Back off and give me some room." She elbowed him out of her way. "And for God's sake, be quiet." Dawn realized she'd abandoned her Spanish accent along with her cover as a helpless little woman. Come to think of it, Quince's voice had changed, too, under pressure.

Someone was coming down the stairs now and in a hurry.

"Dawn?" Eric called out.

She released a deep breath, only now aware she'd been holding it. "In here! Behind the bar," she answered.

He appeared then, a welcome sight as he dodged into the room, wheeling left, then right in a shooter's crouch, the AK-47 he carried braced to fire. He landed behind the bar with them. "Ali must have signaled a boatload of friends," he announced. "They just came ashore."

"Impossible!" declared Quince.

Eric shot him a dry look. "I didn't get a head count, but two are down outside."

Dawn's heart stuttered when she saw blood on his shirt. "You were hit?"

"No." He looked past her, his gaze focused on the open doorway. "They won't wait long to breach the house. They'll be coming in to find Ali. Among other things." He glanced at Quince. "Where'd your men take him?"

"There's a basement below the kitchen."

"With outside access?" Eric demanded.

"No."

"Any way out of this place without using the front or back door or the French doors onto the terrace?" The downstairs windows were barred, decoratively, but also efficiently.

Quince shook his head. Then he swallowed hard. "The place is wired to blow. If we can get out after they come in to search the house, we can get them all."

Eric sighed. "Where did you train, Quince, Utopia? They won't *all* come in. Some will be out there waiting for us to show. And they're armed to the teeth. Besides, you have employees in here. Conroy, the cook—"

"I'm blowing it anyway," Quince declared, muttering as

if to himself. "Ali's people can't be allowed to get what they're after."

Eric tossed Dawn a questioning look and she answered by patting her cleavage. He smiled. "I wouldn't worry about that."

"And if they shoot us?" Quince snapped. "What then? All they have to do is locate the safe and figure out how to crack it."

Eric's worried gaze locked with Dawn's as he repeated, "The *safe?*"

"Yes! It will only be a matter of time until they find the hidden office. It only took me two hours!"

Dawn's heart sank. The little aluminum device between her breasts suddenly felt cold, not comforting as it had moments ago. If the flash drive with the radar-shield plans was locked in Quince's safe, what was she carrying around in her bra?

Eric was glaring at Quince now. "Why would *you* have had to search for the office in your own house?"

Quince backed away in a crouch and looked behind him as if hoping to discover an escape route opening up.

"I'll get answers, Quince, but now's not the time," Eric said. "I locked the front door when I came in, but that won't keep them out for long. We need to set up a defense." He motioned to Dawn. "Make sure the kitchen entrance is locked. Find Conroy and the servants and put them in the walk-in fridge where they'll be safe. Quince and I will go for the weapons."

He turned to Quince. "Where are they?"

"The study," Quince answered. "Why are you doing this?"

"You have to wait for answers, too," Eric told him. "Just keep in mind that you aren't all that necessary to me, so your best bet is to cooperate. Let's go."

Dawn rushed down the hallway to the back of the house, her pistol ready. Conroy and the others weren't likely to follow her orders without it.

When she neared the kitchens, she approached the door with caution, edged up to it, then whirled into the opening in firing position. She sensed she wasn't alone, but saw no one. Carefully, she crept into the room, shifting the direction of her aim every couple of seconds.

This reminded her of a training exercise back at The Farm, where target villains appeared at random right along with pop-up friendlies. Conroy, the cook and the other servants were around somewhere, probably hiding behind something just as she, Eric and Quince had been doing in the lounge. She thought about calling out a warning.

"Drop it," said a quiet voice, devoid of its usual lilt.

"Sean?" she asked, turning. "Is that you?"

"Me and my Uzi, love. Lay down your gun."

She didn't do that, but she did lower the pistol, trying her best to look relieved to see him. "Where have you been? I am to find Mr. Conroy and the others and put them somewhere safe. Will you help me?"

He chuckled. "Appealing to my gentlemanly instincts, Aurora? I have so few of those. Put down the pistol or I will shoot you where you stand." She had to believe he meant it.

She placed the gun on the countertop. "There are men here on the island who intend to kill us all. Why are you treating *me* as the enemy?"

"Because everyone here *is* an enemy, love. Haven't you figured that out yet?"

She sighed and shrugged. "All I want is to board a boat and leave this cursed place. Why Jarad brought me here with him is a mystery."

He laughed. "Not to me. You handle a weapon like a

pro, which I always assumed you were. There are no in-nocents among us."

"Such bitterness, Sean," she said with a sugary smile. "What now? You'll get rid of me the way you did Carlotta?"

"Not yet. Let's go and find your husband and our friend, Quince, shall we?"

"All right," she agreed with one last longing look at the abandoned pistol on the counter. She was facing Sean and also the window near the back door where shadows moved quickly and quietly. Ali's men. In seconds, they would burst through the unlocked door and she and Sean would be cut down as surely as she stood there. "Sean, they're coming."

"Nice try," he said with a click of his tongue. Then a sound alerted him. He turned.

Dawn grabbed her pistol and dropped to the floor just as the back door flew open.

She heard them swarming in, shouting, firing. It sounded like a whole army. Sean had disappeared.

Two rounded the counter, and she squeezed the trigger. The sound of her shots was lost in the indiscriminate fire-storm of the invaders—two more dashed past on the other side of the counter. They missed seeing her, hidden as she was. She aimed the pistol and pulled the trigger. Nothing happened. Damn. Useless. She laid it aside.

One man shouted in Arabic, probably to those outside. All she could do was watch from the shadows as the sur-vivors headed out of the kitchen and down the hallway.

Dawn waited where she was, helpless to do anything at the moment. When no more shots were fired, she risked crawling to the edge of the counter and peeking around it. More men filed in.

The new wave immediately located the door to the cellar

and were trying to get it open. They broke it down and with a shout of success, headed downstairs.

Dawn scrambled over to the two men she had shot. One was writhing on the floor, holding his leg. Quick as a flash, she grabbed the heavy automatic he had dropped. The other man was obviously dead, his nine-millimeter pistol still clutched in his hand. She yanked it free and stuck it in her pocket. The first one recovered enough to make a clumsy grab for her. Dawn landed a butt-stroke to his head and knocked him cold.

For a moment, she considered shooting him again, but decided a shot might bring the others running. An excuse, maybe. Killing a man who was firing at you was definitely different than dispensing with one who was unconscious.

Eric was her first concern. She headed out the way the others had gone. She moved cautiously even though they were making enough noise to cover any sounds she might make.

She concentrated on her approach, so much so that she didn't realize anyone was directly behind her until an arm encircled her neck and a hand snatched her weapon away. She knew immediately it was McCoy. She recognized his scent.

"In there," he rasped, shoving her into a small storage room. He closed the door. "Now, let's have something straight, Aurora. I need to save Quince. I don't have to kill you. In fact, I could use your help. If you cooperate, I'll get rid of Jarad for you and get you back to the mainland today."

Right, like she would believe that? "Suppose I don't want to be rid of him?"

"It's you or him, love. Choose right now."

"I'll help you." If she could convince Sean she was no threat, at least she might have a chance to warn Eric. Maybe she could get the drop on Sean. She cleared her throat. "But the first order of business is to eliminate Ali's men, agreed?"

He nodded. "Go ahead of me. I want you where I can see you. Get out the Glock you took off the dead guy."

She pulled it out of her pocket, checked the load, clicked off the safety, then led the way back into the hall. The pistol was no match for the Uzi McCoy carried, but she felt a bit less vulnerable than she would have if he had made her his unarmed shield.

Dawn could hear Ali's men running up the stairs near the main entrance, making no attempt to conceal their presence. How many were there on the island? Ali obviously had used some method of contacting them similar to what Eric had brought. Or something even more sophisticated since they had known where to find him.

She stopped and turned. "Quince and Jarad were headed for the study where the weapons are kept."

He motioned down the hall to the left, then gave her a little shove when they neared the study door.

"Don't shoot! It's me!" she called softly, hoping no one would unload in her direction. "McCoy is here, too," she added in order to warn Eric.

Sean was right behind her. He pushed her through the doorway, using her for cover. The lights were off and the blinds were drawn.

"Quince? You there?" Sean called.

Quince stepped out from behind a tall bookcase. "Sean?" he asked softly. "Are you all right?"

"Where's Al-Dayal?" McCoy demanded.

Quince nodded to the opposite side of the room where Eric stood holding a fully automatic in the cradle of his arm, his finger on the trigger, the muzzle pointed up instead of at her.

Now that her eyes had adjusted to the dim light, Dawn

could see in Eric's eyes that he knew McCoy intended to kill him.

"If I were you," he said to Sean, "I'd eliminate the most immediate threat first. That is not me, by the way. Truce until we've cleared up this problem? Then we can haggle over the prize."

"Fair enough," Sean replied.

Dawn didn't trust him to keep his word, but realized there was no choice until she or Eric had a clear shot at him.

"Two of Ali's men are down in the kitchen. One dead and one unconscious," she informed Eric. "Five others have gone down to release Ali and more are searching upstairs. Four, I think."

"I didn't see them disembark," Eric said. "The entire island could be crawling with them for all we know."

Quince spoke up then. "We could try to make it to my boat and get off the island. I told you the place is wired. Why don't we get out and blow it?"

McCoy growled a protest. "Not until I get what I came here for. Get it, Quince. Now."

Dawn thought about giving Sean the attaché she had found in the locked drawer. He wouldn't have time to check the contents. Maybe she could fool him into thinking she had what he wanted, the same way Eric had bluffed Ali. But if she did, McCoy would probably shoot them all and take off. Damn.

However, if the information was locked in the safe, it needed to stay there until Eric's team arrived.

"I can't get it out of the safe," Quince admitted.

"What do you mean? How did you expect to… Never mind, I can get into it," Sean declared. "Haven't met a safe yet I couldn't crack. Let's go."

Quince was nodding, turning and pressing on one of the block designs beside the fireplace.

If they entered the secret passage and closed it behind them, they would be safe from Ali's men. But McCoy could also kill them all in there, get the plans out of the safe, then hide and wait out the small army that was after them. Without a lot of luck or a fortunate accident, those goons would never locate that hidden section of the house.

Dawn couldn't risk letting McCoy get whatever was in that safe. "No!" she cried. "Going there's not necessary. I have what he wants."

"Wait! Don't…" Eric said through gritted teeth. He was frowning at her, his frustration tangible.

Dawn offered him a wry grimace, an apology for probably sealing their doom, and reached inside the front of her blouse. She withdrew the small device. "Here. This is not worth dying for," she said, turning around and handing it to McCoy.

Sean took it in his left hand and gave it a cursory look. "And I'm supposed to believe this is what you say it is?"

Dawn shrugged. "Believe what you like. I followed the secret corridor from our rooms and found Quince's office. This was in a locked drawer beneath his computer station. The plans are on it. I checked." She reached for the device. "Of course, if you don't want it, then I'll…"

He snatched it back and shoved it into his pocket, then faced Quince. "What do you have to say about it, Quince? Is this what I'm looking for?"

Quince was already shaking his head. "No."

"Then let's go!" Sean commanded. "We're wasting time we don't have."

His words were nearly lost as bullets struck the door

frame behind him. Everybody dropped and scrambled for cover.

Ali's men were shouting now, running down the hallway, firing indiscriminately.

Eric popped one when he reached the doorway. The others obviously decided Allah didn't need them yet and stayed back.

Two seconds later, she watched a grenade bounce into the room. The windows were barred. The enemy was outside the door. There was no way out but the secret passage, and it would take too long for Quince to open the panel.

Chapter 15

Eric flipped the heavily padded sofa over the grenade, leapt over it, grabbed Dawn and threw her to the floor just as the grenade exploded. He rolled to his back, already aiming at the hall door when Ali's men came in shooting.

Dawn watched the scene unfold like something out of a silent movie, unable to hear it because the explosion had deafened her. While the action played out at full speed, her own reactions seemed to be in slow motion, her emotions temporarily numb. Then as suddenly as it had begun, the attack ceased.

Only when she saw Sean aiming directly at Eric did her autoresponse kick in. She finger-pointed her nine millimeter instead of taking time to aim and pulled the trigger repeatedly until the weapon emptied and she felt no recoil.

Sean fell flat on his back. Quince crawled out from behind a bookcase and bent over him. Dawn couldn't hear what he was saying, but his face had crumpled and he seemed to be begging McCoy not to die. Eric was checking the bodies of Ali's men. He turned to her. "You hurt?"

Dawn shook her head. She hadn't bothered to examine herself for wounds, but felt no pain anywhere. Her hands and arms were covered with plaster dust and residue from the gunshots. A small nick on her forearm began to sting, but it was only a minor scratch. "I'm okay," she muttered.

Another explosion outside the study rocked the room and collapsed the inner wall adjacent to the hall. Debris blocked their exit. The whole place was wired, Quince had said. It could go up any second.

Eric grasped her arm. "Reload," he ordered. She realized she was reading his lips and couldn't hear anything but a distant roaring.

She looked around and saw the shattered gun case with its drawers at the bottom hanging askew. Finding no clip for the empty nine millimeter, she grabbed another gun out of the shattered case and began to check and load it. A Walther PK, she noted. Dependable weapon.

Dawn forced thoughts to practical things like that, trying to ward off others she didn't want to have just yet. She had killed today. More than once.

Her hands shook. The odor of cordite made her gag. Or maybe it was the smoke that filled the room, almost obliterating her ability to see. Thank God she had seen Sean aim and...

No, she had to think about the gun. Get it loaded. Do what Eric ordered. Follow his lead. The only way out of this was to follow Eric. Her breath caught on a sob, but she held it in, willing her fingers to behave, to do what her brain demanded.

There. The clip was in. She had done it. She began to cough uncontrollably.

Eric's arms came around her from behind and lifted her to her feet. He guided her to a door in the wall, a door that shouldn't be there. The explosion must have triggered Quince's secret panel.

Eric reached into a niche just inside the tunnel door and procured two flashlights, handing her one.

Luckily, the grenade hadn't triggered the explosives Quince insisted were rigged to blow the entire place. Damn him and his stupid island villa anyway. Damn the whole island. Why hadn't the government sent a military team here to clear it? Why civilian Special Ops?

And why not? Things would be right on target if the gadget she had found were the real thing and Eric's transponder worked.

Dawn looked over her shoulder and saw that Eric had gone back to get Quince. He held him by the back of his collar and shoved him into the opening behind her.

She proceeded down the narrow tunnel until she came to a forked passage. When she stopped, Eric gestured to the right with his flashlight and she continued, hurriedly leading them God only knew where.

This was taking too long. Dawn sensed they were headed away from the main structure and that the path they were taking did not lead to Quince's office where he'd said the safe was located. Apparently, the study had had more than one secret panel or else they had taken the wrong fork. The whole place must be a rabbit warren underneath.

Her lungs cleared and she began to smell salt air. Dampness had invaded the poorly framed and unfinished corridor sometime after it had degenerated into a rough tunnel carved out of the lava stone.

She figured they had walked just under a quarter of a mile

since leaving the study and should be well away from the villa by now. In any direction, that should lead to a beach.

Her hearing had returned, at least some of it. Quince's breath huffed in and out right behind her. Their shoe soles scuffed against the irregular rock floor. Daylight loomed ahead.

"Wait," Eric said. "Stop here and wait until I see where we are." He stepped around Quince and came up beside her now that the tunnel had widened. "Keep him covered. If he tries to go back, shoot him."

"I *have* to go back!" Quince cried. "Sean might be…"

"McCoy is dead," Eric told him. "There's nothing you can do for him."

"Here. Hold on to this." He handed her the flash drive she had given to Sean. "I brought this. It might have something on it since it was locked up."

Dawn tucked it back between her breasts.

Quince had dissolved in tears, leaning against the wall of the tunnel with his face covered by his arms; he sobbed inconsolably. Sean had obviously been more to him than simply one of the bidders, but Dawn didn't want to know what, at least not now.

Eric had disappeared out the end of the tunnel. She heard his surprised laughter and another voice she thought she recognized. Clay Senate? Where the devil had he been all this time?

"Dawn? Come on out here," Eric called. "Bring Quince with you."

Thank goodness it was time to abandon their roles as the Al-Dayals. This kind of undercover work was not the fun she'd always imagined it would be. Surreptitious entry was one thing, but becoming someone else for days on end was quite another.

She prodded the weeping man until he staggered along in front of her. They exited the tunnel onto a wide, rocky ledge above the beach. Steps led down to a sandy, sheltered cove.

"Come with me," Clay said to them. "There's a cave over there with all the comforts of home." He smiled at her. "You could stand a little cleaning up."

She touched her face and winced. Her fingertips came away coated black with soot, cordite and dirt. The rest of her must look about the same as her hands. Nasty. Her hair felt as if it were standing on end and her clothes were a mess.

Dawn trudged along with the men, periodically urging Quince so she wouldn't step on his heels. He seemed to be in shock.

They entered Clay's cave. Someone had indeed made it a refuge, probably well before Clay ever arrived on the island. Bedding and blankets were neatly folded against one rough-hewn wall. A fire pit lay near the front, stacked with small lengths of driftwood.

"The prisoners are bound in the back there," Clay told them, pointing to a dark passage that led deeper into the rock.

"Prisoners?" Eric asked with a mirthless chuckle. "Who?"

Clay shrugged. "A really feisty woman I found hanging on to the rocks after she was pushed off the cliff's edge, a couple of guards I managed to disarm, a Russian and an American mercenary I would really like to choke personally."

"We need to contact Sextant and get this wound up," Eric announced. "Unfortunately one of Quince's bidders brought along a small army that seems determined to decimate the villa and everybody in it. See if your transponder's working. For some reason, mine's shot."

They watched as Clay removed a knife from his belt and quickly sliced the tracker from the top of his shoulder before she could think to offer her help.

He wiped it off on the leg of his pants, then tapped the point of his knife to it several times. "There," he said, pinching it between his thumb and forefinger for a minute. He frowned at Eric. "No response."

"You're bleeding." Dawn shook her head in exasperation and looked around for something to pad his wound.

"It's nothing," he replied "I'll go wash it off in a minute." Then he crouched near Eric. "Do you have what we came for?"

"It's still in the house, in the safe, so Quince says," Eric told him. "A safe he can't open. Oh, and the house is rigged with explosives, only he hasn't yet told us how that's set up. I can't read him."

Clay's dark brows drew together in a menacing look directed toward Quince. "Time for a few questions." He tapped the flat of his blade against his other palm. "Shall I?"

"Be my guest," Eric said with a negligent wave of his hand.

Quince seemed oblivious to the threat.

"You aren't going to try to scare it out of him, are you?" Dawn asked quietly. "He's pretty much zoned out. I don't think it would work."

"What's his problem?" Clay asked her.

Dawn considered the question before answering. "I think one of the bidders was more than that to him, maybe a co-conspirator. The guy was killed just before we came out." She had killed him. That was going to bother her, but she couldn't dwell on it now.

"McCoy," Clay declared with a nod.

"You've been keeping closer tabs than I thought," Eric said with a smile. As he spoke, he slid one arm around Dawn and drew her near, sharing his warmth. "Learn anything interesting?"

Clay looked from Eric to her and back again, one black eyebrow raised. "McCoy and the woman struggled and he shoved her off the cliff in an attempt to kill her. But they had a fascinating conversation before he did his worst." He paused, then looked curious. "You couldn't read them, could you?"

Eric glanced down at the floor of the cave, then raised his gaze to meet his friend's. "No."

"And you couldn't connect with me, either. Or Jack and the others? What's wrong, man?"

"Let it go for now, okay?" He released Dawn and stepped away from her, resting his hands on his hips. "Just tell me what you found out."

"Quince isn't Quince," Clay announced. "Or at least not the Quince we thought he was."

"That much I figured out on my own," Eric told them. He reached out to brush Dawn's hair off her brow and tuck the strands behind her ear with his finger. "You sensed that, too, didn't you, Dawn?"

She had, but not fully until they were in the study. "Let's ask him."

Quince was sitting cross-legged on the cave floor, his elbows on his knees and his face buried in his hands. Grieving?

Dawn knelt beside him and placed a hand on his shoulder. "Where is Quince?"

He raised his head slowly, as if he'd been sleeping. "My brother?" He swallowed hard. "Dead. And good riddance. The man was a monster. A traitor to the human race!" He sobbed once, then placed a hand over his mouth to hold it in.

"You took his place for the bidding. Why?"

"No. You don't understand. There was to be no bidding.

I can't even get to whatever it was he had for sale, don't you understand? I would never, ever sell it, even if I could!"

"But you wanted all of the bidders to come here to the island as planned, didn't you?" she asked.

"To die," he agreed. "I wanted to eliminate every one of them and I liked the irony of having them destroy one another." He slid his fingers through his hair and left them there, holding his head as if it hurt. "I have to make up for all Stefan did, all the terrible things he arranged, the terror he abetted." Then he looked directly at Dawn. "I wanted you to help me. You were like me, Aurora, caught up in something you couldn't control by yourself. Trapped."

She nodded and patted his shoulder. "I know. What is your name?"

"George. George Cydonia." He sniffed hard and ran a hand over his face, sighing as he did. "Sean is...was...my son."

"I'm sorry for your loss," Dawn said automatically, trying not to think how she was the one who emptied the pistol into McCoy. She'd had no choice really, and it was counterproductive to waste time sympathizing with a killer. "He was very clever," she offered. "I would have sworn he was Irish."

"He was," George said. "His mother raised him in Dublin. She and I parted ways when Sean was only two. He contacted me a few months ago in Athens. I have a business there," he said absently. "Real estate."

Dawn exchanged a look with Eric who was listening intently. They were dealing with a real estate agent?

"What happened to Stefan?" she asked, guiding the questioning away from Sean's death. She would come back to it, though. It seemed strange that Sean would look his father up after so many years. Maybe he wasn't Sean at all, but someone in league with Stefan. "Did your brother die here on the island?"

George nodded. "I acquired this property for him. He wanted something remote and isolated. Said he was retiring. I've known for years what he did, but was afraid I'd be implicated if I turned him in. Then two weeks ago, he insisted that Sean and I come out to the island with him. Then he wouldn't let me leave. He was afraid I would give away his location. Sean…he was…sympathetic to Stefan's plan. I thought I had dissuaded him, but…Stefan left for a few days last week and then returned."

"And he died here? Was he ill?" Dawn prompted.

George shook his head. "No. He was eating dinner. Choked to death on some calamari."

Or was poisoned? Dawn wondered. Sean's presence at the time made that a distinct possibility.

"He had already set up everything for the auction of the information, which he told me he had locked in his safe. Meeting the bidders face-to-face would give him the edge, he said. Stefan liked games."

"So you decided to follow through and get rid of the bad guys yourself," Dawn said, trying to sound approving so he would continue.

"It was a good idea. Sean said he was…helping me."

Or getting rid of his competition for acquiring the plans himself, Dawn thought. Canny.

Eric came and crouched down on George's opposite side. "Did you wire the place yourself?"

George shook his head. "Stefan did. The entire island. All but one of the boats. He told me that if anything happened to him after the guests arrived, if they betrayed him, that I was to get off the island and send them all to hell along with what they came after. I can do that." He looked up at Dawn, his eyes pleading for understanding. "But it seems such a waste, you know? It is a beautiful place. Worth millions."

"So we were all to kill one another and spare the property," Eric said.

"All but Sean. And Aurora, of course," George admitted. "As I said, she's merely a pawn to you, just as I was to Stefan." He swallowed hard.

"Okay, how were you to blow it?" Eric asked.

George seemed to snap out of his stupor as he glared up at Eric. "I won't tell you. But I still can do it at any time. I will before I let you—"

Eric leapt on George and grasped his arms before the words were out of his mouth. "Search him. The remote. Find it!"

Dawn was closest but not quite fast enough. George twisted free and had the thing out of his pocket and in his hand before she could get to it. He held it up and backed away from her, his back to the rock wall, a threat in his eyes. "I'll do it!"

"Do you really want Sean to end up under a huge pile of rubble, George?" she asked gently. "Wouldn't you rather have a ceremony of some kind? Say goodbye to him properly?" She glanced briefly at Eric, who nodded encouragement.

She reached out, trying to touch George's arm. "Please consider it, George. It is true we want what your brother took and intended to sell, but not for the reasons you think."

Again, she looked to Eric for permission to reveal why they were there. "You see, the three of us work for the American government. We came here to outbid the rest and to capture the terrorists' representatives sent here to buy it. We're on your side, George."

"I don't believe you! It's a trick!" He shook the remote as he pointed with it to Eric. "He...he's Arab, not American. And you..." He stopped, frowning. She figured he must have just realized her Spanish accent had disappeared.

"My name is Dawn Moon. I'm an agent with the National Security Agency," she explained. "This is Eric Vinland and Clay Senate. They are also agents."

George looked confused, but at least he was concentrating on them and not the remote he was holding. "It doesn't matter. If I destroy it, no one can have it."

Dawn sighed. "George, you don't even know what it is."

"It's important!" he insisted. "I know that much. It's vital to the terrorists!"

"Yes," she agreed, keeping her voice as calm as possible. "We need to make sure this gets back in the right hands. And to verify that Stefan brought it here and that it's not out there somewhere for someone else to discover. You never actually saw what he had, did you?"

"No." He slowly sank down to sit on the floor of the tunnel. With a gesture of resignation, he handed the remote to Dawn. "The code is 08-16-53. Stefan's birthday."

She sighed with relief and exchanged a look with Eric. He smiled at her and said a quiet, "Thank you."

She sat down next to George, careful to keep him covered in case he decided to reenergize suddenly and do something they didn't expect.

Clay was busy with the tiny device he had removed from beneath his skin. "This damned thing's definitely not receiving and probably not sending, either," he muttered. "Something must be blocking the signals."

Eric looked at Dawn with regret. "Then I guess we're on our own."

Surrounded by Arab terrorists, the most critical part of

their mission unaccomplished, Dawn wondered what they would do now. She could practically see the wheels turning in Eric's head as he assessed their predicament. That gave her hope. He was the one with all the experience. He would think of something. She watched him amble over to the mouth of the cave and step outside.

Clay crouched down near her and crossed his arms over his knees, his weapon dangling from one hand. He closed his eyes.

She hoped he was broadcasting mentally, trying his last-ditch method of contacting backup. Hadn't Eric said that each of the Sextant team had particular talents in that vein?

A few minutes passed in silence. Then Clay spoke. "I'm too tired to think. How about you?"

"Running on adrenaline," she admitted. "Trying not to crash." Now was a good time to satisfy some of her curiosity. She might not get another chance. "Can you do what Eric says he can do? Do you mind read or whatever?"

His full lips quirked down. "No. I'm supposed to have visions. Not that I can interpret them clearly until after the fact. Lot of good that does."

"Have you had any since we've been on the island?" she asked, only half believing him, but still wondering about the kind of men who thought they had these powers.

He made a sound in his throat, half grunt, half laugh. "I dreamed a bevy of demonic birds descended. Sort of like the old Hitchcock movie. Prophetic and pretty damn useless now, wouldn't you say?"

"You trust Eric's abilities, though, don't you?" she asked, reaching for hope.

Again that sound, this time more laugh than grunt. He opened his eyes and peered at her sideways. "The kid? That's what the team calls him, you know. *The kid.* And no, I don't think he can perform his parlor tricks any longer. Not since he met you."

"He said the same thing. So what'd I do?"

Clay sighed and leaned his head back against the rock, stretching his neck. "I don't know. Probably nothing. You just are who you are."

She reached out and touched his arm. "You mean I've screwed up his psychic abilities? That's what you're saying?"

He nodded and looked her full in the face. "He couldn't connect with you during the interrogation. Or since. I think maybe that's wrecked his confidence or something."

Had she done that? "How?"

"Again, I don't know. But maybe you can fix it," Clay suggested softly. "Try letting him in."

"In?" She almost croaked the word. She had let Eric in all right. Twice now. And that obviously hadn't helped him a lot, at least not in the way Clay meant. It had helped her, though. Or maybe not, now that she thought about it. She had trusted the man with her body, but she certainly didn't trust him with her heart. She hadn't let him in *there* yet and didn't dare.

The low rumble of Clay's chuckle broke her reverie. "Let him into your *thoughts* is what I meant, Moon. It might help." He watched her for a few seconds, looking deeply into her eyes, then added, "Send him a message. Think something to him. Try it."

"What?" she asked in a near whisper.

"Anything, doesn't matter what. Maybe he just needs to know he can still do it."

"And then he might be able to contact our backup?" she asked hopefully.

Clay shrugged, but his concern was evident. "It couldn't hurt to try, could it? But you need to believe in what you're doing when you do it."

Dawn wasn't sure she could, not fully anyway, but was willing to grasp at any straw right now. Eric needed to get his team here one way or another, and they weren't coming until he notified him that he was ready. If Clay thought she could help Eric do that, she would certainly try.

She tried to think of something to project to Eric that wouldn't involve anything personal or private. Revealing how she felt about him wouldn't be a good idea. Maybe a simple command to come back inside the cave would do for a start.

She took a deep breath, closed her eyes and repeated the phrase, Come to me, Eric. Over and over, she thought the words until they filled her mind completely.

To her surprise, she heard his hurried footsteps and opened her eyes.

"He came back in!" she crowed, shooting Clay a look of triumph.

"Damn right I did," he grumbled. "The beach out there is working alive with men. And they aren't ours. My guess is Sudanese. Ali's people. I figure we have less than five minutes before they climb up here and find this cave."

They all leapt to action except George. Clay grabbed him and half dragged him out of the cave. They hurried back into the tunnel that led to the house. There was nowhere else to go that didn't lead down to the beach and certain death.

"This way!" Eric ordered when they came to the passage that forked off the main corridor. "Where does this lead?" he asked George.

"To the roof," he answered when Clay jogged him with a firm shake.

They rushed onward and periodically climbed steps hewn into the rock. Dawn had visions of being trapped up there on top of the villa, besieged like knights in a medieval castle with the enemy crawling up the walls.

After an exhausting run, they reached a trapdoor that opened above them. Clay pushed his way next to Eric and they lifted it a few inches to look around.

"It's clear up here for now," Eric said. "Let's go."

They exited onto the flat rooftop that was, as she had hoped, deserted. A three-foot coping surrounded the edge like the battlements of a castle.

Below, outside the villa, they could hear shouts and thudding bootfalls. Definitely surrounded, she thought, and not as well armed as they needed to be.

"Only one door leading up here out of the house," Eric observed, inclining his head toward the small structure that looked sort of like a freestanding closet atop the roof near the middle.

He ordered George to lie down next to the balustrade and stay there. "Clay, you watch the doors. Dawn, check out the perimeter for access that way," he ordered, pointing to his right. "I'll go left."

They found no way that anyone could get to the roof unless they had brought grappling hooks or came through one of the two doors, the one main stairway from the house proper and the flat trapdoor from the tunnel.

However, there was no other way down for them, either. They were effectively trapped up here. The critical information was in the safe downstairs in Quince's office. That would have to be destroyed if it couldn't be reclaimed. Dawn realized they might have to die here in order to ensure national security.

Once they had reassembled, she felt she had to make a suggestion. "You have to try to summon the team again, Eric. Maybe from up here it'll be a clear shot with no interference. Straight across the water, right? They're out there waiting. Give it another shot."

His smile was wry. "I'm afraid it doesn't work that simply, sweetheart."

"It *might*," she argued, trying to ignore his use of the endearment. He probably called women that all the time. "Have you just given up?" She noted Clay's nod of encouragement and continued. "Give it a go, Eric. At least *try*. When I sent you a message to come back in the cave, you came. No hesitation. I think you were reading me then."

"She's right. You could have been, subconsciously," Clay added.

For a few seconds Eric studied her, then released a sigh. "Try your transponder again, Clay, and I'll do whatever I can, too. Maybe one of us will get through to Jack or Will. If we don't see our guys approach before we're overrun up here, we'll have to blow the house. We can't let anyone get off the island with what's in that safe."

Dawn experienced a chill, hearing him affirm out loud that they could die here. She moved closer and took Eric's hand. "You can still do it. I know you can."

He leaned down and kissed her, just a quick meeting of lips. Then he looked into her eyes. "Thanks, Dawn. For everything. You know how much I care, don't you?"

That near declaration sounded a lot like a goodbye. It made her realize she wanted more from Eric than she had admitted, even to herself. When he let go and started to turn away, she grabbed his sleeve. "Wait!"

"What?"

"Take out the contacts," she whispered. "Please. I'd…I'd like to see your eyes when you look at me for what might be the last… Do you mind?"

He reached up and hastily removed and discarded the tiny bits of brown that had disguised the vivid blue of his irises. Then he grinned at her, that same ingratiating expression that turned her all soft inside. "You never cease to amaze me, Dawn, you know that?"

Dawn couldn't speak; she was too caught up in the moment. Silently she brushed the dark hair off his brow with her fingers and wished it were streaky blond again. She would give nearly anything just to see him once more exactly as he had been before becoming Jarad.

"Now go over there, please," he suggested, pointing across the roof. "Keep watch. When you're this close, I can't think, much less project, okay?"

She let go of his hand and turned her back to him, not caring that Clay had witnessed what was between them or that he'd probably guessed how they'd crossed the line on the mission and become lovers.

What difference would his knowing make if they were all blown sky-high? And if they weren't, she would be glad to stand the consequences of fraternizing on the job.

But Clay wasn't watching. He was sitting down on the roof, his weapon resting across his legs as he used his knife to tap a message on the tiny disk.

She glanced back at Eric, who now crouched against the balustrade that surrounded the flat rooftop and looked out across the Aegean Sea. Was he doing it? Could he actually send thoughts out there and have them picked up by Jack Mercier or one of the others on his team? Apparently, he'd done it before, if they could be believed.

His broad shoulders and back were straight, his head tilted back a little.

God, she was in love with that man. Against her better judgment and all the rules governing what they were doing, she had fallen for him like a ton of bricks. Dawn wished to heaven she could see his face.

At that second, he turned and shot her a smile that made her breath catch. Had he read her thoughts at that moment?

Embarrassed to be caught with what was probably a sappy look on her face, she jerked around and hurried to the far side of the roof. Now was no time to go soft.

"Heads up!" Clay cried, a split second before his automatic spat a volley across the door he was guarding.

A scream, loud shouting and a garble of orders issued from inside the opening, now blocked by the bodies of several enemies.

Dawn crouched, weapon drawn, but held her fire.

Eric had assumed a similar stance across the roof. Every bullet counted now. And unless they could hold off Ali's men until help arrived, they would have to make the ultimate sacrifice.

Her gaze met Eric's, and his look said volumes. Frustration, regret and very little hope. Dawn had never wanted to live so badly in her life as she did right then.

"Any success?" Eric called to Clay.

"Nope. You?"

Eric shrugged. "How much ammo you got?"

"One extra clip."

"Dawn?" he asked.

She held up two fingers. Two clips. Thirty rounds.

He raised the machine gun. "Two clips here and a couple of rounds in a pistol," Eric said. "We'll be okay."

Right. Dawn wondered how many were out there and inside the house. Too many, she feared.

"Take cover," he said as he motioned for her to get behind the projection on the roof that housed the door leading down into the villa.

Dawn did that, careful to choose a spot where she wouldn't be in Clay's line of fire. "This okay?"

Eric nodded. "Watch the trapdoor from there. If it lifts, aim for the crack. Don't let them get it fully open or they could rush us."

"I'm on it," she assured him.

For nearly an hour, they held their positions, taking careful aim as they fired, to conserve ammunition.

But their ammo was slowly and surely running out. And, unfortunately, so was their time.

Chapter 16

Eric knew he'd have to blow the place if they were overrun. The remote in his pocket weighed heavy. He just didn't think he'd be able to punch in that code George had given them.

Sure, he could pay the ultimate price to keep that info out of terrorist hands. He tried to convince himself that going that way would be a better death for Dawn than leaving her at the hands of the enemy. Damn it, he couldn't kill her and he couldn't hand the job over to Clay, either! They had to hold out, somehow.

He crawled up to the side of the door where the bodies of the terrorists Clay had shot were lying. He managed to secure two of the weapons they had dropped as they fell. Almost full loads, he noted.

More men were filing up the stairs. He sent an Uzi sliding across the floor of the roof and watched Dawn grab it. Suddenly, the tunnel door raised, opened a crack and she fired. It slammed down.

Eric quickly scuttled away from the other door so he'd be out of Clay's line of fire when the next wave reached it. He aimed, too.

Both he and Clay were out in the open with no cover available. Dawn remained behind the raised structure, half-visible to Eric. He could see her in profile, every inch the agent she had trained to be. My God, how he admired her courage. Not many men would take this in stride the way she was doing.

She loved him. Eric had seen it in her eyes, maybe even heard her think it. He wasn't sure he had read her mind, but as soon as he'd ditched the contacts and looked into those liquid brown eyes of hers, he'd felt the same close connection as when they'd made love.

Maybe, just maybe, he had reached Jack with his thoughts and the team would get here in time. He tried again, as he had every time there was a lull so he could concentrate.

Come on, guys! Get here. We need backup. We're on the roof of the villa. Outmanned. Outgunned. Hurry!

Despite repeated attempts, Clay had had no success with his transponder and neither had Eric. Strange to get two faulty devices when they had been implanted at different times. They weren't even the same make or model. Could there be some sort of scrambler shield on the island?

Even that shouldn't have affected his own method of contact, though. No, he had lost that ability on meeting Dawn. He seriously regretted the loss, but only because it might now cost Dawn her life.

Doing without his lifelong ability to read the thoughts of others had forced him to rely on his instincts and powers of observation, things he had barely noticed he possessed and had never really needed much until this mission.

She made him a more complete person in spite of what he'd lost, maybe even because of that. For the first time in his life, he felt almost normal, but the price of that was too dear. He might lose her before they had a chance to declare their feelings for each other out loud. He had told her he cared, but it wasn't nearly enough. Eric wanted Dawn to know exactly how he felt.

I love you. His desperate inner shout, accompanied by an intense look, caused her to turn abruptly.

Or had it? Why did she wear that look of horror? Her features blurred even as the sound of shots registered. A flurry of action exploded near the door and rapid firing was the last thing Eric heard.

"Eric's down!" Dawn cried. Clay provided cover as she ran the dozen feet that separated her from Eric. Mindless with fear, she grabbed his feet to drag him to the area where she had been sheltered. She couldn't budge him.

"How bad?" Clay called.

"One hit, upper right chest!" she answered, pressing her hand over the wound. Eric was unconscious. She felt for an exit wound, found it and huffed a breath of relief. At least the bullet hadn't bounced around inside. Maybe it had missed anything vital. She prayed hard while doing all she could to stanch the bleeding.

So far none of the terrorists had made it onto the rooftop alive. The attacks came in waves, from the doorway and from the tunnel exit. Both means of access were blocked with bodies, which also acted as shields when the fresh troops appeared. Clay whipped his weapon back and forth, attempting to cover both the door and the hatch while Dawn checked on Eric. George moaned periodically, but wisely stayed where he was. The situation was rapidly degenerating.

She glanced out to sea. "Damn it, Mercier, get your boats in gear! And send us help! He could die!"

"We could all die if you don't cover that tunnel exit!" Clay snapped. He had changed position and now stood a couple of feet away, still watching the door. "A simultaneous attack could finish us off. How's your ammo?"

"Almost gone," she admitted, still pressing hard on both Eric's wounds.

"Get the remote out of his pocket and give it to me," Clay ordered. "Let me know when we're down to nothing. I'll have to blow it, Dawn."

"I know. Do it," she replied, handing him the remote, then resuming her pressure on Eric's wound. "Nice working with you, Senate."

"Same here, Moon, but we're not dead yet. Lay him on his back and use the floor for pressure on the exit wound while you lean on the entry with your forearm. That way you can still fire if you need to."

She took the suggestion, watching as Clay took the stubby little Uzi Eric had been using. "Empty," he muttered as he crawled away to a better position to fire on the doorway. Although no one else had tried to come out of the tunnel, she watched it like a hawk.

The warmth of Eric's body beneath her arm and against her hip felt reassuring. "I hope Mercier picked up something from you or Clay. We could sure use some company about now." Understatement of the year, she thought with an inner groan.

She felt more than heard Eric grunt, but couldn't look at him and effectively guard the trapdoor. At least he was moving a little and making sound.

"More coming up!" Clay said. "Get ready!"

She felt Eric shift her arm off his body and replace it

with his hand. The realization that he was conscious bolstered her hope like nothing else could.

She trained the Walther on the trapdoor and trusted Clay to take care of the others. "Jeez, you'd think they'd have run out of manpower by now. Must have unloaded a damn troop ship."

"Coming," Eric said, his voice cracking with the effort to speak. "Jack's coming...with the team. Don't let Clay—"

"Jack *better* come," she replied. "I sent him a mental message myself. Told him to get his ass in gear. You just rest and don't worry, honey. We'll be fine."

"Honey?" he croaked. She could hear the smile in his word.

"Yeah, *honey*. Might as well start getting you domesticated while I have some free time. You lead entirely too wild a life, Vinland. Need to lighten up a little."

The trapdoor inched up even as she spoke. She fired at it, cursing when it opened a bit wider. Whoever was in there had a damn death wish. Okay with her. She fired again, putting a few rapid rounds right into the dark space. It slammed shut again as she heard a howl.

Eric was coughing. Or laughing. She risked a glance. A pained smile stretched across his beautiful mouth wide and she could see the gleaming white of his perfect teeth. "Lighten up," he repeated in a croaking whisper. "Right."

She wanted so badly to kiss him. He'd realize it was goodbye, though, and Dawn didn't want him to know it was. "Go back to sleep until this is over," she told him.

It *was* nearly over. She reached in her pocket and felt for the pistol, her last line of defense. The Walther was empty now. If she counted correctly, the Glock had four rounds left. Clay must be as low on ammo as she was since he'd had to fire more often than she had.

Dutifully, she called Clay's name and held up the pistol with four of her fingers raised to show him how close she was to empty. He nodded and raised five fingers.

Great. Down to nine shots. Then he'd have no choice but to destroy the villa, everything and everyone in it, including themselves. Dawn looked down at Eric again, hoping he was asleep. He wasn't. He stared back at her. "Jack's…coming."

"I know," she said gently. "Just rest."

"Tell Clay," he ordered, sounding angry. "Now!"

Dawn wasn't sure what to do. Was Eric hallucinating? Delaying the inevitable? Or did he really feel something, maybe a response to his message to Mercier? She made a snap decision.

"Clay!" she shouted, trying to inject as much belief and excitement as possible into her voice. "Eric says the team's on the way!" She wanted to believe it more than anything ever.

Clay nodded, his eyes still trained on the open doorway littered with bodies. "About damn time," he shouted back. "Go have a look if you can leave him for a minute."

Again Eric moved her hand and replaced it with his own. "Go," he huffed, almost soundlessly.

She scrambled up and ran around the perimeter of the roof, looking out in every direction. When she reached the north side, she whooped and pointed. "There! There they are!" She whirled around and rushed back to Eric's side. "Hold on. They'll be here soon."

Then she remembered how low they were on ammo. Could they hold out until the team arrived? Or would Ali's men keep coming in bunches until they took the roof?

"Chopper," Eric said, his eyes closing. "Hear?"

The *whump-whump* of a distant aircraft gently vibrated the atmosphere. Dawn wanted to turn cartwheels.

"Down! Get down!" Clay shouted. Then all hell broke loose. Three of Ali's men poured out of the doorway, stumbling over their fallen comrades, spraying the rooftop with gunfire. Dawn dropped flat and returned fire just as she saw Clay crumple.

After the burst of activity, it seemed there was total silence. She couldn't even hear the *whump-whump* of the chopper now and wondered if it had veered away.

Clay stirred, then rolled to one side. Dawn blew out a breath of relief. He was down, but not dead.

She felt Eric's hand close over her calf and half turned to look at him. He raised a hand and pointed, reminding her to hurry and retrieve the guns. More ammo. She needed those weapons the new downed crew of enemy had on them.

She scuttled forward toward the door to gather what she could find. It was up to her now to keep Eric and Clay safe until backup arrived. For the first time, she remembered George. He was huddled in a corner by the coping, not moving, but there was no time to check and see whether he'd been hit. At this point, she didn't much care about that.

Dawn had almost reached the fallen terrorists in the doorway when a head appeared above the carnage. A head and a weapon. She pulled the trigger of the Glock and heard nothing but a click. Empty.

She prepared to duck. It was all she could do. The enemy's eyes narrowed as he smiled at her and aimed more carefully.

Dawn's life did not flash before her eyes as she'd heard happened at the moment of death. All she felt was horrible, crushing anger.

A single shot rang out. Had he missed at this range? Impossible. Then she saw the lethal wound in the center of his forehead. He crumpled onto the pile of dead that all but blocked the door.

Dawn grabbed the only weapon she could reach in a hurry, a top-of-the-line H&K automatic. Then she turned and saw Eric, propped on one elbow, pistol still clutched in his hand. He collapsed as she crawled back to him.

The confiscated H&K was nearly empty, a couple of rounds left, and there was no time to dig through the dead to find another gun. Footsteps were pounding on the stairs again.

Quickly she sat back facing the threat, bracing the weapon on her knee, aiming directly at the doorway. "C'mon, you bastards. Do your worst," she spat. She might go down, but she was taking somebody with her.

"Friendlies!" Eric shouted. She could hear the cost of that shout in the way he bit off the word with a groan.

Did she trust his instincts? Was that Mercier's bunch clattering up the stairs? How could they have gotten here that fast? And how could he know who it was? If he was wrong and she waited an instant too long to pull the trigger, they were all dead.

For a split second, she considered firing anyway. But she waited. Eric would never gamble with their lives. Unless he was damned sure of himself, rock-positive, he wouldn't have tried to stop her.

"Hold your fire!" someone on the inside called out. "Vinland? Senate? Moon?"

Dawn nearly collapsed with relief. "All clear!" she cried, tears running down her face, streaks of heat against her breeze-chilled cheeks. "We're clear." The last words rushed out on a sob that she caught and contained. Wouldn't do to get caught crying like a little girl.

A huge shadow with accompanying noise descended to the roof as the chopper set down twenty feet away from her. Dawn put down the weapons and crawled rapidly back to Eric. "Thank you, thank you, thank you," she murmured as she pressed her lips to the side of his face and her palm on top of his hand that clutched the wound.

"I love you, Eric," she added with feeling, knowing the sound was lost in the cacophony of sounds that surrounded them now. She just had to say it, though she knew he couldn't hear her, that he was too out of it with pain to read it in her mind if his ability had returned. He wouldn't die, and she had never been so glad of anything in her life.

Friendlies. What a marvelous word, she thought. They would whisk Eric and Clay to a hospital. They would be safe. They would live.

As for her, she would go back to NSA and do what she did best, identifying and illustrating security leaks. Her one big international anti-terrorist mission was all but over.

Mercier himself lifted her away from Eric as two guys with a stretcher hurriedly checked him out and began to load him up. The men were loading Clay's stretcher next, and another guy was assisting George toward the chopper. In a few moments, they would be gone. She had to go with Eric. "Wait!" she cried, but Mercier held her back. For a second, she struggled in protest, then realized she would only be in the way, and cooperated.

Eric's boss tugged her toward the stairs leading down. "Shake it off, Moon. Come with me," Mercier ordered in a loud voice.

After one last glance at the chopper, Dawn followed. She swallowed her tears and put on her agent's face.

If she did nothing else today, she would make Eric proud of how she followed through with their mission. There would be a lengthy debriefing, a chore he wouldn't be up to completing for some time. And there was still the flash drive to locate.

All she wanted right now was to get that over with and

find transportation to whatever medical facility was treating Eric. Before she went stateside again, she had to know he was recovering. Then she could say goodbye and get on with her life, such as it was.

Things would never be the same for her. Eric Vinland had turned her life upside down and inside out. She would always love him. Not that she intended to tell him so again.

If she did, that meant they would have to decide what to do about it. He might want them to be lovers for a while, she supposed. They were incredibly good together. But then it would end, and she didn't think she could face that.

She had before with the others, but Eric was different. His leaving her, even though she knew he would try to let her down easy when the time came, would be the end for her. Better not to get any more involved, end it now and convince herself that everything she felt for him had been due to forced proximity and hyped by adrenaline.

But not before she saw him once more and made sure he would be all right. Would he? Had the wound been worse than she imagined? What if he died? A chill shot through her.

"This way," Mercier directed as they reached the entrance to Quince's ruined study where the grenade had gone off. Sean McCoy's body lay covered with a blanket, as did the other terrorists' remains. He guided her through the rubble into the hallway and into the lounge, which remained virtually unchanged from the last time she'd seen it.

Once there, he sat her down on the silk striped divan and brought her a drink. Scotch. She drank it and made a face. Wicked stuff, and she hated the taste.

"Now then," he said gently. "We need to get to work."

A question occurred to her, and Dawn figured she might not get another chance to ask it. "Did Eric get through to you?"

"Telepathically, you mean?" Mercier smiled. "As a matter of fact, no."

"Then how…?"

He thumped the back of the divan near her shoulder. "What if I told you it was *you* who connected."

Her? Laughter welled up inside her and spilled out. Hysterical, unstoppable and totally inappropriate as it was, she couldn't stop it. She almost hoped he would slap her so she would stop, but he didn't.

Mercier let her laugh until she collapsed back against the divan with scotch spilled all over her lap and tears running down her face.

"Okay, now that you've got that out of your system…" He took the glass from her hand and set it aside. "Are you ready?"

Dawn sat up straight, wiped her face with her palms and composed herself.

"One of the bidders, a Russian, was under guard upstairs in one of the bedrooms," she told Mercier. She took another sip of the scotch and grimaced. "The one who brought all these guys to the party was locked in the kitchen basement. His men set him free, I'm sure."

"They'll be rounded up, don't worry," Mercier assured her. "No one's getting off this island without my say-so, depend on it."

She knew he meant her, as well as the perps involved.

She allowed herself one last glance out the window, sending a brief, silent and fervent prayer winging after the helicopter that had long disappeared. It was all she could do for Eric now. That, and finish what they had begun together. He would demand that of her and be right to do so.

She nodded succinctly and met Mercier's gaze with a steady one free of tears. "I'm ready."

Chapter 17

Eric railed against the tests that kept him isolated at the unnamed medical facility in the Poconos. Mercier had ordered him flown here directly after emergency surgery in Athens.

"For the hundredth time, I tell you I can't do it," he almost shouted. God, he was weary of making the attempts. "I don't want to do it. I'm sick of doing it, okay?"

"Not okay," Dr. Blumfeld declared. "This should be elementary for you, Eric. It's a simple guessing game. The subject in the other room is thinking one of these things," he said, pushing the large cards with pictures closer to Eric's side of the table. "You could do this with one hundred percent accuracy when you were five years old."

"And now I can't," Eric informed him yet again. "Call Mercier again. I want out of here. If he wants to fire me, fine, but I need to leave."

"You want to go and see that woman, don't you? But she's the one who did this, Eric. She took one of your senses from you. If she had blinded or deafened you, how would you feel then? This is even worse. Don't you understand that?"

Eric stood, trying not to kick his chair backward in a fit of fury. If he acted crazy, they just might throw a straight-jacket on him and put him somewhere even more secure. He forced a sigh. "I need to sleep for a while. My shoulder hurts like the devil. Hey, maybe that's interfering," he suggested, sounding quite reasonable, he thought. "The pain, you know." He rubbed the scar gently. It did still ache a little.

"Of course," the doctor said. "We'll try again tomorrow morning when you're more alert."

Sure they would, Eric thought, hiding his scowl. Damn the whole bunch of them. He was getting the hell out as soon as he could find a way. The trouble was, they expected him to try and were covering all possible exits. They wouldn't shoot him, of course. He was too valuable a subject for that. But they would restrain him.

Obviously Jack didn't realize the obsession these people had for ferreting out the intricacies of *gifts* like Eric's or he would never have sent Eric here for evaluation. Or perhaps he did. Maybe Dawn wasn't the only one who'd been betrayed by a superior.

The staff here were agents, too; even the docs were trained and badged. They weren't bad people, only overly dedicated. All the agencies had reps present while the research went on. They'd been at it too long. Eric had been brought here time and again since he was a child, giving them more data and answers to their questions than most of their subjects did. Funny how he had never minded before.

Now all he could think of was leaving, forgetting all this,

finding Dawn and thanking her for putting his life in better perspective.

Well, he hoped to do more than thank her, he thought with an inner smile.

He entered his room, a pleasant place even if it was a bit clinical. They had attempted to make him as comfortable as possible so he would be content and perform. Like hell.

The window was barred. There were four locked, guarded doors between him and the outside of the building. A high wall topped with concertina wire surrounded the property. For his protection against enemy agents who might come looking for him, so Dr. Blumfeld had said in a hushed voice. Did they think he was still five?

"Psssst!"

Eric looked around. His door was closed.

"Psssst! Here!"

He leaned back and looked up, astounded. "Dawn?"

"Get me a screwdriver," she whispered. "A flat-head. Mine broke."

He laughed, not bothering to lower his voice. "Where the hell would I get a screwdriver? They won't even let me have a dinner knife in this place. What are you doing here?"

"I came to bust you out. Or would you rather stay?"

"This is not a sanctioned insertion, I take it?"

"Are you kidding? Get me a damn screwdriver or neither one of us is going anywhere, and I don't plan to live in this freakin' maze of heating vents the rest of my life, okay?"

"Okay, hang on." He looked around the room for something that might do. "Ah, here we go." He lifted the thick folder Dr. Blumfeld had furnished of all Eric's former test results. Doc had let him read it to give him his confidence back. The pages were punched and held together with a flat metal clip and slide. He carefully removed it and tucked it up through the white painted vent.

He had tried the vents before, but they were securely screwed down from the inside where he couldn't get to them. Bless her heart, she had come for him. Wonders would never cease where that woman was concerned.

"How's your wound? Healed?"

"Fine," he answered.

"Clay's okay, too. I saw him last week. He told me where you were."

"Good man." Eric couldn't see Dawn through the slanted slots, but he could hear her shuffling around, grunting a curse now and then. "I hope you're quieter than this when you're really working," he said, unable to resist teasing her.

"Oh, shut up and push up on this thing, will you? Do I have to do everything?"

"Wind up one little mission by yourself and it goes straight to your head! How'd that turn out, by the way?" He bumped the vent with the heels of his hands and it popped out.

She peered down at him, grinning, her face streaked with dirt. "Good guys won, of course. Clay's recovering nicely and getting lots of TLC from your buds at Sextant. George is facing a conspiracy charge, but he's trying to cut some kind of deal by furnishing some of his brother's contacts. Sean was scamming George about being his son, just like we figured."

"I'm glad for George's sake."

"Yeah, he was, too. The radar info was on the flash drive I found in that drawer, by the way. It's now secure. Boris is on his way back to the Russian authorities and Ali bought it in the firefight along with most of his troops. The rest are in Uncle Sam's custody. Nothing left for you to do, Sport, but play Houdini and disappear from here."

She stuck out her hand and beckoned. "You coming or what?"

"Is Aristophanes Greek?" He dragged the desk chair over and climbed up on it, willing to follow her anywhere, the same way she had once followed him.

Moments later, she was leading him through the vents at a fast crawl. She hadn't paused to kiss him hello. Or tell him why she had come to his rescue. If discovered, her career would be over. His probably was anyway, since he'd lost the skill that made him valuable to Sextant.

Eric didn't care about that. What he had found was so much more than he'd ever had before. Dawn.

She had made him a normal person. Somehow, she had banished his enormous burden of carrying the dark secrets of others, of sometimes inadvertently invading the private thoughts of friends. His mind was his own now, the peace and quiet a blessed relief he had never expected and treasured above anything. Except Dawn.

"Did I ever tell you I love you, Moon?" he asked, huffing with exertion after six weeks of virtual inertia. He hurt, and the pain was exquisite.

"Not in so many words," she answered, still crawling forward. "Pick up the pace, will you? We don't have all day."

"How do we get over the wall unnoticed?"

"Leave it to me," she ordered. "We're coming up on the laundry area behind the kitchen. Just trust me and do what I do."

Trust her? She had placed her trust in him when trust should have been impossible for her. How could he do any less?

A moment later when she dived through a hole in the

ceiling, he had to question blind trust. Then he shoved forward and dropped headfirst, just as she had done.

He felt around. They landed in a bin of warm, recently dried bed linens ready for the morning pressing. The room was dark as pitch and smelled of detergent and bleach. Dawn lay beside him, but she wasn't moving.

When he ran his hands over her to see if she was all right, her hand grasped his neck and drew him closer. "We wait right here," she whispered. He watched her press the dial of her watch, which glowed green for a second. "For at least half an hour," she continued. "The workers in the next room will be leaving in precisely ten minutes, but we'd better stay put until we're sure the area's clear. Then we make our exit."

"Over the wall?" he asked, tracing her face with his fingers, dying to kiss her.

"Are you crazy? We change into whites like theirs and go out the service entrance."

"Well, how was I supposed to know your plans? What do you take me for, a mind reader?"

She pinched his cheek. Right through his jogging pants. "Don't get cute. I know you were telling the truth about that."

He pinched her back with both hands while pulling her flush against him and loving every subtle squirm she made. "A believer, are you?"

"I found the ring, right where you said it would be, stuck in the drain of the pool where I used to swim."

"So I can find things. That's not mind reading, Dawn. I can't do that any longer."

"Because of me?" she asked, sounding contrite. And a little defensive, he thought. "Clay said so, too."

"No, because I don't *want* to anymore," he answered truthfully.

Maybe Dawn hadn't been the primary cause of that loss, but only his motivation to ditch it. What did it matter? All he wanted, he had in his arms right now.

"I know what you're thinking," she said with a smile in her voice.

"Yeah? Want to do a little research in that area?" he asked, nipping at her neck. She tasted salty, a little dusty and pretty wonderful. "Tell me and let's see if you're on the money."

"You're thinking you'd like us to work a little late in the wash room, right?"

"God, Moon, you're good!"

"Damn straight I am." She kissed him soundly on the mouth. "You want to take me away from all this, keep me safe and make a wife out of me, that's what you're thinking now."

"Got it in one." He kissed her back until he had to come up for air.

"I'm not going to let you. You know that, don't you?" Her hands began to wander, driving every thought from his head except where they were going.

He reached for the hem of her shirt and began to lift it. "Okay, all but the wife part. Gotta insist on that."

"Fair compromise, I guess," she said, breathless. "Helluva proposal, Vinland."

Eric framed her face with his hands and wished with all his heart that he could see her right now, dirty face, wild red hair and all. "Hey, I don't mess around when it comes to romance. Privacy, a little sweet talk, total commitment, the works."

"Not to mention clean sheets," she added. "What more could a girl ask for?"

Epilogue

"I now pronounce you man and wife. You may kiss your bride."

Dawn thought she had never heard more beautiful words in her life. She felt beautiful, dressed in ivory satin, hair red as before and gaining back its natural curl.

She couldn't say that her personality had changed all that much in the three months since their big adventure when she'd reverted to her former appearance. As she had informed Eric last night, she retained entirely too much of Aurora's meekness. He had laughed out loud.

But now, right now, Eric was kissing her more sweetly than ever, restraining the passion that usually raged between them every time they came together. Anyone

watching the ceremony might think they were pretty con-
servative lovers, she guessed. Ha.

Eric led her down the aisle of St. John's chapel, beaming
as if his dreams had all come true. Dawn knew that hers had.
What a golden treasure he was in any guise he chose! So what
if she couldn't figure him out. She'd just keep him guessing,
too. He had risked everything for her, just as she had for him.
Love was the ultimate risk, but she was taking it gladly.

Eric's parents didn't seem to know what to make of her,
but then they didn't seem to know what to make of Eric, either.

They were a handsome couple, a bit older than she had
expected and obviously uptight, which she *had* expected.
Eric had said he didn't mind, that he loved them anyway.
Dawn knew she would embrace them, too, whether they
were comfortable with that or not.

She wondered if they knew him at all. He'd said he had
spent more time in research facilities while growing up
than he had at home. His grandmother had been the only
one to offer much love and understanding after he began
to exhibit his psychic gifts.

Well, he wouldn't lack for love and understanding from
now on, she silently promised him.

Later, at the reception in the church's social hall, Jack
Mercier, his wife Solange, Holly and Will Griffin, Joe and
Martine Corda and Clay Senate were congregated at one
of the tables. The Sextant team and spouses, Eric's work
family. He danced her over to join them.

"Congratulations, you two," Jack said as he rose and
kissed Dawn lightly on the cheek. "When can we expect
him back at work, Mrs. Vinland?"

She noticed Eric's smile falter a little. He had misjudged
Mercier's intentions in sending him to the clinic in the

Poconos. No one had any idea they would treat Eric the way they had.

He had also been mistaken about Jack's hiring him for the Sextant team only because of his ability to read minds. He'd been right about the loss. He couldn't do that anymore and seemed relieved about it. However, he still had other psychic tricks up his sleeve, like locating missing objects and people. Besides, his normal abilities as an agent far outweighed even those psychic tools.

The caring that his fellow agents had shown when he came home had humbled him as much as a guy like Eric could be humbled. She grinned at him just because he was who he was. Hers, with all his quirks.

"You can have him in three weeks, not a day sooner," Dawn told his boss, accepting a kiss from the rather stoic Clay Senate as she spoke. He offered her a rare smile. She felt a special affinity for the man who had shared the most dangerous day of her life, so she kissed him back. That earned her a comical frown from her new husband and laughter from the others.

"Eric says he needs to show me Greece the way it should be seen. No bullets, no bad guys, no secret plans hidden in my Wonderbra." She patted her bodice and made a face. George had been wrong. All along, the radar info had been on the flash drive she'd found and was now safely back where it belonged.

Eric slid his arms around her waist from behind and rested his chin on her shoulder. "Nope, no derring-do on this trip. Just sea, sand and…sightseeing." He hesitated a full second before the last word and it came out in a flat tone unlike the others.

"Well, I should hope so. Jack says the mission was an unqualified success," Solange said. "How fortunate that it brought you two together. Jack and I met on a mission, too. So did Joe and Martine."

"I'll be forever grateful we did, too. But I never want to participate in one like it again!" It was enough that Eric had agreed she should continue her work at NSA. She was suited for that, and he would continue to work for Sextant.

"Time to go," Eric reminded her, pointing at his watch and tugging on her elbow. "We fly in two hours."

"Cutting it close," Jack said, reaching out to shake his hand. "Have a great honeymoon, you two."

Eric nodded his thanks to each of them, looking very serious.

"Are you all right?" Dawn asked him as soon as they got into the limousine. He didn't seem his usual happy-go-lucky self, certainly not the beaming bridegroom he'd been earlier. He had changed while they were talking to the team. "What's wrong?"

"I felt something," he told her. "Back there, when I touched you, put my hands on your waist. For a minute there, I sensed…something. Rapid, like a heartbeat, but too fast. *Way* too fast." He bit his lips together, then turned to her and grinned. "For an adult, it was too fast. Hey, I know it's probably too soon to tell for sure, but, do you think…?"

Dawn gasped, meeting his gaze with wonder. "Wow, Vinland, you're amazing! You just might have located something a lot more precious than my grandmother's ring!"

INTIMATE MOMENTS™

NEXT MONTH LOOK FOR THE NEW
SIX-BOOK *ROYALTY* SAGA FEATURING
GLAMOUR, PASSION AND BETRAYAL...

CAPTURING THE CROWN

**With the monarchy in upheaval,
who will capture Silvershire's crown?**

THE HEART OF A RULER

BY MARIE FERARRELLA

**AVAILABLE APRIL 2006
AT YOUR FAVORITE RETAIL OUTLET.**

Visit Silhouette Books at www.eHarlequin.com   SIMTHR

Signature Select™

She had the ideal life…
until she had to start all over again.

National bestselling author

VICKI HINZE

Her Perfect Life

Don't miss this breakout novel!

$1.⁰⁰ OFF

your purchase of
Her Perfect Life by Vicki Hinze

RETAILER: Harlequin Enterprises Ltd. will pay the face value of this coupon plus 8 cents if submitted by the customer for HER PERFECT LIFE by Vicki Hinze only. Any other use constitutes fraud. Coupon is nonassignable. Void if taxed, prohibited or restricted by law. Void if copied. Consumer must pay any government taxes. Mail to Harlequin Enterprises Ltd., P.O. Box 880478, El Paso, TX 88588-0478, U.S.A. Cash value 1/100 cents. Limit one coupon per customer. Valid in the U.S. only. Coupon expires May 9, 2006. Redeemable at participating retail outlets in the U.S. only. Limit one coupon per purchase.

VHCOUPUS

5 65373 00076 2   (8100) 0 11209

Signature Select™

She had the ideal life...
until she had to start all over again.

National bestselling author

VICKI HINZE

Her Perfect Life

Don't miss this breakout novel!

$1.⁰⁰ OFF

your purchase of
Her Perfect Life by Vicki Hinze

RETAILER: Harlequin Enterprises Ltd. will pay the face value of this coupon plus
10.25 cents if submitted by the customer for HER PERFECT LIFE by Vicki Hinze
only. Any other use constitutes fraud. Coupon is nonassignable. Void if taxed,
prohibited or restricted by law. Void if copied. Consumer must pay any government
taxes. Nielson Clearing House customers—mail to Harlequin Enterprises Ltd., 661
Millidge Avenue, P.O. Box 639, Saint John, New Brunswick E2L 4A5, Canada. Non
NCH retailer—for reimbursement submit coupons and proof of sales directly to
Harlequin Enterprises Ltd., Retail Marketing Department, 225 Duncan Mill Rd., Don
Mills, Ontario M3B 3K9, Canada. Coupon expires May 9, 2006. Redeemable at
participating retail outlets in Canada only. Limit one coupon per purchase.

52606830

VHCOUPCN

www.eHarlequin.com

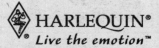
HARLEQUIN®
Live the emotion™

©2006 Harlequin Enterprises Ltd

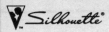

INTIMATE MOMENTS™

Night
Guardians

This Navajo Brotherhood
stands watch in the night at any cost.

The woman Kody Long
rescued from an attack
shouldn't even be on the
Navajo reservation—not
with the mythic, shape-
shifting Skinwalkers preying
after nightfall. But Regan
Wilson refused to leave
without her missing father—
which meant Kody had to
guard her after dark!

SHADOW
FORCE

AVAILABLE APRIL 2006 AT YOUR
FAVORITE RETAIL OUTLET.

Visit Silhouette Books at www.eHarlequin.com   SIMSF

I N T I M A T E   M O M E N T S™
Sparked by danger, fueled by passion!

Passion.
Adventure.
Excitement.

**Enter a world that's
larger than life, where
men and women overcome
life's greatest odds for
the ultimate prize: love.
Nonstop excitement is
closer than you think...in
Silhouette Intimate Moments!**

Visit Silhouette Books at www.eHarlequin.com

SIMDIR104

INTIMATE MOMENTS™

Jordan Wells always knew falling for a smoke
jumper was a mistake. All she wanted was
stability and safety. Then a wildfire reunited
her with Cade McKenzie, the very man she
wanted to forget. They end up racing for
their lives—and rekindling their love.

FACING THE FIRE

AVAILABLE APRIL 2006
AT YOUR FAVORITE RETAIL OUTLET.

Visit Silhouette Books at www.eHarlequin.com   SIMFTF

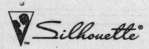

COMING NEXT MONTH

SIMCNM0306